THE CURSE OF GREG

THE CURSE OF CURSE OF GREG

— Book Two of —
AN EPIC SERIES OF FAILURES

CHRIS RYLANDER

putnam

G. P. Putnam's Sons

G. P. PUTNAM'S SONS
an imprint of Penguin Random House LLC, New York

G. P. Putnam's Sons is a registered trademark of Penguin Random House LLC.
Visit us online at penguinrandomhouse.com

Library of Congress Cataloging-in-Publication Data
Names: Rylander, Chris, author.
Title: The curse of Greg / Chris Rylander.
Description: New York, NY: G. P. Putnam's Sons, [2019] |
Series: An epic series of failures; book 2
Summary: "The saga continues as Galdervatn spreads throughout
the world, calling forth mythical monsters and new challenges for
Greg and his Dwarven crew"—Provided by publisher.
Identifiers: LCCN 2018041654 | ISBN 9781524739751 (hardback) |
ISBN 9781524739768 (ebook)
Subjects: | CYAC: Dwarfs (Folklore)—Fiction. | Magic—Fiction. | Elves—Fiction. |
Monsters—Fiction. | Adventure and adventurers—Fiction. | Fantasy. |
BISAC: JUVENILE FICTION / Fantasy & Magic. | JUVENILE FICTION /
Action & Adventure / General. | JUVENILE FICTION / Monsters.
Classification: LCC PZ7.R98147 Cur 2019 | DDC [Fic]—dc23
LC record available at https://lccn.loc.gov/2018041654

Printed in the United States of America.
ISBN 9781524739751
1 3 5 7 9 10 8 6 4 2

Design by Eileen Savage. Text set in Apolline Std.

For anyone who has ever felt cursed

CHAPTER 1

A Kid and His Talking Ax
Hit the Town for Some Fajitas

If I told you it was Thursday when I literally set my own pants on fire while being chased by a Gargoyle with a bad haircut, you likely wouldn't be surprised.

That's because surely you know by now that all Dwarves are born with a Thursday curse. But lately things have gotten so bad our pants could spontaneously ignite pretty much any day of the week and nobody would even bat an eye.

It all started with the return of Galdervatn.

Or, at least, sort of. I mean, that's definitely when it started, but what we didn't know was that Galdervatn only *sort of* came back. Which means the Dawn of a New Magical Age hasn't quite arrived the way I thought it had when I was standing on Navy Pier several months ago, watching the city go dark right after defeating my former best friend, Edwin.

But right now you're probably just wondering how in the world I ended up with my pants engulfed in flames and an angry Gargoyle with a mullet chasing close behind. I wish I could tell you it wasn't my fault, that I wasn't responsible for getting myself into such a predicament. But then I'd be lying, and Dwarves don't lie.

We were in downtown Evanston (a suburb directly north of Chicago) on our first-ever Monster Pacification Mission (MPM).

According to the Council's guidelines, MPMs have just two simple rules:

1. Avoid violence at all costs (befriending the monster is better than beheading it).
2. Don't make a scene.

You already know I broke rule number two. Since, by most people's standards, a pudgy kid running down a street screaming with his pants ablaze in bright flames would constitute something of a "scene." And, coincidentally, the vicious Gargoyle flying right behind me certainly meant I was likely to break rule number one as well.

Turns out that knowing you're a Dwarf doesn't exactly help you avoid *failing* like one. But we definitely hadn't expected things to go *this* poorly.

Maybe if I go back to when we first arrived in downtown Evanston earlier that night to help explain how I got myself into this mess, it won't seem quite so bad? Maybe it'll even seem like we did the best we could and that breaking the only two MPM rules was pretty much inevitable?

But first I should probably clarify why Monster Pacification Missions were even a thing at all.

The short version is this: Galdervatn (or "Ancient Separate

Earth Magic" to your average layperson) is coming back and it can't be stopped, we know that. It appears in the form of a colorful vapor, and as more and more of it gradually seeps from the Earth's core back toward the surface, we're seeing an increase of magical-monster sightings across the globe. And also reports of random rolling blackouts; cell phones dying and never coming back to life; stalled cars, construction equipment, and kitchen appliances; and generally a lot of confusion and chaos among Humans.

MPMs are the Council's solution (for now).

They identify a possible fantastical-monster sighting, then send out a squad of specially trained Dwarves to neutralize the threat to Humans—either by befriending the creature and bringing it back to the Underground, or, if need be, by destroying the thing entirely. But "strange sightings" are being reported so frequently lately that the Council was forced to draft a squad of Dwarven kids to assist. Since Lake, Eagan, Ari, Glam, Froggy, and I were nearly done with our training *and* already battle tested from infiltrating an Elven hideout to rescue my dad, we were the first lucky kids chosen for a mission.

Which is how we ended up on a commuter train that night headed out to Evanston, where earlier that day several Humans had reported power outages and sightings of a strange flying object downtown.

"It's so quiet," Ari had said as we descended the steps from the train station sometime around midnight.

"Yeah, suburbs usually are quiet this late," I said, forgetting yet again that they hadn't spent most of their lives among Humans in the modern world like I had.

"So where was this thing supposedly spotted?" Glam asked,

her faint mustache bristling with excitement as she flexed her bulging biceps under the streetlights. "I'm going to smash it into oblivion . . . whatever it is."

"Glam!" Ari said. "We have to try and befriend it first. Rule number one, remember? Besides, fighting monsters in a downtown suburb definitely won't help us with rule two either."

We all stopped at the bottom of the steps, under the train platform. Our weapons (to be used in case of emergency only) were stashed in two large hockey bags (surprisingly, the perfect size for stowing battle-axes, swords, and other Dwarven armaments) slung over one each of Glam and Lake's shoulders.

Glam set her bag down and threw her hands up in frustration.

"Who cares if Humans see us fighting a monster!" she said. "They're all going to find out the truth eventually. A lot of them probably already know something weird is going on. So why are we working so hard to hide it from them?"

"Because the Council said it's not the right time," Eagan explained. "Besides, do you really think if a bunch of people who've been living underground for centuries suddenly emerge and tell the world that all the blackouts and strange occurrences lately are not related to solar flares and climate change and government conspiracies, but rather to the impending return of an ancient, mythical, long-lost *magical essence*, that the collective world of seven billion people will just go, 'Oh, yeah, okay, cool. Makes sense.'"

"Pfft, they'll *have to* believe it when they eventually see it," Glam muttered.

"Aye, lest it be known so sayeth ye Elders doeth such that magic draws nigh!" Lake added.

"Stop it, you guys, we're wasting time," Ari said. "The Council's decision was to avoid attention and to let the Humans discover the truth in due course. So that's what we'll do. Which means no *smashing* unless we have to!"

"Ugh, *fine*," Glam finally relented. "You just don't want to have any fun . . ."

I'm with her, the Bloodletter added from the hockey bag at her feet. *Let's make this a party while we're all the way out here! I mean, then we can prove wrong everyone who says the suburbs are boring! We'll chop up a monster, destroy some stuff, then still have time to hit Uncle Julio's for all-you-can-eat fajitas!*

"No, we're not going to chop up anyone or anything," I said, looking down at the hockey bag. "I already told you that on the train when you tried to talk me into cleaving that ticket guy in two just to see if METRA line employees are actually real people and not robots."

"Talking to your ax again, huh?" Glam asked with a smirk.

I rolled my eyes, but grinned back.

"Guys, let's stay on track!" Ari said. "Now, according to the police reports, an unidentified gray object was seen flying above downtown Evanston just after sunset. It mostly stayed near the Carlson building on Church Street. Which is just three blocks east of here."

"Hence alloweth thyne party receiveth th're posthaste!" Lake said, pointing east dramatically.

Glam picked up her hockey bag of weapons and we followed Lake down the silent, deserted suburban street toward the heart of downtown Evanston.

After a few steps, three squirrels charged ferociously at us from the base of a nearby tree.* I sidestepped one of them and Glam quickly booted it like a football. The other two squirrels squeaked in terror and retreated back toward the tree (which was an Amur cork tree, in case you were curious).

The squirrel Glam kicked recovered quickly and dove into the safety of a bush, screeching what I can only imagine was a long string of squirrel obscenities.

"Geez, will animals *ever* stop attacking us?" I asked. "I mean, just yesterday a pigeon nearly ripped my whole ear off."

"Well, in its defense, you *do* have pretty ears," Glam said.

I rolled my eyes and grinned. It was normal for Glam to try to flirt with me or comment on how cute I was at least three or four times a day. But at this point, I think it was more of an ongoing joke than anything serious—she just liked to make me uncomfortable (had even said I was especially cute when I was embarrassed).

"They definitely won't stop attacking us if we're kicking them around like soccer balls!" Ari said, glaring at Glam.

"Was I just supposed to let it bite me?" Glam shot back. "It probably had rabies."

Since Ari didn't really have a good reply, she merely sighed.

As a rare vegetarian Dwarf (in fact, the only one in existence as far as we all knew), Ari had been particularly hard-hit by the ongoing battle between Dwarves and animals. I wasn't sure what hurt her more: the inexplicable nature of animals' hatred for Dwarves, or the fact that many of us were being

---

* In case you forgot, the return of magic also led to the reemergence of a savage, inexplicable hatred of Dwarves by pretty much all animals. And it'd only gotten worse in the past few months.

forced to defend ourselves in increasingly aggressive ways. Not that we particularly enjoyed fighting off the attacks—but you really don't know fear until you've woken up to find a whole army of spiders trying to crawl into your head through your nostrils.

"*Anyway*," Eagan said as we recovered from the squirrel attack and continued walking toward downtown Evanston, "the fact that the potential monster was flying helps narrow down the options of what it might be."

In the months since the night we rescued my dad from the secret Elven lair inside the huge downtown skyscraper formerly known as the Hancock building, we'd not only continued our magic and combat training, but had also started learning about all sorts of other things, including Dwarven history, Elven history, and all the different monsters and creatures (there were a lot of them) that once roamed Separate Earth and might some-day return with magic. For the most part, the classes were pretty similar to those at my old school, the PEE. Except that there, my Humanities and Math teachers weren't constantly telling me that my life would one day depend on memorizing the Pythagorean theorem or knowing the names of the artists who emerged during the Early Renaissance period.

Unsurprisingly, Eagan was near the top of the class for most subjects.

"Narrows it down to how many?" I asked.

"Well . . ." Eagan paused, doing some calculations in his head. "There are at least one hundred twenty flying magical creatures known to have existed in Separate Earth. And that's only counting the ones documented, so I guess it actually could be even more . . ."

"Yeah, that really narrows it down," Glam said.

"It's a start," Eagan said, but he didn't sound very optimistic himself, even for a Dwarf.

"Well, we know more than just that it flies," Ari said, referencing some printed transcripts of 911 calls.* "Witnesses also said it was gray. So how many flying gray monsters do we know once existed in Separate Earth?"

We all turned and stared at Eagan expectantly. He threw his hands up.

"Guys, I don't know!" he said. "I'm not a walking monster encyclopedia! You're all in the same Monsterology and Creature Classification class as I am, you know. I don't always have all the answers."

"T'couldst be'est a Harpy?" Lake suggested.

"Yeah, Harpies can fly," Ari agreed. "And are generally thought to be gray."

"Okay, what else?" Eagan said. "Who can remember more?"

"I hope it's a Langsuyar Vampire!" Glam said. "They supposedly take the form of *beautiful* women, but how beautiful can they be? They don't even have facial hair! Pfft. I'd love to use my fist as a wooden stake and punch a hole right through her ugly torso!"

"Gross, Glam," Eagan said. "But remember rule one: 'avoid violence at all costs.'"

"Yeah, yeah, I know," Glam said, rolling her eyes.

It could be a Krystallinsk Wyvern, the Bloodletter suggested (only to me, of course, since I was the only one blessed/cursed with the ability to hear it). *Ooh! I hope it is! For eons, I've been*

---

* Not all Separatist Dwarves live in the Underground. In fact, the Council assigned a number of Dwarves to live and work in high places among Humans, such as 911 dispatchers or local government officials.

longing to feel my blade once again slice through their supposedly impervious diamond-encrusted skin! After it's all over, I'll even tell you how to make a Wyvern-skin coat! They used to be quite popular back in Separate Earth, you know. Only the most glamorous people had them.

Next, Ari and Lake each suggested a different hybrid: possibly a Griffin, or maybe a Chimera, respectively.

As we neared the city center, we passed a homeless guy slouched in an alley. I realized he must have heard a good portion of our conversation, because he looked at us like we were walking, talking toasters.

Downtown Evanston was made up mostly of modern, sleek, glass buildings, separated by a few gray stone relics from the early twentieth century. That night, the area was deserted, aside from that homeless guy, and a few cars cruising past on the mostly empty streets.

Our eyes searched the night sky, hazy and orange from the glowing reflections of the nearby streetlights. We collectively looked for signs of a Griffin, Chimera, Krystallinsk Wyvern, Langsuyar Vampire, Harpy, or any other yet-to-be-mentioned monster. But nothing seemed out of the ordinary.

The first sighting had been reported just over four hours ago. After that, a few more trickled in until just after sunset according to our copy of the Evanston Police Department report log. There was no reason to suspect the monster had suddenly vanished. Unless it was one of the few fantastical beasts that could list "spontaneous disappearing" among its powers.

"Maybe it was a Kolossal Dagslända?" Eagan suggested, apparently thinking the same thing. "They supposedly have a life span that is measured by the hour. So maybe it showed up, freaked out some Humans, laid a hatchling somewhere, and then died? Perhaps we need to be looking around for a Dagslända hatchling instead?"

"No," Froggy said calmly.

We all spun and stared at him.

It was often easy to forget he was with us. Even now, after being reunited with his dad (who was also our combat instructor, Buck) and making more friends than he'd ever had at the PEE, he still rarely spoke. In fact, I sort of figured he sometimes didn't even listen to our conversations at all since his ears were often plugged with a pair of earbuds connected to an ancient MP3 player.

"What do you mean, *no*?" Eagan asked.

"It wasn't a Kolossal Dagslända," Froggy said. "It was a Gargoyle."

"What makes you so sure?" Ari asked.

That's when Froggy calmly pointed up toward the roof of an old gray building across the street. Perched on the ledge was a dark gray beast with gnarled wings and glowing red eyes that peered down at us in a decidedly predatory fashion. The creature opened its mouth and let out an anguished shriek before unfurling its massive wings and leaping off the roof.

The demonic red eyes seemed to grow bigger by the second as they soared right toward us.

CHAPTER 2

That One Time When I Accidentally Set My Own Pants On Fire

I f it weren't for Glam, I'd probably be dead.

I was so stunned at the sight of the massive Gargoyle dive-bombing at us that I just stood there with my hands in my pockets and a dumb expression on my face while it swooped in to slice me up like deli meat with its huge claws. But Glam reacted instantly, throwing down the hockey bag full of weapons and unzipping it before I even had to time to fully register what was happening.

The next thing I knew, she was tossing me the Bloodletter. I managed to swing it up just in time to deflect the huge Gargoyle to my left, toward Ari and Froggy. They dove out of the way as sparks erupted from the Bloodletter's black blade.

The flying beast crash-landed just past us, skidding across the sidewalk.

I didn't remember much about Gargoyles from Monster class. In fact, what I particularly remembered from the day our instructor introduced them was Lake distracting me with a steady stream of notes with ancient Dwarven sayings on them. You know, stuff like: *The early bird gets the worm*, or *Time to face the music*, but just Dwarven versions. Like: *Lurbumlir Largefeet's beard isn't getting any thicker* (which means: *Hurry up!*), or: *It smells like fifty rotting Boongrucks died in here* (which means: *It smells awesome in here!*). Lake knew about a thousand old Dwarven idioms and they cracked me up. So he frequently passed them to me scrawled on notes to see if he could get me to burst out laughing in the middle of class. And he usually succeeded. That day, I'd actually laughed so loudly that I snorted involuntarily, choked on my own phlegm, and then got kicked out for disrupting the class.

But before I left the classroom, I'd somehow managed to catch and retain a few details about Gargoyles. Such as: I knew they were made of stone, even when animated. Which partially explained the sparks and why the Bloodletter's blade had glanced harmlessly off it.

The two hockey bags were now empty and we held up our weapons as we formed a half circle around the fallen Gargoyle. It rolled onto its hind legs and spun to face us. Up close, the glowing red eyes were almost hypnotically intense, so bright it was impossible to stare directly at them, but equally impossible to look away.

The beast crouched as we surrounded it. Standing at full height, it would have been close to six feet tall. Its cracked gray wings were huge, likely well over fifteen feet across at full expansion. It had Human-like, wiry muscular arms and legs, talons for feet, and gnarled hands that ended in curved claws that could have gutted any of us quite easily. The Gargoyle's head appeared to be too large for its lithe body, in part due to the massive ram horns on each side of its skull, set below large pointed ears. Its face came to a point, almost like a bird's beak, with a huge grin that revealed dozens of sharp, jagged teeth.

And then there was the beast's hair. Which was a sight unto itself. It graced its head like a crown, despite looking nothing like one. It was short on top between the curved horns, but flowed wildly down to its neck in the back in what can only be described as the world's most frightening hipster mullet.

The mulleted Gargoyle shrieked again.

Glam quickly passed around a flagon of Galdervatn. Although more was leaking up to the earth's surface every day, most of the time it still wasn't enough to allow us to perform magic without directly ingesting the stuff first. That would change in time, of course, but for now it was better safe than sorry, and so we drank greedily from a bison-hide flask emblazoned with the Shadowpike family crest.

Though "drank" doesn't quite adequately describe the experience of consuming Galdervatn. It's more like a vapor than a liquid, for one, and so the only way you can even tell you're swallowing anything at all is the icy freeze that shoots down your esophagus and into your stomach—that, and your whole mouth going numb for several seconds. I also used to think Galdervatn was flavorless, but as we've had more and more of it over the past few months during our biweekly magic training sessions with Fenmir Mystmossman, I've noticed that it does have a very faint, earthily bitter aftertaste.

Unfortunately, Glam and I were the only two who managed to drink any before the Gargoyle launched its next attack, promptly knocking the flask of Galdervatn from my hand with a burst of water that spewed from its mouth like a fire hose. It was forceful enough to send me sprawling back into the narrow trunk of a small American hop-hornbeam tree.

The Gargoyle (who I'd decided to name Mullet) screeched in between more fire-hose bursts of water, its wings flapping madly as it hovered above us. It was like it knew we couldn't take it down. I was reminded then, as the monster blasted Glam backward with a stream of water, of another Gargoyle fact I'd learned in class that day before getting the boot: one potential danger of reanimated Gargoyles was their ability to drown victims by vomiting insanely powerful blasts of water at them.

Lake and Ari swung their swords at the beast, but the blades just glanced away harmlessly amid showers of sparks. Even Dwarven steel couldn't penetrate the Gargoyle's magical granite skin. Which meant we were pretty helpless to fight this thing.

I climbed to my feet as Glam struggled for a desperate gasp of air under the never-ending waterfall gushing from Mullet's mouth. I lifted the Bloodletter, but Froggy, Eagan, Lake, and Ari were already ineffectively pelting the beast with an array of swords and throwing axes. I realized that one more kid taking useless hacks at the Gargoyle's stone skin was not going to save Glam.

Go for the eyes, Greggdroule, the Bloodletter said.

"Please don't use my full first name," I reminded him for probably the hundredth time, as I strapped the ax onto my back and instead pulled free my dagger, Blackout. "But thanks for the tip."

Well, you have a wonderful name, Greggdroule, the Bloodletter said. *Nothing to be ashamed of, Greggdroule.*

I scowled and the Bloodletter laughed, as I ran toward Mullet the flying monster. I did my best to summon a gust of wind using Dwarven magic as I leaped toward the hovering beast's back. After several months of lessons, using magic was getting easier—though it was still far from an exact science. For example, just three days ago during our last magic training class, I accidentally turned our instructor Fenmir Mystmossman's wizard robes into molasses while trying to conjure a set of tree-trunk steps up to the roof of the warehouse. Nobody knew a spell to turn the pile of sticky sap under his feet back into wizard robes, and so class ended early that day, much to our disappointment. But we all agreed later it was worth it to see Fenmir standing there helplessly in his Mickey Mouse *Fantasia* boxer shorts (yes, really).

This time my intended spell worked, and a rush of wind carried me up onto Mullet's back. I grabbed at the small stone horns on the tips of his wings to steady myself. He flailed wildly, but I hung on. I summoned all my remaining strength and flung my right arm around the side of his head.

And plunged Blackout into Mullet's left eye socket.

I know, I know.

Rule number one of MPMs: *Avoid violence at all costs.*

But at the same time, I couldn't just stand there and try to make nice with a creature while it was seconds away from successfully drowning one of my friends! Besides, maybe Gargoyles were quick to forgive and forget? Maybe after all this was over, I could apologize swiftly, and still become buddies with it later? We could all move on, and perhaps Mullet could even come with the Bloodletter and me to Uncle Julio's for fajitas?

It's certainly possible, the Bloodletter said. *You have no idea, over the eons, how many foes my owner and I went and had mead with at a local tavern shortly after chopping off one of their limbs. It's quite remarkable, actually. But maybe losing a hand simply makes one thirsty? I wouldn't know, for obvious reasons.*

I didn't have time to remind the Bloodletter to stop reading my thoughts (something he'd been doing more and more lately), though it likely wouldn't have made a difference anyway. But I was too preoccupied with Mullet's anguished scream of rage and vigorous efforts to fling me off his back by wildly flapping his huge stone wings from side to side. I tried to hold on, but eventually lost my grip.

I went flying, the world a spinning wheel of dark concrete and dim streetlights.

Thankfully, my strong Dwarven bones didn't break when I crashed onto the hard pavement next to Glam. She was drenched and gasping for air. Mullet loomed over us, shrieking, with Blackout's handle sticking out from his left eye socket.

"Um, I think—I think you've got a little—uh—little something in your eye there," I said to the Gargoyle, not able to help myself. "I guess maybe this was an *eye-opening* experience for you, huh?"*

Mullet responded with another cry of rage as he ripped the dagger free and tossed it aside. His glowing eye, which was nothing more than an empty socket emitting red light, looked unharmed. But that didn't mean he wasn't still rightly pissed off about the whole being-stabbed-in-the-eye thing.

"Greg!" Eagan shouted from behind me somewhere. "Run! Run as fast and far as you can. Gargoyles only stay animated if they're near their original perch. If you can get him to chase you long enough, you might be able to run him into suspended animation."

I nodded and quickly climbed to my feet just as Mullet reared back to launch a burst of water at my face.

---

* Even though my friendship with Edwin was basically dead and buried, I still loved lame puns. Unfortunately, my new Dwarven friends didn't find them nearly as funny as Edwin used to.

But I dove out of the way just in time, then ran directly underneath the hovering Gargoyle. And I just kept running. I didn't need to look back to know he was chasing me—I could hear his stone wings flapping behind me like some kind of terrible death-march drumbeat.

I ran as fast as I could. Which, although it was pretty fast for me, still wasn't nearly fast enough to outrun a flying statue with a fifteen-foot wingspan. The Bloodletter confirmed as much seconds later.

You'd better do something! it shouted in my head. *He's going to catch you!*

"Well, aren't"—huff—"you"—huff—"supposed to be"—huff—"some sort of"—huff—"all-powerful"—huff—"weapon?" I gasped out my response.

Sure, but I'm still just an object, Greggdroule! I need a handler! Someone who's supposed to be a hero, remember?

I continued wheezing and huffing for breath, racking my brain for anything that might get me out of this. The flapping wings were so close now I expected to feel sharp talons tearing into my back or a burst of water sending me sprawling. That's when it came back: the very last thing I heard that day in class before our Monsterology and Creature Classification instructor, Thazzum Craghead, kicked me out.

"Gargoyles, heh, just hope you never run into one," he'd said. "They can be notoriously tough to take down. Nearly indestructible. Their stone exterior becomes enchanted and therefore nearly impervious when animated. In fact, two of the only known methods of stopping a Gargoyle are said to be getting it a certain distance from its lair, *or* putting it in direct contact with sunlight."

Of course I was already trying to run him away from his

perch, but I apparently hadn't gotten far enough away yet. Which left one other option: sunlight. But it was well after midnight with a 0 percent chance of sunshine for at least four more hours.

Use magic, you Orc-brained Polywiggle.

While I didn't appreciate the name-calling (or the mind reading), the Bloodletter was right.

Of course, I'd never summoned the sun (or sunshine) with magic. In fact, I wasn't even sure there was an actual spell for that at all. Then again, Dwarven magic was about manipulating the universe and its natural elements, and so it at least seemed academically possible. Fenmir Mystmossman had said a number of times during our magic class that the potential of Dwarven magic was theoretically limitless.

And so:

I focused all my energy on the sun.

I thought about its bright rays bursting through the clouds.

I thought about its heat radiating down from millions of miles away.

I thought about its fiery surface.

I thought about its explosive solar flares.

I thought about its raw energy.

And then my pants suddenly ignited, bursting into flames.

CHAPTER 3

Glam Smash!

Remember earlier when I said Dwarven magic was still far from an exact science?

And also when I said that knowing you're a Dwarf doesn't help you avoid failing like one?

Yeah, well, I think magically setting your own pants on fire while trying to save your friends from a Gargoyle with a mullet is pretty good evidence of both of those statements.

So there I was, running down the main drag of downtown Evanston, my pants ablaze, screaming bloody murder while a huge winged beast was closing in, ready to pounce and put me out of my misery. I wish I could say that in that moment I came up with some ingenious plan to save myself. But honestly, my attempts to escape death really just boiled down to a lot of flailing and screaming.

Thankfully, Gargoyles' favorite method of destruction was water, which tends to put out fires. Meaning, before I could run screaming for too long, a powerful stream of water suddenly hit me from behind. It knocked me off my feet and sent me sprawling forward, rolling across the pavement like a damp log.

It also immediately put out the fire.

A burst of steam erupted from my pants, pluming above me like a miniature mushroom cloud. As luck would have it (I know, I'm as shocked as you are that I actually found some good luck on a Thursday[*]), the steam caught Mullet off guard. With a mighty screech, he swerved wildly to avoid it, briefly startled and disoriented.

That's when I saw my chance.

While Mullet struggled to slow midflight so he could circle back around, I summoned one Dwarven spell that I knew I could do properly.

I rolled to a kneel and put every ounce of my magical will into the gusty breeze blowing in off Lake Michigan, which was just a few blocks away. A torrent of wind collided with Mullet's flapping stone wings. They caught like sails and he soared down the street, away from me and his perch at least a hundred feet in just a few seconds. He likely would have been able to break free from the gust eventually, but it was too late: the damage had already been done.

Mullet suddenly dropped from the air like a stone statue and crashed onto a small Nissan parked on the curb. The roof of the car collapsed as the lifeless Gargoyle rolled off it and smashed onto the asphalt. A single horn and part of its wing broke on impact.

I wasn't sure exactly how far away a Gargoyle needed to be from its stoop to turn it back into inanimate stone, but apparently this was it.

---

[*] Though, technically, being after midnight, it was now Friday. Which maybe helps explain my gloriously fortunate break.

I climbed to my feet, marveling at my good fortune: I'd actually set myself on fire trying to stop the Gargoyle from drowning me. And yet, somehow it had worked. Maybe this should have been taken as a sign that our luck was finally changing—that Dwarves wouldn't always be doomed to failure.

If my former best friend, Edwin, were still around, I could use this to finally prove to him that our constant failure wasn't a self-fulfilling prophecy, after all. But the last time anyone had heard from Edwin was a few months ago, when I'd used that very same wind spell to launch him out into Lake Michigan. Sometimes I wondered if he might have drowned in the harbor by Navy Pier. I had nightmares about it actually—ones where I'd wake up with my clothes soaked in sweat as if I'd drowned in the lake right along with him. My stomach ached even just thinking about those dreams. But I knew they couldn't be true. For one thing, he had Elven magic that surely would have saved him. Secondly, Edwin was a *great* swimmer—he was even on the school swim team at the PEE. But most of all, I knew he was still alive because the Bloodletter kept telling me so, kept reminding me (on an almost daily basis) that I still had a score to settle with Edwin. That as long as he was still alive, *vengeance* for what had happened to my dad had not been realized.

But the Bloodletter couldn't tell me where Edwin was or what he was doing or why nobody had heard from him in months. My leading theories were that he was either moping around in shame somewhere, or in hiding, secretly plotting his next nefarious move. It's weird to say now, but part of me almost wanted to forgive him. To forgive and forget and move on—maybe even someday reconcile our friendship in some flawed, but real way. That was impossible, though, I knew that. My life would never be the same because of what his parents had done. And beyond that, Edwin still surely hated me.

I remembered the look of pain and hatred I'd seen in his eyes back on the pier after our battle. People don't just get over that level of anger. If anything, it only deepens, becomes more resolute. A permanent fixture in someone's mind.

No, wherever Edwin was, whatever he was doing, we were likely still enemies.

But now, out in Evanston, despite having pants scorched down to a few tattered, blackened shreds, I was otherwise, quite surprisingly, unharmed. I figured the fire being of my own magical doing had something to do with that. It sort of fit with everything Fenmir Mystmossman had been saying about the purity of Dwarven magic and how it's rooted in need, not desire, and in protection, not harm (including to oneself).

My five Dwarven friends ran toward me, their expressions a combination of worry and glee. Lake, once he saw I was okay, basically busted a gut giggling over the whole thing. Glam peered down and smirked at my bare legs.

"You call those legs?" she scoffed playfully. "My three-year-old nephew has more muscle than that."

I felt myself blushing, but just shook my head.

She's right, you know, the Bloodletter said. *You've got remarkably skinny chicken legs. Sort of makes you look like a huge lollipop.*

"Man, you're worse than the kids at the PEE," I muttered at the Bloodletter under my breath.

Don't ever compare me to Elves! he said. *Take it back!*

I ignored the ax as Glam took off her still-soaking deerskin jacket and handed it to me.

"Here you go, Princess," she said.

"Thanks," I said with a grin, as I wrapped the soggy sleeves around my waist like an apron.

"Greg, you did it!" Ari said. "You took down the Gargoyle!"

"How did your pants catch fire?" Eagan asked, as he gingerly poked at the now inanimate Gargoyle with the tip of his shortsword. "Gargoyles aren't supposed to be able to create fire."

"Umm . . ." I said, struggling to come up with an answer that wasn't *I stink at Dwarven magic.*

Eagan grinned as he waited for me to admit it was my own fault my pants caught fire, but thankfully Ari kept us on track.

"Guys, sorry to interrupt," she said, looking up at a nearby high-rise apartment building, where curious faces were peering down at us from several windows. "But we need to get out of here."

Sirens wailed to life in the distance, punctuating her point.

"What are we supposed to do with this thing?" Eagan asked, kicking at the stone Gargoyle. "We can't just leave him here, can we?"

"Whence shall ye rival fiend realizeth reanimation?" Lake asked. "Or henceforth nevermore?"

"I guess I don't know if or when they come back to life," Ari said. "Eagan, do you know?"

He shrugged desperately.

"Gargoyles can and will come back to life," Froggy said, startling us all. "But only if they're on their stoop. And, of course, only with more magic."

"So if he never gets put back on his building, then he'll never come back to life?" Eagan asked.

Froggy nodded.

"Whoa, wait," Ari said. "You're not suggesting we just leave him here? After all that?"

"What else are we supposed to do?" Eagan asked. "The cops will be here any minute. We can't just take him back with us on the train! We'll be seen carrying him away for one. Plus, we won't be able to stay out of sight and flee from the cops lugging around a huge statue. If we can even lift it at all . . ."

"But you know as well as I do that more magic surfacing around here is inevitable," Ari argued. "It might not be tomorrow, or even this month, but it will happen again eventually. So if the city mounts him back on his building, then it's only a matter of time before he comes back to life again and all this was for nothing."

"Yeah, but by then the Humans in Evanston will have bigger problems than a single Gargoyle," Glam argued.

"Guys, Froggy said it would also have to be back on its perch," I said.

Froggy nodded.

"So?" Ari asked, looking up in a panic.

By then there were at least a dozen faces staring down at us from the nearest buildings, and the sirens sounded like they were just blocks away.

"So we can solve this permanently if we make sure the city doesn't even bother trying to remount it," I said.

"But how?" Ari asked. "It's nearly indestructible."

"I think that was only in the presence of magic, while alive," I said. "After it became a statue again, the horn and wingtip snapped off pretty easily when it fell."

"He's right," Froggy confirmed.

He was apparently a way better student than we all realized. At least when it came to learning about fantastical creatures.

"Okay, yeah, okay." Ari nodded. "So we just need to find a way to destroy this thing?"

But Glam was already a few steps ahead of us. Eagan cried out in surprise, stepping quickly out of the way as she charged over toward the Gargoyle. Her fists had already magically transformed into two massive boulders.

"*Glam smash!*" she squealed gleefully.

The rest of us dove for cover.

CHAPTER 4

The One Place Where Wearing Wet Deer Pants Gets You Ignored

You'd think that a kid wearing a hunk of damp deer hide around his waist like a kilt would draw a lot of stares and funny looks.

Well, not on a commuter train in Chicago at two in the morning. If anything, most of the people riding the Chicago METRA trains at that time of night actively *avoided* looking at one another, no matter how unusual someone was acting. In fact, the weirder you seemed, the more likely you were to get ignored.

"You really did a number on that poor Gargoyle," Eagan said as we settled on the top floor of a mostly empty train car. "I don't think there was a single piece of the statue left bigger than a baseball."

Glam blushed and ran a finger along her feathery mustache. Her hand then trailed to the dozens of braids dangling around her head. She flicked them back off her shoulders casually.

"I like smashing," she said.

"Clearly," Ari added, but I could tell that she, too, was impressed with the way Glam had basically gone berserk on the stone Gargoyle.

Without her, we'd never have been able to destroy the thing with enough time left over to slip away into a dark alley—all before the cops showed up.

WE could have done better, Greggdroule, the Bloodletter said. *You and I could have made the stone BLEED.*

I rolled my eyes and tried to ignore it. I didn't want to talk to the ax in front of the others again. I had a feeling it sort of annoyed them. So instead, because I knew it would read my mind anyway, I shot back a thought: *Yeah, just like you were able to break through Mullet's skin when he was flying at my face with his claws! And here I thought my talking ax was sharper than any object on earth.*

Ouch, Greggdroule, that hurts my feelings!

"I still wonder if it was worth coming all the way up here to Evanston at all," Eagan said. "I mean, you could argue that we caused the city more damage than we did good. We destroyed a car and a piece of a historical building, and surely at least twenty eyewitnesses saw some part of that."

"No, it was definitely still for the greater good," Ari said. "I mean, who knows how many people the Gargoyle might have harmed had we just left him there to his own devices."

"We'd be better off simply revealing the truth to Humans now," Eagan said. "Dwarves shouldn't be shouldering the burden of suppressing all the monsters cropping up across the globe. I overheard my uncle and Dunmor talking the other night: In some areas of the world, the local sects are stretched so thin for combat-ready Dwarves that they've already recruited some Humans to train—after being sworn to secrecy, of course.

And in a few places, like Peru and New Zealand, they've simply let the monsters roam unchecked for weeks now!"

"I know," Ari said. "But the Council voted. And the side that won were those who want to minimize the damage caused to the Human world rather than tell them what's really going on. So for now, our job is to neutralize the danger of these monsters around Chicagoland as much as we can."

"You're right, of course," Eagan said. "In time, the Humans will need to know the full truth, but for now we have to trust that the Council will know when that time is."

"Yeah, just like they trusted us when I told them I knew where the Elves were holding my dad captive," I said, knowing it was petty to still be upset about that.

After all, that was months ago now, ancient history (relatively). I should have been over it. But I wasn't. Had the Council sent a team of fully trained Sentry warriors to save my dad, things might have gone differently. Perhaps Edwin's parents would still be alive and hope for our friendship would still exist. But I'll never know because they didn't trust me. Or maybe they just didn't trust in themselves as Dwarves?

Ari shrugged. I knew she hated taking the Council's side, but ultimately she believed in the system.

"We all know this decision was about more than just protecting Humans," Eagan added. "We'd be naïve to believe as much. It's so obvious—the Council is determined to try and make allies of the monsters before the Elves do. It has more to do with that than with protecting Humans—as harsh as that sounds."

Ari nodded reluctantly.

"I just wish I knew what those greasy Pointers were up to!" Glam said, slamming her fist into an open palm.

"I thought we were going to stop stooping to their level," I reminded her.

I'd been trying lately (mostly unsuccessfully) to get the Dwarves around the Underground to stop calling the Elves by any derogatory slang names. I often used the argument of how offensive we found it when they called us *Gwints*, and how Edwin hadn't quite understood just how offensive the word was to us. And likely the same was true for our derogatory words for Elves (like *Pointer*, *Langey*, and *Bowster*, to name just a few).

"Sorry, Greg," Glam said half-heartedly, even though I could tell she was more sorry for disappointing me than for actually calling them a disparaging name.

But what she had said was still true: Nobody quite knew what was going on with the Elves. They'd been mostly quiet as a group since our attack on the former Hancock building (an event that had come to be known among Dwarves as the Battle of Hancock Tower). A lot probably had to do with their leaders, Locien and Gwen Aldaron, perishing during the chaos of that attack. And their son and heir apparent, Edwin, disappearing entirely in the meantime. All things that weighed quite heavily on me. I was, after all, part of the reason those things had happened. Even though I hadn't been directly responsible for their deaths, if I hadn't initiated the attack, his parents would almost certainly still be alive. And despite their not exactly being the nicest people, I still never would have wished for their deaths in a million years, even *after* finding out they were responsible for abducting my dad and destroying our family store. Plus, Edwin would still be around—and as hard as this is to imagine now, we might even still be friends.

I'm not really supposed to know this, but secrets are hard to keep in the Underground (likely due to Dwarves being bad and unwilling liars): Recently, Dwarven spies reported back that the Elves were in complete disarray without unified leadership. Several different factions were vying for power and the infighting was making them weak and disorganized. It seemed as though the Elves had never considered losing their leadership a remote possibility, and so few contingency plans were in place. But many Dwarves suspected they would eventually regroup, find a new leader, and come back as strong (and angry) as ever. So the more monster allies the Dwarves could accrue in the meantime, the better.

At least, that was the prevailing logic among many Council members.

Which was why, despite having taken out the Gargoyle, stopping it from hurting any innocent Humans, I still was going home feeling a bit like a failure. We'd broken both of the rules on our first MPM, and had failed to bring back a potentially powerful ally. It felt good to have prevented possible violence against Humans by the Gargoyle, but it wasn't enough to make up for failing the MPM's main objective.

I just hoped my dad—who, though not completely okay, was actually still alive, in case you were wondering—wouldn't be as disappointed in me as I was.

CHAPTER 5

Why You Should Always Bring a Piano with You in Python Country

G reg!"

My dad greeted me the next morning with a huge smile the moment I opened my eyes.

He'd been snoring when I'd gotten back to our small Underground apartment the night before, and I had decided not to wake him for a number of reasons.

"Hey, Dad."

"You made it back alive," he said. "And on a Thursday! What a feat."

"Yeah, well, technically the mission ended early Friday morning," I said.

"Of course!" he said dramatically. "We Stormbellys do our best work on Fridays."

"I just wish we'd been more successful with our mission."

"What do you mean?" he asked as he turned toward our small kitchen to pour me some tea.

My dad was still just as obsessed with tea as ever. Even

after everything that had happened since the time he drank Galdervatn-spiked tea in front of me, unwittingly setting off the crazy chain of events that (at least in part) led us here. And though a lot had changed with him (which I'll get to), it was still amazing to have my dad back even if he wasn't quite the same. Because he still loved tea and still loved chess, and he was actually around a lot more now than he used to be. Our store was gone and there was no need for him to gallivant all over the world in search of our lost magic since, you know, he'd already found it.

"I mean, our mission was to befriend the monster," I said, sitting down at the table. "Not destroy it. Which is what ended up happening."

"Well, that's okay, Greg," he said, setting a teacup in front of me. "You did your best, I'm sure, and that's all that matters. At least it won't be able to hurt anyone now."

He sat down and took a swig of tea. The table was already covered with a nice spread for breakfast: a pan of scrambled eggs laced with brisket and cheese, half a roasted ham, several pounds of homemade bison sausage, a platter of maple-glazed bacon, and a small bowl of grapes.

"Thanks, Dad," I said, taking a sip of tea before scooping a generous portion of food onto my plate.

"But some advice for next time," he said, quickly standing back up like he had something so important to say, it couldn't possibly be said sitting down.

I groaned.

"If you're going to dance with the beast, make sure you bring it a sandwich first!" he declared without any trace of irony. "Preferably pastrami, but anything will do, really."

"Dad, you *have* to know that doesn't make any sense!" I said, almost pleading with him to be reasonable for once.

"Sure it does, Greg," he said, patting my hand as he sat back down. "Sure it does. When you really think about it."

He took another sip of tea and proceeded to stare dreamily up at the stone ceiling of our Underground studio apartment.

That's the thing about my dad now: he may have survived the Elven poison, but he's not exactly *completely* okay. Let me go back and tell you what happened (though, really, there isn't much to tell).

Right after I defeated Edwin on Navy Pier, then got over the shock of seeing almost all of downtown without power (an incident a city official later dubiously explained away to the public as "a circuit malfunction"), I hurried toward one of Edwin's parents' houses. It was the main reason I'd just left Edwin out there in the lake—my dad had been poisoned and was perhaps just minutes from death. I ran nearly the whole way, almost four miles. Or, at least, I would have if I hadn't ~~stolen~~ borrowed a bike about half a mile in. (Hey, you'd probably borrow a stranger's bike, too, if your dad's life was on the line!)

Anyway, after getting there and finding the house deserted, I looked right where Edwin had told me I might find the antidote to the ancient Elven poison. Inside a small compartment behind a huge Chuck Close painting in his parents' bedroom was a stash of Separate Earth Elven artifacts: scrolls and potions and the like. I grabbed everything, stuffed it all into a bag, and then hurried back to the Dwarven Underground.

Foggy Bloodbrew, who was my dad's friend, a Council Elder, *and* the Chief Dwarven Physician of the Underground, examined all the contents I'd brought back. She determined two small vials of strange liquid to be the possible antidote. But there was no way to be sure which was the antidote and which was something else, and there was no more time to spare. My dad could have died literally any second. So I gave her the okay to give him both substances.

And, to this day, we don't know if the *change* was a side effect of the antidote, of the poisoning itself, or of the mysterious, unknown third substance. But either way, the antidote technically worked and he made a remarkably quick recovery from the poison. Except, of course, for the aforementioned *change*.

See, since then, my dad has been kookier than ever. I mean, for the most part he can function and have normal conversations. But at the same time, roughly every hour or so (on the good days), he suddenly feels the need to share what he calls *Kernels of Truth*. Which is something he's never done before.

First, he'll get all mystical and announce some grand bit of *advice* to anyone who will listen. Then his eyes fog over and he just stares longingly at nothing for five or ten minutes, before finally snapping out of it. It wouldn't be so bad if the advice was *good* advice, or made any sense at all. But the fact is, 100 percent of the time it's total nonsense.

And it wasn't just me noticing the effects either. My dad was still a Council Elder, after all. And it's hard not to notice something's up when one of your elected leaders keeps finding the need to interrupt the middle of Council Sessions to announce:

"What we really need to do is: Start bathing our shoes. Yes. Yes, I think if we give our shoes baths at least once a week, that will solve the problem we're having with the ants."

OR:

"A word of advice: If you meet a python, don't play dead, play fast. A piano, I mean, of course. Play it fast!"

OR:

"A *Kernel of Truth* for you all: Red is the best color for foods to be."

I wish I was making those up, but they're really things my dad has loudly announced in the middle of Council Sessions in the past few months. Eagan even heard rumors that Dunmor was considering relieving my father of his position as an Elder. And I had to admit: I wasn't sure I blamed him.

But the problem was that Dunmor *couldn't* actually do that. Or technically he could, as the Council Alderman, but he probably never *would* because it'd be a massively unpopular move. One that would almost surely get Dunmor voted out of his own position during the next round of Council Elder elections a year away.

That's because of the strangest development of all:

My dad was now a Dwarven celebrity.

A living legend.

After everything that happened, he'd become one of the biggest icons in the modern Dwarven world. Everywhere we went in the Underground (and even above in the Human world), Dwarves would stop and stare at him as he passed, whispering excitedly among themselves. If phones were allowed in the Underground, I can only imagine he'd be stopped to take a selfie with someone at least fifty times a day. He was the lone Dwarf, after all, who had predicted the return of Galdervatn. He was the Dwarf largely credited with taking out the Elf Lord and his wife (which was fine by me—I didn't *want* any more guilt for that on my conscience, I felt enough of that in my nightmares as it was). And last of all, my dad was the Dwarf who had cheated death by surviving an ancient Elven poison.

He was a *hero* in the way Stormbellys were supposedly destined to be.

Sure, the other Dwarves noticed he was stranger than ever. But they only took that as further evidence of his genius. After all, he'd always been a little quirky. People had called him nuts for years, when he rambled on and on about Galdervatn and the return of ancient magic—which until recently had been considered nothing more than a wild conspiracy theory. But then he'd been proven right. So now who were they to argue with his increased weirdness?

It wasn't completely bad logic, but just the same I knew my dad and this wasn't him at his best. Something was definitely wrong. And I didn't know when or *if* it could ever be fixed. Foggy Bloodbrew didn't either. She'd been spending all her free time studying trace amounts of the two ancient Elven substances leftover in the vials. But without access to old Elven alchemy texts, it was hard for her to learn much about them. Separate Earth concoctions were governed more by holistic mumbo jumbo and magic than the laws of modern chemistry.

A loud pounding on the door broke both my dad and me from our own reveries.

I jumped up and answered it.

"Fynric!" I said.

"Greg," he grunted with a thin smile.

Despite the fact that he'd been my guardian (and roommate) for a while when my dad was being held captive by the Elves, he still wasn't exactly a chummy sort of guy. In fact, he'd gotten even grouchier somehow than when he used to work at my dad's old store, Egohs (Earthen Goods and Organic Harmony Shop).

"Dad, Fynric is here," I said, turning around and stepping aside.

"Actually, Greg, I'm here to see you," Fynric said.

My dad looked at us from the table, not moving, with a sense of calm that suggested he already knew Fynric was here to get me and not him.

"*Me?*" I asked incredulously.

Fynric nodded.

"Dunmor wants to see you right away," he said. "And he's none too pleased. Not happy at all."

I sighed, figuring I knew exactly what this was about. Behind me, my dad whistled long and low. He was shaking his head slowly.

"Greg, a *Kernel of Truth* for your meeting with Dunmor," he said. I slapped my palm to my forehead. "Talk to him as if you're raking leaves. Raking leaves in the fall. And a squirrel is there, too, watching you both."

Fynric and I exchanged a hopeless glance.

Then Fynric sighed and, with very little humor, said, "Well, come on, then, Greg. Let's go rake some leaves with Dunmor."

CHAPTER 6

Of Course Yet Another Fantastical Mystery Is Explained by a Mystical Object with a Lame Name

It turned out I was right when I said I knew exactly why Dunmor was so angry.

"Tell me again," he demanded of us. "What is rule number one of an MPM?"

Glam, Eagan, Lake, Ari, Froggy, and I were all sheepishly sitting across from him, around his huge stone desk in his Underground office. We stared down at our feet. He'd already made us repeat the rule twice now: *Avoid violence at all costs.*

"It was either that or let it kill us!" Ari said.

"So perhaps you had no chance to befriend the beast," Dunmor admitted. "But did you have to make *such* a scene? What *is* rule number two?"

"'Don't make a scene,'" we all mumbled.

"Well, guess what?" Dunmor asked, moving his hand to his large red beard—almost like it was helping him drive the point home. "You made a scene. Not only in front of eyewitnesses, but several people caught it on camera!"

"They did?" Eagan asked, looking sick.

Dunmor nodded.

"Yes, a video of Glamenhilda smashing the Gargoyle to pieces with boulder fists apparently went bacterial," Dunmor said. "On the Interweb."

"A video of Glam smash?" Glam asked, looking sort of proud.

"Went *viral*?" Ari clarified.

"Yes, whatever it's called," Dunmor said with a dismissive wave of his hand. "Luckily, most of the public, including the major media outlets, are declaring it a fake. Crafty visual effects done by a few Northwestern students."

"For what's it's worth, I'm sorry," I said. "It was all me. It wasn't their fault. *I* caused all the ruckus."

"I know you're sorry, my boy, I know," Dunmor said, his features softening. "The fact is, I normally wouldn't be handling this at all. We've got other people in charge of MPMs. You're not the first Dwarves to violate MPM rules, and you won't be the last. But you *are* the first *children* to go on an official mission. Which is why I wanted to speak to you all personally. There's a lot riding on you six as the trial group for recruiting and sending Dwarven youth on MPMs.

"The fact is: the number of reported monster sightings in the Great Lakes region this week alone is up 40 percent. And a full moon is due in a few weeks, which almost certainly will lead to a great many people finding out they're Werewolves. It's more than we can handle. And so we'd like to start mobilizing more Dwarven youngsters who are as deep into their training as you are. But we have to be sure you can handle it first. And I really believe you can. So you're all getting another chance to prove me right."

"We are?" Ari asked.

"Yes, and soon," Dunmor said. "You'll leave first thing in the morning. Forgive me, I know that's not a lot of time, but as I said, we simply have no other choice. Magic's presence is finally being noticed, and it's getting harder for Humans to dismiss. Tomorrow we'll be sending a seasoned MPM veteran along with you to supervise. And also to help get you there, since it's a bit of a drive."

"Wh're art thy terminal destination?" Lake asked.

"Wisconsin," Dunmor said. "Near the Dells. There have been reports of a strange creature roaming the forest, killing wildlife, throwing boulders at cars on rural highways. We suspect it may be a Rock Troll, with which you're all familiar, I would hope. They're large, destructive creatures, but generally dim-witted and usually easily fooled. Study up this afternoon and then get some rest. You'll meet your chaperone and driver at the west Underground entrance at sunrise."

For a few seconds, there was total silence. I wasn't sure whether it was from excitement, shock at getting another MPM so soon, or utter fear of facing down a possible Rock Troll in the woods of Wisconsin. For me it was partially a mixture of all three, but also something more. Something that had been bothering me lately.

"Thank you," Glam finally said. "For the chance to smash a Rock Troll to dust."

"Glam!" Ari said. "Rule one!"

"Oh, yeah . . . I mean—of course—I meant only if I *have* to."

Dunmor sighed and put his face in his hands.

"Please don't make me regret giving you another chance," he pleaded.

"Before we go, I have a question," I said, not able to hold

back my curiosity any longer. "How do you know all of this? I mean, I'm not trying to doubt you, but just a few months ago nobody even knew magic existed at all, let alone how or when it would come back. But now we have monsters popping up everywhere, MPMs, and all this knowledge about how quickly magic is returning. How do we know all this? And why now? Why is magic suddenly coming back after so many thousands of years?"

Part of me expected my friends to groan with embarrassment. Or nudge me to be quiet and not question our Dwarven World Leader so openly. Or maybe they'd laugh at my ignorance? But they didn't, instead they all turned their cautiously curious gazes toward Dunmor.

He surprised us all by grinning.

"I'm shocked that it took you so long to ask," he finally said. "Especially as Trevor's son. Of course, in his current condition, I sort of understand why perhaps you hadn't thought to ask him these same questions . . ."

I dropped my head—it was true: Though he was still my dad, I barely asked him any real questions anymore. Because most of the time his answers were total gibberish. I didn't know how much I could trust of anything he said anymore.

"It might help me to answer your question if I explain how the Fairies banished magic in the first place, all that time ago," Dunmor said somberly.

At that introduction, my friends leaned forward and I knew right then that this was one ancient Dwarven tale that even they weren't fully familiar with. As if the banishment of magic had been some dark secret that nobody ever wanted to talk about. At least, that is, until we all found out it was coming back.

"The Faranlegt Amulet of Sahar is key to this story," Dunmor began. I tried not to groan at the fact that *of course* it was an enchanted amulet with a mysterious-sounding name that had caused all this. "It was created by the gods upon the very inception of the earth. In fact, some say that it formed the very seed that once was the core of our planet, and that all life and existence grew from it. And the amulet was only later removed from this spot by the Fairies in a time of desperation. Either way, the heart of the ancient amulet was made from a rare, now extinct enchanted gemstone called *Corurak*. It was a stone that apparently glowed and sparkled with many translucent colors all at once, depending on the eye of the beholder. The amulet's whereabouts for many tens of thousands of years was unknown. But what is known is that the Fairies used it to banish magic near the end of Separate Earth."

"How is it possible that one small amulet could do that?" I asked.

"Patience, Greg, I'm getting to that," Dunmor said. "It was foretold that the amulet possessed the power to transform magic into another form. And indeed the Fairies used the amulet to convert magic into what we now know as Galdervatn. But according to the legend, back then Galdervatn wasn't a fog-like substance at all. It was the *Fairies themselves*. They embedded magic into their very souls. And seeing the global destruction magic was causing in the escalating war between Elves and Dwarves, they sacrificed their lives, traveling together as a whole race of beings deep into the Earth's core, burying magic along with themselves in the process in an attempt to save the world. But they could not have foreseen the epic geothermal shifting, the changes to the earth that have transpired over the last few eons. Or that these geological vicissitudes could somehow release magic from its resting place deep within the earth. Nobody did, except for your father, of course.

"But now the Fairies' souls, the strange mist that we call Galdervatn, are escaping, drifting through the cracks in the earth's dying shell, back toward its surface. We know this is happening because we can *see it*. Sometimes the swirls of purple fog can be spotted drifting up from the sewers, or in the burst of a geyser in a national park. And furthermore we can see the signs: the formerly extinct magical creatures. They could not be returning without magic—it's essential to their existence."

"Where is this amulet now?" Eagan asked.

"Nobody knows," Dunmor said. "It's assumed to have been destroyed. But there are some writings among the remnants of the ancient Annals of the Fairies that indicate that before they banished themselves to the earth's core, they hid the Faranlegt Amulet of Sahar inside the magical realm of a cave in an unknown, remote forest. But most consider this to be Orcdung."

"But why?" Ari asked. "So much of the rest has turned out to be true. Why would that part be so easily dismissed?"

"Because it's a paradox," Dunmor said. "It can't be true." He glanced at our confused faces and then sighed before elaborating. "The hidden realm of this forest requires magic for entry. But if magic hasn't existed for years, and technically was already banished when they hid the amulet in this forest . . . then, well, you can do the math on that, I'm sure?"

We all paused to think over what was surely meant to be a rhetorical question.

"But it stands to reason," Eagan started, surprising us all, "that if magical creatures are coming back with magic, then surely so could the magical realm of a secret forest."

Dunmor smiled and nodded.

"That is indeed sound logic," he agreed. "But even if it's true, the sections of the Annals of the Fairies that chronicle which forest it might be, where it's at, how to find it, etcetera, have not been found, and were likely destroyed by the ravages of time, along with most of Separate Earth's other ancient records. And *even if* those records do exist and are found, they still wouldn't fully explain how to find the secret cave within this magical forest, or how to get past the alleged guardian of the amulet. The reality is that the Fairies did not want it to be found ever again—and so if they were, in fact, unable to destroy it, then they did the next best thing: hide it in a place so inaccessible that it would surely never see the light of the sun again. In fact, many believe they simply brought the amulet with them into the Earth's core, and that there is no magical forest or cave at all. Either way, as much as it might be nice to find it, allowing us to harness the power of magic in unimaginable ways, it's not something the Council considers even a remote possibility. The Fairies did not want it found, and thus surely did everything within their power to ensure it never would be. But that's enough for today, I have a lot to do. So off with you now."

We all nodded and then collectively stood to leave.

"Not you, Mr. Mooncharm," Dunmor said. "I have another matter to discuss with you."

Eagan paused at the door, looking equal parts worried and confused.

"It will only take a few moments," Dunmor assured him.

Eagan shrugged at us, stepped back inside Dunmor's office, and then closed the door behind him.

CHAPTER 7

❖ ⟫⟨ ❖

We Knock Around Some Skulls with Other Bones Just for Fun

What was that all about?" Glam asked as the rest of us gathered in the Arena to hang out and relax.

Though Dunmor had told us to spend the day studying, and we intended to, we also needed at least an hour of fun to unwind first.

"Getting a new mission so soon, or Eagan staying behind?" I asked. "Or the whole story about the amulet?"

"Everything!" Glam said.

"Well, I'm just glad we're getting another chance to prove that we can successfully complete an MPM," Ari said.

"Can we, though?" I asked, as I started racking up pool balls in the game room.

Ari glared at me.

Playing games in the Arena had become something of a ritual for us. Almost every day after long hours of magic training with Fenmir Mystmossman, combat training with Buck, or classes with one of our Separate Earth Studies teachers, we'd come to the Arena and play a game of pool. It wasn't just about ignoring or escaping the pressures we were facing, including the impending chaos of magic's return. And it wasn't because pool was symbolic of hanging on to some semblance of the modern world.* I mean, sure, it had become a nightly ritual partially for all those reasons, but also because we *were*, ultimately, *still kids*. Just because a New Magical Age was quickly approaching didn't mean our whole lives had to revolve around combat training and school lessons, did it? We could still make time for fun, right?

Plus, it was helping me learn more about my Dwarven friends. I mean, we had bonded quickly from the start, but I'd still only known them for about three months and so there was a lot about their lives I didn't know.

For instance:

Ari—When I first met her, half her head was buzzed short, with wild, silvery-purple hair on the other side. And I loved it. But it turned out she changed her hair more than once a month, and it was always something fun and different. Presently, her whole head was clipped short and dyed blue, except for a tiny pink rat tail dangling a few inches down her neck. It wasn't my favorite of the four different hairstyles I'd seen her in, but I still loved how boldly different and fun it was.

Eagan—Turned out he was a huge gamer. Despite living Underground, in a place where most modern electronics were

---

* In fact, modern pool and billiards are thought to have been derived from an old Dwarven Separate Earth game called *skalleknuser*. Except in that game, the pool cues were actually sharpened Dragon tibias and the balls were polished Imp skulls. And you don't even want to know what the playing table was made from, or what the real rules used to be. Trust me on that.

banned (though this was rarely enforced since Dwarves believed in personal freedom above all else), Eagan was obsessed with video games. Whenever we weren't all hanging out (and sometimes even when we were), his face was often buried behind a black-market phone or handheld game console, his fingers scrolling deftly across the screen or buttons. He sheepishly called it a *guilty pleasure*, but the rest of us figured a guy who read and studied as much as he did deserved a break from academics from time to time..

Froggy—We all knew he loved music deeply. But we also recently found out that he was somewhat of a horror movie buff, too. He's seriously seen or at least knows about every horror movie ever created. He made us all watch this obscure (and very gory) Italian movie (it's even poorly dubbed in English and everything) from the 1970s called *Zombie*. It was mostly just gross, but there was one very cool scene where a zombie fought a tiger shark underwater!

Glam—She didn't talk about herself very much, so it was harder to find out more about her aside from that she loved smashing things, eating meat, and checking out all the "cute" Dwarven boys in class. But just recently, I found out that Glam played hockey. She used to sneak out at night on Tuesdays in the winter and go to the outdoor rink on Midway in Hyde Park to play pickup games (sometimes even former and current Blackhawks players would show up). She wasn't the best puck handler, but apparently more than held her own on defense, where she could violently crash into other players until her heart was content.

Lake—Because of Lake's insistence on using an English translation of ancient Dwarven, he might have been the hardest of all to get to know. But just a few weeks ago, when everyone else but Lake and I was busy after class with a variety of other duties, I discovered that he loved chess! Ever since, we've tried to play at least one game every Sunday. It wasn't the same as it was with Edwin. Partially because Lake was, quite frankly, terrible. However, it was still fun to play again and to have something unique to bond with Lake over.

"Well, anyway, we will try to do better at the MPM tomorrow," I said, as I continued racking the pool balls.

"We *have* to do better," Ari said. "The Humans need us, even if they don't know it."

Glam nodded and proceeded to break the racked balls with a thunderous CLACK.

"So why do you guys think Dunmor needed to talk to Eagan?" I asked.

"Oh, so you're the only one Dunmor ever needs to talk to privately?" Ari asked. "Do you think you're *special*?"

"No, of course not, I just—just . . ." I stammered. "I mean—I thought—I guess—"

"Relax, Greg!" Ari grinned. "I'm only messing with you."

I forced out some nervous laughter.

They teased me a lot for being a "Chosen One." So far, the Bloodletter was the only recovered magical relic from Separate Earth that had "awakened" and selected a new owner. It was said that many of the powerful, enchanted weapons from Separate Earth had this ability—almost as if they had minds of their own. But only the Bloodletter had confirmed these legends thus far. I was definitely getting the feeling lately that my friends were secretly jealous. The Bloodletter had even suggested as much (quite frequently, I might add). Which of course just made me uncomfortable. I'd never asked to have a telepathic talking ax as a friend, after all. In fact, most of the time, Carl (as the

Bloodletter referred to himself), could be quite annoying. He was always trying to talk me into destroying things just for fun and whatnot.

"Haply Eagan receiv'th companions anew?" Lake suggested.

"No, why would they assign him new classmates?" Ari said. "That wouldn't make any sense. We make a really good team, surely the Board of Dwarven Education can see that."

"Yeah, no way," Glam agreed. "He's probably just thinking about turning vegetarian and Dunmor wants to talk him out of it. They're all worried Ari's propaganda is finally getting to him."

Ari made a face, but didn't say anything. She and Glam were always going back and forth about eating meat. Glam would constantly find ways to eat meat in front of Ari (like the time she sat right next to Ari and gnawed on a massive smoked turkey leg during our Dwarven Civics class). But to Ari's credit, she would simply pretend it didn't bother her. Most Dwarves agreed with Glam that plants were actually more sacred than meat, which only made the whole thing more intense, and almost made me want to take Ari's side, even though I personally loved meat. But I really respected how much she stuck to what she believed, no matter how unpopular it was among her peers.

"Nope, that's not it," Eagan said from the doorway. "And I don't really appreciate the implication!"

Glam's face turned a shade of red I'd never seen before.

"I didn't mean it, like, literally," she said quickly.

"It's fine," Eagan said, striding into the room.

I couldn't help but notice that he was walking differently. Like, he suddenly had more purpose than before. I know that sounds dumb, but it's hard to explain.

"So what was it, then?" Ari asked.

"Well, first, that I can't go with you on the mission tomorrow," he said.

"No!" Glam said angrily, gripping the pool cue like she was about to stab it into the solid wall of stone behind her.

"That's not fair," Ari said. "We need you."

"Wherefore wouldst those gents doth yond?" Lake nearly shouted.

Eagan paused, then a smile slowly spread across his face. I figured it was because he'd only been kidding around, but then I realized it was something else. Something a lot more exciting.

"It's not what you think," Eagan said. "I can't go with you tomorrow because I'll be getting officially sworn in."

"Sworn in?"

"Apparently I'm the newest elected member of the Dwarven Council," he said.

CHAPTER 8

Boz Brightfinger Eats Seventy-Four Swiss Cake Rolls

I can't believe Eagan is on *the* Dwarven Council!" Ari said for maybe the tenth time in the van the next morning.

I couldn't blame her. It *was* a big deal. I mean, there were lots of smaller Dwarven Councils all across the world (called Dwarven Committees), but those only had local jurisdiction, like State Legislatures or something. The Dwarven Council in Chicago was the universal, official governing body for the entire Dwarven World. It was an even bigger deal than if a fourteen-year-old Human kid became a U.S. Senator or Member of British Parliament or something.

"It was a controversial decision to let the vote stand," Bosgroli Brightfinger said from the driver's seat. "He's now officially the youngest Council member in modern recorded history."

Bosgroli "Boz" Brightfinger was the chaperone Dunmor sent with us to Wisconsin for our second Monster Pacification

Mission. He was also charged with driving us there, in an old gray minivan, our cache of weapons stowed in the back.

For nearly the entire three-hour drive, we'd been excitedly chatting about Eagan becoming one of the presiding 125 members of the Dwarven Council.

Most of our information had come from Boz, since Eagan had been too excited (and still sort of in shock) the day before to really tell us much. Also, shortly after breaking the news, he'd had to run off to start preparing. He said it was going to be a lot more work than any of us would have guessed (and definitely way more work than our Dwarven studies classes).

But basically the story was this: Eagan had been anonymously nominated for the Council seat left vacant when his dad died in the Dosgrud Silverhood Assembly Hall Troll attack a few months ago. Per Council rules, all nominees *had* to be put forward for voting. And Eagan somehow won the most votes among the twenty-three nominees, becoming the youngest-ever member of the Council by seven years, breaking the previous record of age twenty-one (held by my very own father, funnily enough).

"He's going to be great," I said, though I still wasn't sure about that.

My doubts had started the night before when I was lying awake in bed listening to my dad snore.

It should be you, the Bloodletter had said, his voice cutting through the darkness directly into my brain. *You should be on the Council, not Eagan.*

No way, I thought back. *Eagan is the smartest kid I know. And logical and honest and kind—almost to a fault. Plus he's a full year and a half older than me, which I know isn't a lot, but definitely matters somewhat. And he's lived his whole life learning about Dwarves* and our culture. I only just found out what I was less than four months ago! I barely know anything compared to him.

Yeah, but he's not destined for greatness the way you are, the Bloodletter insisted. There's a reason I didn't choose him. I mean, I like Eagan, too, even though he's a little soft for me. But you could, can, and will change the world someday. It should be you.

I didn't respond, letting my mind go blank. The truth was, I wasn't sure I really wanted the gig anyway. Too much responsibility for a kid like me: someone prone to setting his own pants on fire and accidentally getting his (former) best friend's parents killed. But I did know I was going to miss having Eagan with us on this MPM. He was always so logical and knowledgeable about everything. He kept us from panicking when things went south, as they invariably did, us being Dwarves and all.

"Eagan will probably be an Elder before he's eighteen!" Glam said proudly from the backseat of the van.

"Well, I don't know about that," Boz said, wiping his brow with his sleeve.

Boz Brightfinger wasn't much older than us. If he were a Human living in the modern world, he'd probably still be in college. He was a round guy, barely fitting into the driver's seat, the steering wheel pressed into his solid gut. He had an exceptionally long black beard (for being so young) that was tied into twin braids that hung nearly to his belt. Boz seemed like a nice guy, but he also produced enough sweat in an hour to turn Lake Michigan into a saltwater sea. And he ate Swiss cake rolls like they were going extinct. Which, shortly after pounding down his fifth package, he reminded us they were.

"I'm going to miss these," he said as dry crumbs of chocolate fell into the tangles of his black beard under his lower lip. "Soon after magic fully comes back, they'll be just another dying remnant of the modern world. A tragedy."

In addition to sweating and eating Swiss cake rolls, he also really liked to talk about all the doom and gloom that he thought the New Magical Age would bring. Or at least that's how I perceived it. I found his stories of freeways packed with motionless, rusted-out cars and roving bands of Humans with torches and shovels battling giant scorpions (savage Separate Earth creatures that he called Jattemawr) dark and terrifying. But I think Boz found this vision of the future exhilarating (except, of course, for the inevitable demise of Swiss cake rolls).

We'd been hearing stories like this from older Dwarves for weeks now. Stories of what the new world would look like. How scary and dangerous it would likely be. But many of them also seemed excited, because they saw a world where Dwarven magic would put us back on top. They saw a future that was terrifying, yes, but also one where Dwarves would once again be in control. We would be the people who rose up and defended the weak, slayed the evil beings, and made the world a safe and wonderful place to live (in theory).

To me, this all felt too grand, too different from what I'd known my whole life—even counting the past few months—to consider it possible. It all still felt like a story they were telling us at bedtime to give us nightmares, and not like something that would actually happen someday soon. I mean, four months ago I'd thought I was just a relatively happy kid, a nobody, another face in the crowd going on with his life as best he could. A life very few people would ever know about. But now I was embroiled in (and to those Dwarves who still believed in prophecies, *involved in*) a world-changing series of events as a fantastical, magic-wielding Dwarf. It was more than I could wrap my head around, telepathic ax aside.

Eventually Boz exited the van off Interstate 90 onto a rural highway.

We were in the Wisconsin Dells now, an area full of forests, lakes, and rivers in the middle of Wisconsin that drew tons of tourists every summer. In fact, I'd once heard some of my old classmates at the PEE call it *the Las Vegas of camping*. I'd never actually been out here before, except to drive through. My dad had never had time for camping in the past because of the store (and, you know, his lifelong hunt for magic).

Boz drove us past the main town, filled with impressive themed hotels (like Mt. Olympus Hotel or Polynesian Water Park Resort). He drove us nearly an hour deeper into the woods and then finally pulled over on the side of a two-lane highway in the middle of nowhere.

"We're here," he said, cheerily wiping away more sweat from his brow.

"Uh, where?" Ari asked.

"At the site of the last reported sighting of whatever creature is roaming these woods," he said. "Yesterday morning something in the forest threw a deer carcass at a passing car right in this very spot. The car managed to avoid an accident, but the driver told police he saw a dark shape running off into the shady cover of the trees. The county sheriff department dismissed it as a hoax. But since we all know that monsters are, in fact, real, we also know it likely wasn't a hoax. Okay, then, out with you, go find the beast!"

"Aren't you coming?" I asked.

"Negative," Boz said, carefully unwrapping another Swiss cake roll. "My instructions were to drive you here and monitor the situation. Only to intervene in case of emergency. This is a test of your skill, remember? To see if the Council was right to enlist the help of Dwarven youth for MPMs. If I come with you, it won't really be a valid test, will it?"

"Pfft, we don't need your help anyway!" Glam scoffed, pulling the van's sliding door open. "Come on, everyone, let's go crush this beast into bone powder—if it even has bones!"

Boz grinned and shook his head at Glam as we all climbed out of the van.

"Someone please try to control her," he said, but we could tell that he didn't mean it—he clearly rather enjoyed her zest for destruction the way most other Dwarves did.

"Yeah, we'll try!" Ari said, sliding the rear passenger door shut.

We retrieved our weapons from the back of the van.

Greg and Carl: together again! the Bloodletter said in his best movie-narrator voice as I placed him into the battle-ax sheath on my back. *Who will perish this time? Will it be another Gargoyle? Or perhaps a whole village of Wood Sprites? Either way, no one can save the large pepperoni pizza they will destroy afterward to celebrate!*

I rolled my eyes, but couldn't suppress a smile. I will say this about my talking ax: Despite its penchant for death and destruction, it was surprisingly cheerful. A welcome change after having spent so much time around Dwarves. Not that my time around Dwarves was all bad. In fact, quite the opposite. In spite of some of our less pleasant characteristics (the negativity, the funky body odors and general refusal to shower more than twice a week, the crass and blunt way we often talked to one another, etc.), I still had to admit that I'd never felt more at home. Living among Dwarves was just so much, well, *easier*, than existing in the modern world above.

For one thing, Dwarves didn't worry about image—we were genuine almost to a fault. Status and wealth generally meant nothing to Dwarves. We were notoriously hard to impress and so nobody really bothered trying. There was no point. Dwarves *are who we are* as individuals, for better or worse. What you see is what you get. But more than that, I'd never felt like I'd had so much purpose in life since moving to the Underground. The training, the classes, it all felt so much *bigger* than anything I'd learned at the PEE. And now MPMs gave me an even more specific purpose, an application for my new skills and knowledge: We were helping to keep peace and order in the world. And I never could have imagined how fulfilling that would feel.

Which was why I was so eager to hop out of this van and do it all over again no matter the dangers ahead (need I remind you of the flaming-pants situation?).

After we geared up with our weapons, we turned toward the dark forest, standing in a line in the ditch by the minivan. We weren't sure what we were about to face. But at least this time we were in such an isolated spot that we didn't need to worry about rule number two: *Don't make a scene.* Then again, should things go awry way out here, our only hope of rescue was a particularly rotund and sweaty Dwarf currently sitting in a minivan putting away Swiss cake rolls and listening to popular-music hits from the 1980s.

So what? the Bloodletter said, reading my mind again. *Let's just storm on in there and chop up everything that moves.*

Geez, Carl, I thought back. *Calm down.*

Hey, just trying to get you all riled up, the Bloodletter said. *Like a fiery coach from a cheesy sports movie.*

How many cheesy sports movies can an ancient Dwarven ax possibly have seen?

Hey, you forget how much time I spent in the living room of that couch-potato Buck.

Fair enough, I thought with a grin.

While I wasn't about to kill a bunch of innocent animals, the Bloodletter was right that I didn't need to be afraid. After all, we'd already infiltrated a secret Elven base *and* rescued my dad together. We'd just destroyed a supposedly indestructible Gargoyle less than forty-eight hours ago. Surely we could handle whatever this was as well.

I was about to make a rousing, inspirational speech to the group to urge them to follow me into the dark and scary woods when I realized my companions were no longer next to me. They were already several feet into the thick of the trees, picking their way fearlessly forward.

"What are you waiting for, buttercup?" Glam called back to me. "A nice walking path to a picnic spot? Come on, let's go!"

I jogged into the forest after them, ignoring the Bloodletter's jeers.

Of course what I didn't know was that we were about to come face-to-face with a savage monster we'd already met once before.

CHAPTER 9

We Become Fancy Dinner Party Hors D'oeuvres

We wandered aimlessly through the forest (dodging savage attacks from birds and little critters along the way) for nearly an hour before we spotted the first signs of him.

It started with the discovery of a dead animal. What kind of animal was impossible to tell based on the condition of the carcass. It had been relatively small, smaller than a deer at least. What was left of it now was just a heap of fur and crushed bones.

"Gross," Ari said, looking away.

"Yummy," Glam said, clearly just trying to make Ari uncomfortable.

Looks like my ex-wife's cooking, the Bloodletter said.

"What would do something like this?" I asked, ignoring my ax's lame joke.

"Tis be but Eagan be'est in thyne company," Lake said longingly. "Ye gent's knowledge of ye pantheon of beasts runneth vast."

He was right, maybe Eagan would know. But he wasn't here. So we'd need to rely on ourselves. Besides, it was like Eagan always said: We were in the same classes as he was, there was no reason we couldn't have collectively learned just as much. Plus, Eagan always insisted he wasn't even the top student in our Monsterology class. I had an idea as to who might be, though.

"Froggy?" I asked, turning toward him. "You seemed to know a lot about the Gargoyle during the last MPM. What do you think?"

He shrugged and said, "Could be a lot of things. This isn't much to go on."

"Maybe it was a Nekimara?" I suggested. "Based on the lack of blood around the carcass."

"No, those are too small," Ari said.

"How do you know it's bigger?" Glam asked.

"Well, the eyewitness accounts, for one," Ari said. "And also that."

She pointed to a pair of trees that had clearly been smashed apart to create a walking path for something huge. At least as large as a bear, but probably a lot larger. Beyond the Y of the split-open trees were several more uprooted ones that had been hastily shoved out of *something's* way.

It was a trail to follow, of sorts.

And at the end we'd find something big enough to smash apart full-grown hemlock trees like tissue paper. And savage enough to crush small animals into unrecognizable piles of fur and bones.

So naturally we headed toward whatever that something was.

Glam took a drink of Galdervatn from her small bison-hide flask, then passed it back to me. I took a drink and handed it to Ari. After taking a sip, she replaced the stopper and handed it back to Glam. Since Lake and Froggy didn't have the Ability to do magic, there wasn't a need for them to drink any.

We followed the creature's destructive trail for nearly a quarter of a mile, deeper into the woods. The terrain slowly sloped up a hill and grew rockier. As the trees became sparser, we would have lost its track (since it no longer needed to smash trees out of its way to get past) if it weren't for the missing rocks.

Every few feet, we'd come across a huge hole that had once presumably housed a massive boulder or two. In some cases, we could even see where a section of stone had been sheared away from an exposed chunk of bedrock by unimaginably brute force.

Pfft, I could do that, too, the Bloodletter said. *Easily.*

Either way, it became abundantly clear that this thing was collecting rocks.

"It's like Dunmor said," Froggy said as we stopped near a particularly massive hole in the dirt with the unmistakably angled impressions of a missing boulder at the bottom.

"What do you mean?" Glam asked.

"He's referring to when Dunmor said they suspect it's a Rock Troll," Ari answered. "Guess they were probably right."

"Do any other creatures like rocks besides—"

My words were cut off by a shadow crossing my face. A shadow cast by a huge boulder soaring through the air, blocking out the sun. Heading directly at my head.

I froze, too stunned to even attempt magic, and surely

would have been smashed into Greg soup if not for a gust of wind hitting me right in the chest. It blasted me backward, out of the way of the boulder just before it slammed into the ground with a fat THUMP!

The hard, gnarled roots of an old Red (Norway) pine tree broke my fall. I wasn't sure whether to thank Glam or Ari for the magic that had just saved my life, but there wasn't really time to ask. A thunderous, gravelly voice screaming from the top of the hill interrupted all customs of polite gratitude.

"DISPERSE!" the voice bellowed. "NO MISAPPROPRIATE STONEY SILICATE MINERALS!"

We let our gazes trace the path of missing stones up the hillside, which ended in a mostly treeless, rocky precipice. Beyond it was a much steeper drop-off leading to a shallow valley of uninterrupted pines and firs, hemlocks and spruces, among others. A dark, massive shape shifted behind the shadow of the tall rock formation at the height of the cliff.

"We don't want your rocks!" Ari shouted up at the shape. "We just want to talk! *Promise!*"

"FABRICATOR!" the voice bellowed. "ENTIRETY MORTALS, STONEY NOTWITHSTANDING, PREVARICATORS AND DECEIVERS!"

"The vocabulary on this thing!" Glam said. "Are we sure it's a Rock Troll? I mean, Dunmor and all the ancient texts say they're pretty dumb."

The beast at the top of the hill cried out in a thunderous rage.

Welp, I've heard enough, the Bloodletter said. *Come on, Greggdroule, let's get on up there and hack this thing to bits. Little tiny bits that we can use as a garnish on our chicken salads.*

The creature finally stepped forward into the sunlight. It was indeed a Rock Troll, as the Council had suspected, large vocabulary or not. At least twelve feet tall and nearly as wide. Its skin was gray and brown earth tones, angular and cleaved like stone.

But Rock Trolls were not actually made of stone, at least not according to the old Separate Earth cryptozoology texts. Obviously no living Rock Trolls had been examined or studied since the times of Separate Earth; according to ancient books, their skin felt like hard stone, but it was made of a wholly organic material, not too dissimilar from elephant or rhino skin, though certainly much tougher. In fact, back then, some Dwarven sects used to make armor from Rock Troll hides, claiming it to be stronger than most metals. The old texts also claimed that Rock Trolls had the brain capacity of a three-year-old Human, at best (though I certainly had never met a toddler who knew the word *prevaricator*—heck, I didn't even know what it meant and I'd gotten into a prestigious school on an academic scholarship). The old books also claimed that Rock Trolls were mostly good for manual labor, that is if one could find a way to properly control them. One suggested method had been offering them rocks and gems to appease them, the rarer the better (with a few exceptions).

As he stood at the top of the hill glowering down at us, suspected thieves, I realized I recognized this Troll. It was the very same one that had tried to kill us all just a few months ago during the Battle of Hancock Tower.

"Kurzol?" I asked.

The Rock Troll cocked his head at me. Then he leaned back and roared at the sky so savagely that several dozen birds took flight from the trees in the valley below.

"NOOOOOOO KURZOOOOL!" he screamed.

He charged down the hill right toward us. A massive boulder was gripped in each hand, ready to bash several small Dwarves into a fine paste that would be spread on crackers and served at fancy Rock Troll dinner parties.

CHAPTER 10

Glam Settles Some Unfinished Business

This time I did not freeze.

It helped that Kurzol wasn't a very fast runner. As he lumbered toward us, he lifted up one of the boulders in preparation to launch it. But I summoned a spell that I had been relatively good at in class and other times of imminent peril.

Several tree roots magically sprouted up from the earth in front of the Rock Troll. They clipped his feet and he fell. He tumbled end over end the rest of the way down the hill. But now we had a huge Rock Troll and two large boulders rolling freely toward us like we were bowling pins.

A pretty typical end result for a Dwarf trying to help.

"Jump!" I shouted.

We all dove separate ways into the surrounding forest, just as Kurzol and the two boulders smashed into a cluster of black spruce trees immediately behind where we'd been standing.

Before Kurzol fully recovered, Lake came charging at him from the woods, swinging a small ax madly around his head in wild circles, a maneuver our trainer Buck had dubbed the *Executioner's Windmill*.

"Lake, no!" Ari yelled. "Rule one!"

But it was too late.

Lake's swinging ax collided with the Rock Troll. The blade clanked harmlessly off Kurzol's midsection. He yelled out in rage and swatted Lake with a quick backhand—sending him flying at least thirty feet into the forest.

"ERRONEOUS DESIGNATION KURZOL!" the Rock Troll screamed, climbing fully to his feet.

Greggdroule, what are you waiting for? the Bloodletter said. *Unsheathe me and fell this beast before he harms one of your friends!*

I willed myself to ignore the Bloodletter, as hard as that was to do. I wasn't going to give in to violence so easily this time. We had to try to calm this thing down before we simply destroyed it. We owed it to Dunmor, at the very least, for giving us a second chance.

Don't be a fool, Greggdroule! He'll kill you all!

Kurzol grabbed his face, still howling in frustration. Then he spotted me. He ripped a young eastern white pine tree free from the ground by its trunk and started swinging it around like a flyswatter as he charged at me.

"Stop!" I yelled. "Stop, Kurzol!"

But this only made him angrier.

"NO *KURZOL!*" he yelled, his gravelly voice almost shrill now. *"KURZOL INCONGRUOUS NOMENCLATURE!"*

I dove out of the way of his tree club. The roots smashed into a bush behind me as I scrambled to my right. What was with this guy? What did he mean by *Kurzol incongruous nomenclature?*

Who cares? Just fell the thing with my blade and be done with it! We may still even have time to grab that pizza later.

"I don't think he likes his name, Greg!" Ari yelled as she grabbed me by the shirt and helped me dodge another wild swing from the Rock Troll's tree club. "Stop calling him Kurzol!"

"I remember you now!" Glam yelled, standing in the middle of the clearing. "Come on, Fluffy, let's finish what we started!"

She threw down her two massive broadswords and motioned for the Rock Troll to come at her.

Oh, yes, this girl gets it, the Bloodletter said excitedly. *I should have chosen HER.*

"Glam, no!" Ari shrieked. "Rule one, guys! Rule one!"

Kurzol grunted, looked at his tree, and then tossed it aside, apparently accepting Glam's challenge to duke this out Dwarf to Troll, no weapons. He charged at her. Glam readied herself, her fists transforming into Glam-smash boulders.

At the sight of her rock hands, Kurzol skidded to a stop, confused and amazed.

"IGNEOUS INTRUSIVE FELSIC ROCK!" he said (even his confused voice sounded like a scream—it turned out Trolls had only two volumes: loud, and deafening). He pointed at Glam's hands. "APPENDAGES MUSCOVITE GRANITE! MY METACARPALS GRANITE?"

He's distracted, now's your chance, Greggdroule! the Bloodletter squealed. *Slay the beast and then we'll build a cool fort with its carcass! No girls allowed, of course.*

"No, not yet," I said under my breath.

Though I knew if Kurzol recovered his wits and killed Glam in the next few seconds, it would all be my fault.

Yeah, it will be, the Bloodletter confirmed.

Glam wasn't sure what to do with the confused Rock Troll now just staring at her hands. She raised the boulder fists and motioned for him to charge again.

"Yeah, you!" she sneered. "I'm going to use these to smash your face, Fluffy! Let's see what you got. Come on."

"RELINQUISH GRANITE APPENDAGES!" Kurzol roared.

"No, get your own!" Glam said. "No Kurzol smash! These Glam smash!"

"KURZOOOLLL NOOOO!" he screamed, and reared back a massive Troll fist.

Glam was ready, taking a defensive position. But it didn't help. Kurzol's fist slammed into her chest.

FLUMP!

Glam grunted as she flew backward into the forest.

"Everyone, stop calling him Kurzol!" Ari yelled.

At the sound of the name he apparently hated, the Rock Troll spun around, glaring at Ari, his pure black eyes barely visible behind the rock-like crags of his forehead and eyebrows.

"You are not Kurzol!" she said quickly. "We know that."

"KURZOL," the Rock Troll thundered calmly. "THRALL-DOM MONIKER."

"Kurzol was your . . . slave name?" Ari asked.*

"ELF IMPOSE MISNOMER KURZOL," he agreed.

"What is your real name, then?" Ari asked, pointing at him and then herself. "I'm Ari."

"STONEY," he said.

"Stoney?" Ari asked, pointing back at him.

"STONEY!" he yelled, pounding his chest.

"Stoney, we just want to talk," Ari said.

"DISALLOWED!" he yelled. "FALSIFIERS. STONEY CANDID. OTHERS UNSCRUPULOUS."

---

* Honestly, I had no idea how she was understanding this thing. He was like a walking thesaurus.

68

This is getting nowhere, Greggdroule, the Bloodletter pleaded, sounding desperate, almost whiny. *Grab me. Chop off his leg. Then the other one. Ooh, we can cut off all his limbs and build a raft with them!*

Ari was about to plead her case again, but it was no use. Stoney (the Rock Troll formerly known as Kurzol) was convinced that everyone but him was a liar. And having lived with Elves for who knows how long, it was hard to blame him. He took several threatening steps toward Ari.

"DECEIVERS!" he shouted.

But he stopped because Froggy had appeared out of nowhere and stood right in his path. He was unarmed. In fact, he wasn't even wearing his combat belt lined with throwing axes anymore. Instead, Froggy held only a single rock in his hands. It was roughly the size of a golf ball, black and shiny.

Froggy said nothing, but simply held out the rock toward Stoney as an offering.

"OBSIDIAN," Stoney said. "BESTOW STONEY?"

Froggy nodded.

Stoney took another step forward, then delicately reached out with fingers the size of Froggy's legs and deftly plucked the pebble-size (to him) stone from Froggy's outstretched hand. He examined it carefully, his face twisted into an odd expression that I could only imagine was a Rock Troll's version of a smile.

Then he suddenly reached forward and wrapped his arms around Froggy and lifted him up. He squeezed him to his chest as we all cried out in alarm. Were it not for Froggy's half-Dwarven bones, he'd surely already have been crushed like a paper cup. But just the same, his face was turning red from the pressure and his silent gasps told us he couldn't breathe.

Stoney was going to squeeze Froggy to death.

Greggdroule, help him! the Bloodletter screamed.

My hand instinctively drew back and gripped its handle. As soon as my fingers grazed the cold metal, I felt an overwhelming urge to pull it free and cleave Stoney in two. I was suddenly convinced that if I didn't, Froggy would die. I envisioned myself swinging the wicked blade at the Troll, slicing it effortlessly through the air.

Glam, who had recovered from the massive punch to her torso, drew her sword, also ready to rush in to the rescue.

"CONSIDERABLE GRATITUDE!" Stoney cried out as he kept squeezing.

He wasn't trying to hurt Froggy; he was merely hugging him to say thanks. Hugging him to death, though. I let go of the Bloodletter (much to its dismay) and my bloodlust faded. The ax sighed sadly.

"Okay, okay, Stoney!" I shouted. "You're hurting him now."

Stoney cocked his head at me like he didn't get it, but his hug loosened, as evidenced by Froggy's desperate but now audible gasps for air.

"CONTRARY STONEY OBJECTIVE!" he said, sounding alarmed.

"We know you didn't mean to," Ari said. "He accepts your thanks."

"You can put him down now," I said. "It's okay."

"Alloweth wend ye gent posthaste!" Lake shouted. "Lest thy gratitude doth procure ye gent's premature demise!"

Stoney nodded and finally released Froggy.

He fell to the ground, wheezing. Glam sheathed her sword.

"STONEY EMBRACE NATIVE MAMMALS!" the Rock

Troll said, sounding sad. "GESTICULATION CEASES. STONEY EMBRACE, VITALITY TERMINATES. WOODLAND AGGREGATE POPULACE ABHORS STONEY."

"Omigods, guys," Ari said (apparently secretly a walking thesaurus herself). "He wasn't out here killing deer and other animals to be vicious. He was just hugging them. Not even aware of his own strength! He was literally loving animals to death."

"Heh, pretty funny," Glam said.

"No!" Ari said. "It's so sad! The poor animals. And poor Stoney."

I helped Froggy to his feet as Ari walked toward Stoney.

"You must be so lonely!" she said, reaching out to pat the Rock Troll's arm.

"ISOLATED STONEY," he said. "STONEY DONATE IGNEOUS MINERALS AUTOMOBILES. ENDOW WOODLAND CREATURES AUTOMOBILES. AUTOMOBILES ABSCOND."

Ari translated for us, and then we all looked at one another in shock (and maybe a little sick amusement). The reports of him throwing dead animals and rocks at cars: He wasn't trying to cause any harm or damage. They were gifts. He had been trying to make friends with the people in the cars.

"STONEY UNQUALIFIED ACQUIRE COMPANIONS."

"*We* like you, Stoney," Ari said. "Don't we?"

"Oh, yeah, for sure," I said.

"Heh, Fluffy and I could become wrestling buddies," Glam said.

"Ye gent couldst becometh thyne wondrous companion merely a fortnight's watch!" Lake added.

"FABRICATION," Stoney said. "PROPAGANDA."

"We're not like the Elves that held you captive," I said. "We don't lie . . . well, not as much, anyway . . ."

"INVENTIONS CONCEAL LIES TO MANUFACTURE AUXILIARY FALSEHOODS."

"Come with us," Ari said. "We can show you a better life than they did."

"STONEY REPUDIATES INCARCERATION," he said, his already thundering voice rising again. "RENOUNCES MISERY REPLICATION."

"We won't hold you prisoner the way the Elves did," I said.

"DENIAL!"

"We have rocks in Chicago," Ari said. "Lots of *rare* rocks and gems."

"PRECISE WHEREABOUTS?"

Now he seemed interested.

"Uh, the, uh . . . the Field Museum!" I said, suddenly remembering a Thursday field trip the PEE had taken there last year. "They have a whole exhibit there. Called, umm . . . the, uhh . . ."

"Grainger Hall of Gems," Froggy filled in.

"We will take you there to see them," I said. "Diamonds, rubies, emeralds. Other rare rocks. Lots of them! We'll take you."

"FICTION," Stoney said.

Then he turned and started trudging back up the hill toward his rock outcropping. I was about to call after him to say it wasn't a lie, but then I realized it was. It *was* a lie. There was no way we could just take a huge Rock Troll to a city museum and not cause total pandemonium.

"You're right, it was a lie," I said, walking after him. "But I didn't mean to. I *want* to take you there, but we can't."

"WHY?"

"Well . . . um . . ."

"STONEY PRESENCE DISTASTEFUL," he said, not stopping.

"Wait, please!" I said, running to keep up with his huge steps. "That's not it . . . it's just complicated. Look, I know how you feel. For a long time I had just one friend. Or I thought I did, but it turned out he wasn't really my friend at all. So I was alone just like you for years."

He stopped but didn't turn around.

"LIE," he said.

"No!" I pleaded. "I really was . . . well, okay, so yeah, I guess I had my dad but he wasn't around as often as I wanted and . . ."

I sputtered out, realizing again that he was right. Even if you didn't count my dad, you had to count Edwin. Being alone is about how you feel in the moment. Whether Edwin was or wasn't my real friend all along didn't matter. I had thought he was and so I truly never felt alone in the way that Stoney surely must now. Plus, I think part of me knew deep down that in spite of how everything ended between us, there was a time when Edwin and I truly were friends. Maybe that was easy to overlook after everything that had happened, but I'd only be lying to myself—and Stoney in the process.

What was this thing? A walking, talking, rock lie detector?

"Okay, but you won't be alone if you come back with us," I said. "That's not a lie and you know it. Since we'll be there with you. Plus, I promise we will go outside and collect rocks for you every day. They may not all be rare, but we will do our best."

Stoney hesitated, still just standing there halfway up the mountain, but also still not looking back at me either. Then he shrugged one of his massive stonelike shoulders.

"STONEY RETAINS ABUNDANCE COMMON IGNE-OUS ROCKS," he said. "STONEY COVETS EXTRAOR-DINARY MINERAL."

"What extraordinary mineral?"

"ANTECEDENT ELVEN SUBJUGATOR HOLD DIS-COURSE ASSOCIATED RECIDIVIST CONCERNING," he said, finally turning around. "SCARCEST MINERAL. SOLITARY. ENDANGERED. UNIQUE. PURPLE GLEAMING MINERAL. RED SHIMMERING MINERAL. GREEN GLIS-TENING MINERAL. ORANGE SPARKLY MINERAL. VOLU-MINOUS HUES. LUMINOSITY. ONE ONLY. ONLY ONE."

"Where is it?" I asked, not really understanding half of what he was saying—the combination of his broken grammar and extensive vocabulary making his speech like a code to decipher. "We can help you find it."

"STONEY PINPOINT," he said. "LOCALITY DIAGRAM."

He pointed at his head.

"You have a map memorized?"

He nodded.

"Well, let's go get it, then!" I said.

"DISTANT," Stoney said. "ISOLATED. STONEY PLUM-MET SALINE TOMB."

Saline tomb? As I stood there trying to figure out what exactly he meant, Stoney turned to start back up the hill again.

"You want the truth, Stoney?" I yelled after him.

He spun around quickly like a dog that had just heard the word *treat*.*

"TRUTH!" Stoney bellowed excitedly.

---

* Or like a dog hearing the word *Dwarf*, apparently, these days. As the four healing bite wounds on my ankles from the past few weeks alone could attest.

"Here's the truth," I said firmly, staring right into his all-black shining eyes. "Others like us will come here to destroy you. That's a fact. I don't like it and don't want them to, but it *will* happen. I won't lie to you. *But.* Come with us, back to Chicago, and give us a chance to be your real friends. I won't let anything harm you to the best of my ability. Come with us; listen to what our leaders have to say. If, after a few days, you don't want to stay with us anymore, then I promise. *Promise.* Promise that we will let you leave. I will break you out myself if I have to. You have my word. This is the truth. The only truth I really know is what I know I will do."

Pretty corny, Greggdroule, the Bloodletter said. *That's some grade-A-Wisconsin-quality cheese right there.*

I ignored the ax and kept staring at Stoney. He gazed right back for several seconds. Then he dropped to one knee and leaned forward so his huge, craggy nose (which was the size of my whole head) was just inches from my own. I did everything in my power to stay firm and not back away. His hot exhales blasted my face with a surprisingly fresh and earthy pine scent.

I'd never seen a stare quite like Stoney's.

He didn't blink. Not once. And without irises or white parts to his eyes (they were literally glistening pools of pure black), I couldn't tell what they were doing or where they were looking or what they were searching for. His gaze opened me up like a bad surgeon looking for something he wasn't sure was there.

No, the Bloodletter said. *He's just a dumb Troll. It's like you're having a staring contest with a crab.*

But I knew that wasn't true. Sure, Stoney didn't exactly strike me as someone who would want to get into the nuances of astrophysics with you. But he also didn't seem nearly as stupid as the old Separate Earth texts attested. His vocabulary, for one thing, probably surpassed that of even the brightest college students. Also, his insistence on all things *truthful* (though perhaps a bit naïve) spoke of great emotional intelligence at the very least.

Finally, the Rock Troll nodded and stood back to full height.

"ACCEPTABLE," he said. "STONEY ACCOMPANY."

Then he brushed past me and started walking back toward the clearing where my friends were quietly celebrating. But as I followed him down the path, I realized that convincing him to come with us without violence was just the first phase of a successful MPM. And maybe even the *easy* part this time around.

Because of rule two: *Don't make a scene.*

How in the world could we possibly transport a twelve-foot-by-ten-foot, thousand-pound, walking, talking pile of rocks two hundred miles back to Chicago with nothing but a small minivan and a sweaty, Swiss cake roll–eating driver named Boz without making a scene?

CHAPTER 11

We Learn That Scooping Poop Could Make Us All Rich

Stealing is wrong.

I know that. You know that. We all know that. But sometimes what's wrong is the right thing to do. Does that make sense or does it merely sound like a desperate attempt to rationalize a guilty conscience?

Well, either way it doesn't matter because the fact is we stole a semitruck.

But we had to. The minivan clearly wasn't going to work. Why they sent us in a minivan in the first place still baffles me—though it surely had something to do with their very Dwarven assumption that we'd fail to befriend the giant monster stalking the woods.

Our attempts to get a Rock Troll home started with Boz suggesting we simply strap Stoney to the roof of the van like a canoe or something. Which, though we were all skeptical, Stoney was game for, and so we gave it a try anyway. A few minutes later we were looking at a crushed, smoking heap of a gray minivan with four flat tires, no inside cabin, and a very sheepish-looking Rock Troll lying on top of it.

Then I suggested that we find a fan bus full of Milwaukee Brewers fans headed to Chicago for tomorrow's Cubs game. Because surely if we threw a Brewers jersey and hat on the hulking Rock Troll, he'd fit right in among the other Brewers fans on the bus. But nobody else was much of a baseball fan and so they didn't really get on board, even after I assured them that there were definitely Brewers jerseys large enough to fit a thousand-pound Rock Troll.

And so it ended with Boz, Glam, and Ari walking to a truck stop a few miles down the road, while Lake, Froggy, and I kept Stoney company in the woods and out of view. A few hours later (a few hours filled with Stoney telling us all about different kinds of rocks he had owned or wanted to own) a massive eighteen-wheel semitruck came barreling down the two-lane rural highway, horn blaring.

I didn't know how they'd stolen it, or from who, and frankly I didn't *want* to know.

The point is: it worked. The truck was built to withstand carrying cargo as large and heavy as a Rock Troll. We opened the back and, with Stoney's much-needed help, ditched enough of the old cargo (massive boxes filled with bottles of some beverage called Spotted Cow) onto the side of the road to make room for all of us.

Boz flawlessly drove the huge machine back to Chicago like he'd been moonlighting as a truck driver since he was ten.

During the three-hour drive, it quickly became obvious that Stoney hadn't had a friend to talk to in a long time—perhaps ever. Because he had a lot of pent-up stories to tell. Despite struggling with syntax, and using words so big we often had to think about them for a bit before getting what he meant, Stoney spent the entire time breathlessly telling us all sorts of rock-related stories.

There was the time he found a pointy rock that he used to scratch his back.

And the time he tripped over a rock but couldn't get mad at it because, you know, it was a rock.

And then there was the time he found a huge diamond the size of a baseball but threw it away because to him, "EXCREMENT DIAMOND. DIAMOND FECES MINERAL."

And of course we can't ever forget about the time he found a buried stash of gold bars. "DELECTABLE," was his comment on that.

Yeah, so it turned out part of why Stoney loved rocks so much was because he ate them. Not all of them, though. We couldn't really get to the bottom of which ones he ate and which ones he merely collected, but it seemed to have something to do with how soft they were, what he referred to as a "MOHS SCALE RATING" or a measurement in "VICKERS UNITS." But regardless, we definitely discovered that gold was his favorite food. And also that when he finished digesting rocks, they, uh, came out the other end as diamonds.

Stoney ate rocks and pooped diamonds.

I couldn't make this stuff up.

But more than all that, he really wanted to talk about the special rock he'd mentioned earlier. The one he had heard his Elven masters talking about. The rarest rock in the world.

"ROCK ONE," he said for the tenth time—he was clearly obsessed with this stone that he referred to as *Rock One*. "STONEY PROCURE. FORTHCOMING. STONEY DETECT ROCK ONE. STONEY DISCERN ROCK ONE WHERE-ABOUTS. DISCOVERY ABSTEMIOUSLY IMMINENT."

Through all his stories, I had to shut out the Bloodletter's insistent voice.

Just cleave this thing here and now, Greggdroule. My blade can pierce his skin. Do it now before it's too late. You don't know these things like I do. You never saw Separate Earth like I did. You can't trust it. He will only cause destruction in the end.

I did my best to ignore it. To pretend it couldn't be right. But the Bloodletter had a point: The ax had seen probably tons of Rock Trolls in its thousands and thousands of years of exis-tence. It *should* know more about them and their nature than I did. At the same time, perception can distort reality. If Separate Earth Dwarves and their weapons were all told from day one to think only one thing about Rock Trolls, then how were they ever supposed to see past that?

Now that we had a real, live Rock Troll with us, I hoped Stoney could change these preconceived notions.

By the time we got back to Chicago, and successfully snuck our new Rock Troll friend into the Underground, none of us ever wanted to see or hear about another rock or stone or gem or mineral ever again. But it had been sort of fun watching this massive Troll (who we'd all assumed was a murderous, raging beast) chat excitedly with his new "CONSOCIATES" about rocks.

But for now, I only hoped that the other Dwarves in the Underground would see Stoney the same way we did. That they would see past what they thought they knew about Rock Trolls. Because I had made a promise to Stoney. To protect him and keep him happy, and not harm him the way the Elves had.

And I intended to keep that promise no matter what.

CHAPTER 12

———————— ❖ ————————

I Learn the Subtle Art of Name-Dropping

I was right to have been worried.

Stoney's reception in the Underground was, well, less than welcoming. As he lumbered along with me, Ari, and two armed guards through the halls toward a large chamber that was to be his room, almost every Dwarf we passed eyed him warily. Or crossed over to the other side of the hallway, as far from him as they could get.

Some even said stuff like:

"Ugh, I can't believe the Council would allow this."

"They better not be keeping that thing near *my* quarters."

"Stupid rock eater."

Stoney, to his credit, either ignored them or just let it roll off his back. Because he remained nothing but calm and courteous. Maybe a little nervous, but I knew he trusted me and so he listened to my every request and stayed composed.

The room they had found for Stoney used to be an armory. Now it was an empty chamber with high ceilings that dripped cold water sporadically and had no furniture of any kind. There was enough space for him to lie down and pace a few steps this way and that. A trough had been set in the corner for his waste (*diamonds*, in case you forgot), and a large pile of rocks (his food, I assumed) was heaped into another corner of the room.

At the sight of his bare, uninviting quarters, my heart sank.

"This is, uh, your room," I said. "It's, um, not much, but . . ."

Stoney pushed past me and looked around the unadorned cavern with dripping walls. Then he shuddered a few times and I thought for a second we were about to get squashed like naïve, overly trusting bugs (proving the Bloodletter had been right all along). But then he spun around with that twisted, awkward stone smile on his face.

"STONEY PROPRIETOR?" he said.

He gestured around him.

"Yes, Stoney," Ari said. "This is *your* room."

"MAGNIFICENT!" he boomed. "STONEY ACCOMMO-DATIONS SANS MANACLES!"

"Manacles?" I said.

"Handcuffs or restraints," Ari said. "The Elves must have made him sleep chained up when they weren't using him as a mindless weapon."

"STONEY SLUMBER UNRESTRAINED!"

One of the guards took a step back, looking nervous.

"I'm glad you like it, Stoney," I said.

He nodded.

"Say, uh, guys?" the guard said. "Can you let me know when you're ready to go so I can lock up?"

"What do you mean *lock up*?" I asked.

The guard scoffed.

"Hey, kid, you can't possibly think we're just going to let this thing roam the Underground freely, can you?" he said.

"But I promised him," I said, clenching my jaw so hard it felt like my molars might crack in half.

"I don't care," the guard said. "That's between you and him. I got my orders. Orders are orders."

Stoney growled.

"GREG VERBAL CONTRACT!" he bellowed. "STONEY AUTONOMOUS!"

"I know, I know," I said to him. "And I meant it. I did. I will take care of this."

Stoney was heaving in anger. He looked seconds from throwing a tantrum, which could have easily caved in the entire chamber.

"I *promise*. I'll take care of it right now," I said. "You trust me, right?"

Stoney nodded.

"And I'll stay," Ari said. "I'll stay here with him while you go talk to Dunmor."

I shot her an appreciative smile.

"Is that okay, Stoney?" I asked.

Stoney nodded again.

"Okay, fine," I said to the guard. "Do what you gotta do. I'm going to go fix this."

"Okay, sure, kid, whatever," the guard said as he followed me out of Stoney's chamber.

The loud echo of the door's lock clacking into place chased me down the hallway.

◆Ⅰ◆

It was probably a little stupid to think I could just show up at the office of the Council Alderman (basically the president of all Dwarves) unannounced and expect to get an immediate meeting, even considering my history with him.

So I shouldn't have been surprised to be turned away by his outer security detail several times. I was about ready to give up when one of Dunmor's assistants happened to be exiting the offices and saw me standing there, looking dejected.

"Foluda, don't you know whose kid this is?" the assistant said to the head of security. "It's Trevor Stormbelly's son."

"You're Trevor Stormbelly's kid?" Foluda asked in shock. "So sorry about that. I—I didn't know. Why didn't you just say so?!"

Okay, so I was having a hard time getting used to my dad being a celebrity. I hadn't quite learned the power of name-dropping yet. Part of it was surely my dad's new condition—I just didn't see how anyone could revere him while he was basically losing his mind right in front of us all. But either way, once they knew I was a Stormbelly, they immediately admitted me into the administrative wing of the Underground. Almost an hour later, Dunmor's secretary, a young bearded guy named Whukgrek Jadehand, was able to arrange a short meeting with Dunmor.

"Ten minutes tops!" Whukgrek said before ushering me into Dunmor's office.

It seemed the approaching return of magic had turned the Alderman's office into pure chaos. As I'd waited for the meeting, there had been people running this way and that with armfuls of scrolls and ancient books, as if everyone was a panicked sixth grader running late for class on their first day of middle school.

"Greg, you can't just do this every time you need something," Dunmor started as he sat down in his small wooden chair, looking flustered. "I have so much going on right now, plus your father is back and so . . ."

His normally well-groomed beard looked stringy and frazzled at the same time.

"This is important," I said.

"Yes, well, so is all of this."

He gestured at the heaps of parchment and scrolls scattered about his desk in piles so disorganized the word *pile* would be offended to even be associated with the mess.

"Okay, I'll get to the point," I said.

"Please."

"It's about Stoney."

"Who?" Dunmor asked.

"The Rock Troll we just brought back from Wisconsin," I said.

"Oh, yes, that," he said. "You will get your credit, do not worry. You kids did an incredible job, just incredible. With that incident alone I should be able to finally talk the Council into allowing more kids to volunteer for MPMs. Rest assured we will show our appreciation in time, but—"

"It's not that," I interrupted. "It's about where Stoney is being held. I promised him he wouldn't be our prisoner. We can't lock him in his quarters."

For a moment, Dunmor just stared at me. His eyes seemed to run circles around my head as he pulled a piece of elk jerky from his pocket and absently chewed on it. My stomach rumbled at the sight of it. Then he finally sighed and placed his empty hand under his sad, damaged beard.

"Right," he said slowly. "Greg, you have to realize that we can't possibly just let a Rock Troll, one who only recently was allied with the Elves no less, roam the Underground at will. It would be irresponsible, negligent even. He needs to be debriefed first. We need to know he can be trusted before freedoms can be granted. I'm sure you can understand that we must look out for the safety of all Underground residents first and foremost?"

"I get that, I really do," I said. "But I wouldn't exactly say he was *allied* with the Elves. *Imprisoned* is a more fitting way to describe the association. He won't cause harm. You have *my* promise. Stoney means well, he really does."

"Greg, please don't take this the wrong way, but we can't govern our society based on the promises of thirteen-year-olds," Dunmor said. "We must instead rely on prudence, intelligence, and history. Besides, it's not my decision to make. This isn't an autocracy. It's a democracy. There are established procedures for *all* incoming potential assets. Every monster or creature or other being brought in after a successful MPM must remain in lockdown until it is fully interviewed, assessed, and determined to be nonthreatening to the general Underground public. Only a Council vote can unlock his chamber door, Greg. I'm sorry."

"How long will that take?" I asked.

Dunmor shrugged helplessly.

"This is relatively new for *all* of us," he said. "Some MPM creatures have been cleared in as little as twenty-four hours. Some still haven't been cleared at all. The Council has been meeting once a day to discuss and vote on every pending case. And so your Rock Troll's case will be discussed and voted on tomorrow along with all of the others."

I nodded and let my shoulders relax a little.

"But I must warn you," he continued. "He *is* a Rock Troll.

And so it's highly, highly unlikely he will be cleared tomorrow. Maybe not ever, given our history with others of his kind."

"What history?" I demanded. "None of you had even seen a Rock Troll in your lives before we brought him here."

"Greg, you know what I meant," Dunmor said. "I was referring to our long, well-documented struggles with these creatures during Separate Earth times."

"So you're going to make decisions based on things that happened hundreds of thousands of years ago instead of based on what you see and hear and witness firsthand now, today?" I asked, hardly believing what I was hearing. "If you don't trust him, he'll never trust you. Keeping him locked in his room will ensure that he never gets cleared. He may even . . ."

I stopped just short of telling him that Stoney could simply break his way out of his room quite easily if he wanted to. Did they really think two locked wooden doors could hold a huge Rock Troll in check?

"May even what?" Dunmor asked, eyebrows raised.

"Nothing," I said, knowing that threatening violence on Stoney's behalf would not help his case at all.

I'd have to figure something else out.

"I'm afraid I'm out of time to discuss this, Greg," Dunmor said shortly. "Will that be all?"

I sighed and reluctantly nodded. This was over for Dunmor for now. But it certainly wasn't over for me.

Not yet.

CHAPTER 13

Fairy Wings Make Wonderful Snacks

My dad was seated at the dinner table when I finally got home. Spread out in front of him was a small feast: a huge bowl of smoked-whitefish mousse, tallow-fried beet chips, a platter of beef tartare, assorted cheeses, and a plate of roasted bone marrow with bacon-and-fig jam.

"Smells good," I said, my stomach growling angrily.

My dad's mouth was stuffed too full of tartare to speak, but he motioned at the other seat, a plate already set out for me. I sat down and scooped a big spoonful of bone marrow onto a beet chip. I hadn't really eaten a proper meal since breakfast. I mean, we did stop at a fast food place on the drive home from the Dells, but three Big Macs and a twenty-piece McNuggets only gets you so far.

After eating enough to calm my angry belly, I finally explained to my dad how the MPM went and what was going on with Stoney.

He nodded sympathetically.

"It's a tough spot," he said. "But it sounds like you did well."

"Yeah, but I didn't," I said. "Not if I can't fix this. I gave Stoney my word, and it will be broken if we have to keep him locked up. I just don't understand Dwarves sometimes, Dad. I mean, we claim to be all enlightened and not like the Elves, who judge people and look out for themselves first. But then in the next breath we're talking about how savage and stupid Rock Trolls are when nobody living has ever really met one before now. I mean, my experience with Stoney doesn't even come close to what the old texts say Rock Trolls are like. It makes me wonder how much of anything I can trust in those dusty, ancient Separate Earth books."

My dad was silent for a few moments and my stomach sank as I fully expected the onset of another round of nonsensical talk. But then he nodded slowly as he took a bite of smoked-whitefish mousse on a beet chip.

"Everyone is misunderstood," my dad said, mumbling with his mouth full. "I've always said that." He paused to swallow his food and take a drink of tea. "You know, I think that if everyone in this world understood each other perfectly all the time, then pretty much nothing bad would ever happen."

I nodded. I wanted to ask him for more. In these rare, brief clear moments, I fully appreciated just how smart my old dad really was. How kind and generous and thoughtful. Things I'd perhaps always taken for granted. I was desperate for his advice, but I was afraid to ask anything at all. His weird new *Kernels of Truth* quirk had been sort of funny at first, if annoying. But lately I'd been finding his lapses into vacant, meaningless wisdoms sort of frightening. It's like he wasn't even my dad anymore when he was having an *episode*. Like he wasn't even a real person. They were creepy and disturbing in the same way as seeing someone sleepwalking.

But I had to keep trying—maybe that was what would finally help him get better?

"What should I do, Dad?" I ventured quietly.

Right away his eyes glazed over the way they so often did these days, and my heart sank into my belly.

"Sage words of wisdom you seek," he said darkly. "And I shall nobly comply with this *Kernel of Truth*: To be without friend or foe is to be at peace. But what is peace without meaning?"

He paused, waiting, as if he actually wanted an answer to his overwrought question.

"Um, maybe—"

"It's bull-horn stew!" He cut me off, raising a finger into the air dramatically. "Boiled and boiled and boiled down to nothing. Until all that's left is the Fairy wings. Which, might I add, are wonderful for snacking. Wonderful indeed. Ah! Don't be so aghast! I am no brute, no barbarian. For they grow back! Ho-ho! I bet you didn't know that, did you? Ha. You did not! Well, it's true: Fairies shed their own wings naturally every few months. Now where was I? Oh, yes, the best way to skin a Barbegazi without poisoning yourself. First, you'll need a yellow lance with blue stripes, a wooden bucket, preferably oak, and a wide-gap grundledung. Then you've got to go to a frozen pond and . . ."

Shaking my head, I was unable to keep a mournful groan from escaping my lips.

I needed to fix this. I could no longer sit by and watch him get worse. Witness him slowly lose his mind. Once I figured out this Stoney problem, and once this MPM stuff calmed down, I would devote everything I had, every last ounce of energy, to finding out what had happened to my dad and how (if at all possible) I could fix it. I couldn't go on like this. Watching my dad become this shell of a Human being was slowly tearing me apart. Even if it meant going to the Elves and begging for their help (since it was their potion that had caused this), I'd do it.

But it would have to wait, since I still somehow had more pressing problems at the moment. Namely: I needed to figure out how to keep a solemn promise I'd made to a new friend.

I stood up from the table, my dad still chattering away to nobody. He wasn't even looking at me anymore. He gazed across the room at a blank wall while he spoke nonsense.

"Thanks for dinner, Dad," I mumbled.

He ignored me and continued his ranting as I left. I had one more stop to make before returning to Stoney's quarters to relieve Ari. It was becoming increasingly evident that I wouldn't be able to fix this tonight. That Stoney would be a prisoner at least for one day.

But I wasn't about to let him spend it in jail alone.

Eagan answered the door in a T-shirt and flannel pants, rubbing sleep from his eyes.

"Greg," he said groggily. "I heard you guys were successful in getting the Rock Troll back without incident. I meant to stop by to congratulate you, but I'm just so tired. There is a lot to learn, being on the Council."

He gestured behind him, where dozens of huge tomes as thick as my head were piled all over his desk and around his bed.

"What are all those books?" I asked.

"The Annals of the Council," he said wearily. "All new Council members are expected to read the entire recorded history of the Council within one month of taking their appointed seat."

He sighed.

"Oh man," I said.

I'd always liked to read, but those books were so thick (and surely super-boring), that they probably added up to more than I'd read my in whole life, times a hundred. Maybe even a thousand.

"Yeah," Eagan said. "I'll be okay, though."

He didn't sound very convinced.

"Well, now I feel bad for bothering you," I said.

"No, no, it's fine," he said. "Come on in."

He stepped aside and motioned for me to sit at the table. It was piled so high with the Council Annals that I couldn't even see the chair across from me. Eagan heaved a huge stack of books onto the floor, creating a sort of window for me to look through. He sat down across from me, his weary face framed by a canyon of weathered books.

"So what's going on?" Eagan asked.

I was still so shook up from what had happened with my dad, I almost led with that. I wanted to tell Eagan how I'd finally reached a breaking point, and maybe even ask him for help. After all, if there was any Dwarf around here who might be able to successfully negotiate with Elves to find out what was wrong with my dad it'd be him (with the Mooncharm family historically being the most effective lobbyers in Dwarven history and all). But that wasn't why I'd come here tonight. Besides, he probably wasn't the right person to complain to about my "kooky" dad, since his dad had actually died* and was gone forever.

So instead I laid out what I'd come for, explaining my predicament with Stoney.

"Can you help?" I asked at the end.

"Well, I can *try*," Eagan said, but he didn't sound very confident. "I mean, I am the youngest Council member ever. And the newest. I have so much more to prove than anyone else. Already probably at least half of the Council won't take me seriously because of my age. But I'll do everything I can to appeal Stoney's case at the MPM Council Session tomorrow."

"Thanks, Eagan," I said. "It means a lot."

And it did. Given the fact that a Mountain Troll had basically orphaned him, it would be hard to blame Eagan for not wanting to help out another one—even if it was a totally different subspecies altogether.

I had to admit it was comforting to find even a few other Dwarves (Eagan and Ari for sure—and probably Lake, Froggy, and Glam as well) who didn't seem stuck on believing the narrative from Separate Earth about Rock Trolls being stupid, bloodthirsty beasts. It actually gave me hope that we could find others who were open to new ideas based on their actual experiences rather than on unsubstantiated claims passed down to them by their dead ancestors.

---

* Between my guilt over the untimely demise of Eagan's dad, the deaths of Edwin's parents and my lost friendship with him, it was a wonder I ever slept at all these days. Though to be fair, when I did manage to fall asleep for a few hours, it wasn't exactly a pleasant slumber filled with dreams of cupcakes and rainbows . . .

As if to confirm this, Eagan looked at me and said: "What's right is right, Greg."

I nodded.

This was why Eagan was now on the Council, despite his age. He had more integrity than any Human, Elf, or Dwarf, kid or adult, I'd ever met. His ethics could not be compromised, not even by his own emotions. The Bloodletter had been wrong before when he'd said it should have been me on the Council. Eagan was clearly the perfect choice—he certainly made me want to be a better Dwarf, which was precisely the sort of people we should have as our leaders.

So why couldn't I muster more hope that he'd somehow find a way to sway the Council tomorrow? But I had to force myself to believe he could. Because a promise is a promise. And for Dwarves, promises actually mean something. So if Eagan failed to convince the Council, my last option would be to break Stoney free and then find somewhere for him to go.

Which surely wouldn't end well for him.

Or me.

Or Chicago, for that matter.

CHAPTER 14

❖

Ari Convinces Me That Killing Your Friend's Parents Is Almost as Bad as Not Eating Meat

When I finally got back to Stoney's cell, I found him and Ari sitting on the floor across from each other.

Ari was laughing. In fact, her face was so red, it looked like she'd been laughing for the entire four hours I'd been gone. Stoney was waving his arms all about him like he was telling an insane story.

"STONEY CRASH!" he shouted in his gravelly, loud voice. "SHALE FRAGMENT. STONEY DISCERN PUERILE AMPHIBIAN AND BLUE CAKE COALESCING!"

It made no sense to me, of course, but Ari kept laughing like it was the end of the funniest story she'd ever heard.

"Sorry I took so long!" I said.

Ari shook her head.

"It didn't feel like any time at all!" she said. "Stoney is *hilarious*."

"STONEY MOTHER COMEDIC ENTERTAINER," he said.

"Wait, your mom was a Troll comedian?" I asked him.

He nodded with pride.

Ari shrugged.

"There's actually a lot more to his backstory," she said, the smile quickly fading. "And it's terribly sad. For one thing, Rock Trolls don't require magic to exist—they never actually went extinct, like we all assumed, when the Fairies banished magic. The Rock Trolls merely went into hiding to escape the being pulled even further into the growing violence of the war between Elves and Dwarves. From what I can tell, there is, or was, anyway, a whole community of Rock Trolls that lived deep inside a vast, mostly unexplored cave system in the jungles of Vietnam for many millennia. They had a whole sophisticated society and civilization down there. For thousands and thousands of years they lived in this sprawling maze of caves undetected. Until the Elves found them several decades ago, when Stoney was just a child. Most of the Trolls got away, but many others were captured or killed, including Stoney. He hasn't seen his family since. He doesn't know if they're still alive. And even if they are, where they might have gone next. There are more unexplored caves remaining in this world than anyone is aware of. They could be anywhere."

Stoney nodded and then dropped his head.

"I'm so sorry, Stoney," I said.

"STONEY RELIEVED HEREDITARY RELATIONS ABSENT," he said. "DOMESTIC SOVEREIGNTY INTACT."

I nodded—he was glad they were gone so they never had to be imprisoned like he had.

"Well, I have some bad news," I said. "I can't get them to unlock your room. *Yet.* But to show you I meant what I said back in the forest, I will stay in here with you until you have the freedom to leave. I don't want you to feel like a prisoner."

"GREG," Stoney said solemnly.

His head twitched several times like he was having a seizure.

"What's wrong, Stoney?" Ari asked.

"GREG," he said again, mashing his block fingers into his deep eye sockets.

"I think he's crying, Greg," Ari whispered to me.

"GREG COMPASSION," Stoney said, his voice strained. "NO PRECEDING MUNIFICENT DEMONSTRATIONS."

I breathed out, my heart aching. If you'd asked me several months ago when this beast was charging at me inside the former Hancock building, aiming to squash me into oblivion, I never would have predicted this was where we'd end up. Me struggling to not cry (and remember: *Dwarves never cry*), while he openly wept because me staying with him was the ~~kindest~~ *only kind* thing anyone had done for him since he was taken from his family all those years ago.

"It's okay, Stoney," I said. "It's the right thing to do. I made a promise, after all."

"STONEY GRATITUDE!" he gushed, then wrapped me in a Troll hug.

"Stoney, no!" Ari and I both started, but it was too late.

I was already in his grasp being very painfully thanked. And if it weren't for my strong Dwarven bones, I would be nothing more than a pile of Greg jelly right now. But eventually he put me down and I gasped and wheezed to catch my breath.

"I did bring you a present, though," I finally was able to say.

From my backpack, I dug out a large geode my dad had brought me once after one of his magic-hunting trips. It was half a sphere, roughly the size of half a basketball. Rounded sedimentary rock on one side and in the middle where it'd been cut in half was a dazzling display of aqua and purple crystalized minerals. Geodes were relatively common and so I figured Stoney might not find it that impressive. But perhaps the fact that it was a gift from a new friend made it interesting to him no matter what it was, because he lunged forward and snatched it from my hand.

"GREG!" he gushed, looking at the geode, which in his hand was, relatively, the size of a golf ball. "RESPLENDENTLY LUSTROUS! CRYPTOCRYSTALLINE QUARTZ SHELL! EPICENTER MINERALS AMALGAMATED TRICOLOR SMITHSONITE!"

Stoney thanked me with another mercifully brief Troll hug and then sat in the corner examining the geode like it was a suspense novel just getting to the good part.

Ari grinned at me.

"That was nice of you," she said.

"My dad gave me that after one of his trips four years ago," I said. "He'd been in Romania searching for Galdervatn back when everyone thought he was a lunatic conspiracy theorist just wasting his time. Of course I didn't know that back then. I thought he was a lunatic tea and soap maker hunting for weird ingredients, still just wasting his time."

"But he wasn't," Ari said.

"I know that now," I said. "But back then I really resented him for being gone so much. So when he brought back souvenirs like that geode, I used to thank him half-heartedly and then just throw them into the back of my closet."

I sat down on the floor and sighed into my hands, shaking my head.

"I'm sure he knew you still appreciated the presents," she said.

"But I didn't," I said. "At least, I didn't think I did. Mostly I was just happy he was home so I could spend time with him and play chess. But when he was abducted a few months ago and Fynric gave me just ten minutes to pack up my things, I . . . well, the first thing I grabbed was an armful of all the junk he'd brought back from his trips, still buried in the back of my closet."

Ari smiled thinly at me and nodded. Then she sat next to me, our backs to the damp stone wall.

"You're really worried about him, aren't you?" she asked.

I glanced up at her and then over to Stoney, who was still in the corner examining the geode as if he and it were the only two things that existed.

"I am," I admitted.

I told her about his most recent episode and how I was now more determined than ever to find a way to fix him. But then I had to admit I didn't know how to even start.

"I mean," I continued, "my one link to the Elves was Edwin. But even if I knew where he was, he'd probably just as soon skewer me with his sword than listen to anything I had to say. Let alone the laughable idea that he might try to help me out."

"You never know," Ari said.

"You didn't see the look on his face last time I saw him," I said. "Pure hatred."

"Hate comes and goes as quickly as thunderstorms in Chicago," she said. "I used to *hate* my dad every time he tried to force me to eat meat at dinner, and then would send me to my room hungry when I refused. But then once I was alone in my room and had calmed down some, I always realized he only wanted what he thought was right for me even though he was still *wrong*. And then the hate softened. It became something else, something more manageable. And even when I thought I truly hated him, I still always loved him beneath it all."

I nodded slowly.

I knew she had had a rough relationship with her dad. He was a Traditional Dwarf. He didn't like the idea that his daughter might have radical new ideas or that she might not think the way Dwarves were *supposed to* think.

"But not eating meat and someone thinking you killed their parents are pretty different," I said. "Even for a Dwarf."

"True," she agreed. "But let me remind you: Edwin did tell you where to find the poison antidote, right? Even right at the moment when you thought he hated you most?"

I nodded.

"And nobody made him?"

"Well . . . no," I said.

"Then why else would he have done that?" she said. "If he didn't still love you as a friend deep down?"

I opened my mouth to disagree. To say that no way could he still have had any goodwill toward me while staring at me with such fury and disgust. But I didn't say that because I realized it was possible, however remotely, that Ari was right.

That if I could somehow find Edwin, it was conceivable he would still help me fix my dad.

CHAPTER 15

※

Stoney: Master Linguist

The next twelve hours alone with Stoney were more interesting than I expected.

Well, we both slept for at least six of them (it was hard to sleep for much more than that on a hard stone floor). But after Ari left to go home and before we fell asleep, Stoney and I spent a shocking amount of time talking. And the conversation was far from boring in spite of his stilted, yet multifarious (a word I learned from him), English.

For one, English was actually Stoney's *fifteenth* (!!!!) language. He spoke Vietnamese much more naturally, which I had to admit sounded both awesome and hilarious in his deep, gravelly voice. He also fluently spoke ancient Elven, Fairy (an old, pretty language called Gaeaellicaa), French, German, two versions of Mandarin/Chinese, five different Troll dialects (Mountain, River, Lowland, Forest, and of course Rock), and a touch of both Orcish and Goblinese. He even spoke some of his native Rock Troll language for me, which to my ear sounded like stones and gravel grinding together. But just the same, it was still strangely eloquent and complex. Stoney claimed that Rock Troll was one of the most efficient, *emotionally adaptive* (whatever that meant) languages in existence.

Furthermore, Stoney actually did like talking about things other than rocks. *Sometimes*, anyway, since he still found a way to work them into every conversation somehow or other. But more than that, Stoney simply had a lot to say. He *knew* a lot. About the Elves especially. Which, in light of the conversation I'd just had with Ari, piqued my interest quite a bit.

I mean, I still didn't have fanciful visions of tracking down Edwin and then dude-hugging (complete with multiple back slaps) in a green pasture with a rainbow in the background and butterflies dancing around our heads with him tearing up and telling me exactly what was wrong with my dad and then even offering to personally help me fix it. I knew chances of that were virtually zero.

However, I couldn't deny that he was still my best hope, among the Elves, of finding out the truth. He was the only one I could conceivably imagine might help me. And so until some other idea magically appeared, locating Edwin was my first step to solving my dad's problem. Plus, as much as I didn't want to admit it, I also wanted to find Edwin just to see him again. To know that he was okay.

Stoney was the one who first brought up the Elves and his captivity. He told me he had spent most of the last two decades locked away in a dungeon. Being trained like a dog to be obedient to his "ELVEN POTENTATES." The few times he ever saw the light of day it was almost always only to do bad things—usually *violent things*—for his captors. His forced "OBLIGATIONS" spanned the globe. Turned out Stoney had already seen a lot more of the world than I had, even as a prisoner. Not that I envied him, considering the circumstances of his many travels (which he said often occurred down in the dark, wet cargo holds of commercial freighter ships).

But Stoney had *not* actually been beaten into submission. It was all an act. He'd merely been pretending to be obedient all those years, biding his time, hoping to avoid further torture while he waited for the right moment to escape.

That's when Stoney revealed the first of two shocking truths:

He hadn't taken out the Elf Lord by mistake that night. He'd done it on purpose. In the chaos of the battle, he'd spotted his chance to finally neutralize his biggest tormenter of all: Locien Aldaron, Edwin's dad and the Elf Lord. And even though you could argue Aldaron had it coming, Stoney still felt a lot of remorse over the whole thing. And I fully understood where he was coming from, because it was something I hadn't gotten over yet myself, even though my role in his death was obviously less significant than Stoney's.

"NIGHTMARE," he said somberly. "STONEY DREAMS CEASELESSLY TRAUMATIC. STONEY LOATHE FATAL UNDERTAKINGS."

I nodded sympathetically.

He then went on to say that in the chaos of the Elves losing all their leaders, he still hadn't gotten away like he'd hoped. Locien's generals quickly apprehended him and punished him severely for being so "careless" during battle. A few days later he was shipped off to a secret Elven base in New Orleans. There, a new leader of an Elven group emerged. And they were planning something big. Something terrible. Stoney kept repeating the words "VILLAINOUS LEGION" over and over again.

"UNMITIGATED MORTALITY," Stoney said when I asked him to elaborate. "UNIVERSAL ANNIHILATION."

"How soon might this happen?" I asked.

"TWO FORTNIGHTS," Stoney said darkly. "SPECULATIONS INSINUATE. PERCHANCE THREE."

Four weeks? Six at most? According to Stoney, the Elven faction in New Orleans was possibly just one month from executing a plan that might lead to a deadly global catastrophe. My stomach turned sideways as I asked him more questions.

But it was hard to get any more details, because Stoney admitted he didn't really know much more himself. He had still been just a prisoner, not a trusted Elven co-conspirator. His days in New Orleans were mostly spent in a dark dungeon with other prisoners. Much of what he learned was mere hearsay from other captives. In fact, once he was transported to New Orleans, it was almost as if he and the other inmates were largely forgotten. It wasn't until the guards simply stopped feeding them one day (which eventually turned into a whole week without food), that they devised an escape plan out of pure desperation, fearing they would otherwise starve to death.

But regardless, Stoney was sure whatever this new Elven sect was planning would have terrible consequences for the rest of us—Humans, Dwarves, Trolls, and all the other newly emerging creatures alike.

"Edwin Aldaron," I finally said. "Do you know or remember him? Locien's son?"

Stoney shook his head emphatically.

Which, despite my obvious frustration at not getting any leads, was also oddly comforting since it backed up Edwin's story that he truly hadn't known the depths of his parents' unsavory activities (such as abducting my dad and holding him prisoner).

"So you don't know if he's the leader of this new Elven faction in New Orleans?"

"UNKNOWN," Stoney agreed. "COMMANDER ANONYMOUS. SPECULATIONS INSINUATE ADOLESCENCE."

My breath caught in my throat.

So it was certainly at least possible it was Edwin. Part of me still desperately hoped it wasn't if what Stoney said about these Elves' plans were true. It was hard to imagine Edwin organizing anything that would lead to *universal annihilation*, as Stoney had put it.

I sighed.

"GREG ANXIOUS FATHER'S NEUROSIS?" Stoney said suddenly.

My head snapped up. He peered down at me, those pure black eyes somehow conveying concern, empathy, and hope.

"You were listening to me and Ari earlier?" I asked.

Stoney nodded. "GREG TROUBLED."

"Yeah, you could say that," I said. "And the real problem is that I have no idea how to go about fixing it."

That's when Stoney revealed his second shocking truth:

"STONEY RECOGNIZE AILMENT," he said calmly. "STONEY ASSIST."

CHAPTER 16

That Time When Dwarves Continue to Be Dwarves

Ari showed up around noon the next day to hang out with Stoney so I could go to the afternoon Council Session. I had to attend for two reasons:

1. I needed to see what happened with Stoney's MPM case. Would Eagan somehow convince them to unlock Stoney's chambers so he didn't feel like a prisoner and thus also help me keep a promise?
2. I needed to convince the Council to send me and a small army to New Orleans both to save my dad and save the world, not necessarily in that order.

Of course, while most Sessions were open to the Dwarven public, it wasn't commonplace to allow just anyone who showed up to speak in front of the Council and the Elders. There were procedures for that sort of thing—you had to sign up for a designated special Session if you wanted to introduce a new topic on the floor. Special Sessions happened only every two weeks.

But, luckily for me, my dad was not only an Elder, but a legendary celebrity Elder. Plus my good friend was now a Council member. And I had a much more personal relationship with Dunmor, the Council Alderman, than most Dwarves. The point is: these are the types of special details that grant you exceptions to rules.

And so I stood before the Council and the Elders and did my thing:

I passionately explained (part of) what Stoney had told me: that there was a new faction of Elves in New Orleans amassing an army. Planning something terrible. And although we didn't know exactly what that was, Stoney was certain it would bring death and destruction to all of us. I finished by imploring them to send a small squad of Dwarven soldiers (me included) down to New Orleans to investigate. In the end, I thought I stated my case pretty well. And I stood there waiting for murmurs of panic, cries of desperation, and calls for immediate action.

"So what?" Elder Dhon Dragonbelly said after I was finished, breaking the short, potent silence. "Elves are *always* up to nefarious things. Why should this report be any different from all the others?"

"All the others?" I asked weakly.

"Yeah, you don't actually think this is the first story like this we've gotten, do you?" Elder Ooj (and lone Leprechaun Council member) asked incredulously.

"I—well—I mean—" I started. The truth was that I had sort of thought that.

Laughter erupted throughout the Assembly Hall. Dunmor quickly banged down his huge stone gavel and silenced the room.

"Greg," Dunmor explained patiently. "We get dozens of reports every week of various Elven factions up to no good all across the planet. We certainly do our best to investigate them all, and take them seriously, but it's a numbers game. Most of the reports don't really amount to much more than a group of Elves devising an unethical hedge fund scam or some other nonsense. Hardly the things we can worry about right now, given the sorts of dangers all the recent monster sightings pose."

Of course I could have told them the *real* reason I was so desperate to go to New Orleans: because I suspected the answer to what was wrong with my dad was there. I was eager to capture one of the Elves there and make them tell me what was wrong with my dad, by any means necessary (that part had been the Bloodletter's idea).

Maybe it would help to tell you everything Stoney had told me the night before, which unfortunately wasn't as much as I'd hoped for:

He claimed he'd seen my dad's described symptoms before. When he was a prisoner in New Orleans, a fellow inmate (an Elf, surprisingly enough—one considered an enemy of the faction for some reason) developed nearly the same symptoms after a few weeks in captivity. Unfortunately, Stoney didn't know if the condition was reversible, but he was sure the Elves were responsible. Before he went mad, this fellow prisoner Elf revealed that their captors had given him some kind of poison, perhaps were even testing it on him. If that were true, it certainly stood to reason that if these Elves knew how to induce the symptoms, they might know how to fix the condition. Of course, the thought that it could possibly be Edwin leading this group also didn't exactly hurt my desire to get down there and investigate.

But it would all be pointless if I couldn't convince the Council it was worthwhile for other reasons. They likely wouldn't see *fixing my dad* as a dire enough need to require an allocation of precious, limited resources (i.e., trained soldiers). And so I decided to keep pressing them with talk of the Elves' larger plan—hoping it would be enough to make them agree.

"But Stoney said what the Elves are planning is akin to 'universal annihilation,'" I pleaded with the Council. "I mean, surely that trumps whatever other reports you've gotten. This isn't some pyramid scheme to make money. We could be talking about an all-out war!"

"Well, see, that's the thing," Elder Heb Blazingsword said. "Your information came from a Rock Troll. And, well, how do I put this delicately? They're morons, Greg. Big dumb beasts that should hardly be considered reliable sources of actionable intelligence."

"But that's not true," I said. "Stoney is just as smart as you or I. Probably even smarter!"

This was met with a chorus of condescending chuckles, offended gasps, and boos from the Council and the audience of onlookers. Dunmor merely shook his head with a wry, yet frustrated grin on his face.

I couldn't believe this. My worst fears were being confirmed: most Dwarves were indeed just as ignorant and prejudiced as their ancestors. Perhaps living modestly Underground, while admirable, had also shielded them from becoming more open-minded. Not that I could say the Human world was perfect in this area, far, far from it. But at least a lot of Humans were *trying* to be better. This felt like a collectively heartless dismissal of Stoney's value to a society. A stubborn refusal to open their minds beyond their precious sacred texts.

"Just because you *like* this—this *Rock Troll* . . ." Elder Dhon Dragonbelly began saying.

"No," I interrupted. "He can speak *fifteen* languages. How many do *you* speak besides modified ancient Dwarven English and modern English?"

Ooj, the often loud and angry Leprechaun Dwarven Elder, scoffed loudly from the end of the table.

"That barely matters," he said. "Anyone can be taught to repeat words. That's hardly evidence of superior intelligence. Cannot even dogs learn words? Or to 'speak' on command? I mean, really . . ."

I shook my head, not quite believing what I was hearing. Did their prejudice toward Rock Trolls really go this deep? Or did others think as I did but were simply too afraid to voice it? I was flabbergasted, so frustrated that I spoke again without even thinking.

"But the key to fixing my dad is there!" I blurted out.

My dad stood suddenly, looking bewildered, as the crowd settled into an awkward and anxious silence. Though most of them still revered him as the One Who Predicted Magic's Return and/or the One Who Destroyed the Elf Lord, they were still well aware of his new, bizarre ailment. Even as much as they tried to ignore it.

"Greg, what on earth are you babbling on about?" my dad said. "I'm perfectly fine! Tell my son I'm fine."

He looked around at the other Elders. They shifted their gazes away uncomfortably. My dad didn't seem to notice. In fact, his eyes were already glazing over; yet another "episode" was imminent, possibly even brought on by the stress of what I was doing.

At least three of the Elders groaned loudly as my dad's finger shot into the air like he had an important declaration.

"A *Kernel of Truth* for such times as these!" he shouted.

"Now look what you've done," Dunmor said sadly in my direction.

"Whenever ignorance rears back its ugly head," my dad began, giving me hope that perhaps this time it wouldn't be complete and utter drivel. "Which, might I add, looks an awful lot like the head of a panda bear! They say ignorance has no physical appearance, but I assure you as sure as I'm standing here today that it very much resembles a lovable panda. But only with more green grass on top. Now, where was I? Oh, yes, I was describing this narcissistic orangutan in a bad wig I once knew. He was a blowhard for a monkey, which, since monkeys can't talk, is quite a feat, buffoonery notwithstanding. Now, the difference between a wig and a Whig is a bit more nuanced. It begins with . . ."

I slowly sat down as my dad rambled on.

The entire Council knew there was nothing really to do in this moment but wait for him to finish. But as I sat there, defeated, knowing I had no more arguments to make, I was at least comforted by the knowledge that I'd tried. After all, what had I really expected? Dwarves were still Dwarves—constantly driven to inaction by their own negativity. The looming return of magic hadn't changed that. Perhaps no argument I could have made would have changed anything.

The official vote would happen much later in the meeting, of course. It was hard for me to harbor much hope at that point.

Then again, as a Dwarf, I sort of had fully expected to fail. But as a concerned son who had already saved his dad from death once, part of me wanted to believe I was finally overcoming our curse and that a vote to send me and a team of warriors to New Orleans might actually stand a chance. Maybe seeing this most recent episode of his (which lasted almost ten full minutes, I might add) would convince many of them that fixing my dad was worth the resources, not even mentioning the possible malevolent Elven plot.

But for now, I would just have to sit back and wait.

Later in the meeting, during the MPM-review phase of the Session, Eagan stood before the Council and the Elders and did his thing—looking rather important in his new Councilperson robes (which were made from bison hide, bison having long been considered by Dwarves to be the most regal of all animals):

Eagan passionately pleaded for Stoney not to be treated like a prisoner. He said we'd be no better than Elves if we continued treating him like that. We'd also be liars. He really dug in hard on the whole Dwarven pride thing, suggesting somehow that Stoney's case alone could define whether Dwarves really were as virtuous and trustworthy as we all claimed to be, or if we were more like the Elves than we thought: deeply flawed and totally capable of being every bit as self-centered and unenlightened, even if it manifested in different ways.[*]

---

[*] It was easy to see why the Mooncharms were legendary for their powers of persuasion and ability to compromise. And why someone, who'd clearly already known that, had nominated him to fill his father's vacant Council seat.

There was very little follow-up discussion to his speech since there was still a lot of other MPM business to attend to afterward. So we both sat there in our separate seats (Eagan with the other Council members up in the stadium seating behind the Elders, and me at a stone table in front) and anxiously waited through all of it. Finally, at the end, the Council cast its votes on all matters discussed during the long, grueling Session.

And it resulted in both good and bad news.

Which one do you want first?

The good news to soften the blow of the bad news? Yeah, that's what I would have picked, too. Okay, then, the good news:

Eagan succeeded. He somehow convinced the Council to narrowly (by three votes!) approve unlocking Stoney's chambers. It did come with some conditions, however, such as: armed guards would remain outside, in the hallway, at all times; and Stoney must always have an escort with him wherever he went within the Underground, at least for now. I figured Stoney would be okay with this. It was certainly better than being locked up the whole time.

But now for the bad news:

"By the official vote of one hundred eighty-six nays to twenty-nine ayes, motion denied," Dunmor announced. "No action will be taken by the Council regarding the reported Elven activity in New Orleans."

I immediately jumped up and shouted at the Elders before I even realized what I was doing.

"No! This is ridiculous!" I knew I should stop, but I was so frustrated and angry I literally couldn't help myself. "Do you all want to die at the hands of these Elves? Is that it? Are you so self-defeating that you secretly want their plan for 'universal annihilation' to succeed? Huh?!?"

Murmurs erupted throughout the Dosgrud Silverhood Assembly Hall. People began shouting at me to sit down and shut up, which then prompted Foggy Bloodbrew (my dad's best friend on the Council) to rise up from her seat and shout at them about having manners. This elicited more yelling, including at least one nasty insult directed at my dad (apparently some of the other Dwarves *were* starting to lose patience with him, even in spite of his celebrity). We were seconds from an all-out brawl when Dunmor pounded a huge rock onto the stone table and called the proceedings back to order.

"Greg, please sit down," he said. "You can't do this every time you disagree with our vote. That's not how a republic works."

"Not until you tell me why," I said. "I came here with vital information. Everyone's safety, the future of the whole world is—is possibly on the line. I mean, why—why would we ignore this? It just doesn't make sense!"

Dunmor sighed, knowing all about Stormbelly stubbornness. And also likely knowing the truth: that although I was worried about what the Elven sect in New Orleans might have been planning, that was not the main reason I was so upset by the Council's inaction. He knew it was more about my dad and the potential cure for his condition that the New Orleans Elves might possess.

Speaking of my dad, he was seated a few chairs away from Dunmor at the table of Council Elders, beaming at me proudly. He'd always been the sort to stand up for what he believed in, even when everyone else called him a fool (which they had for decades before he'd eventually been proven right).

"We owe Trevor's son an answer," someone shouted.

"Yeah, he's a Stormbelly, after all!" another added.

This was met with a surprisingly thunderous rumble of agreement, showing that (for now at least) the majority of Dwarves were still beholden to my dad's status and willing to overlook his new and disruptive idiosyncrasies.

I was starting to like being the son of a famous Dwarf. Sure, it got me stared at a lot in the Arena by other kids. But clearly it also had its perks.

"Okay, fine," Dunmor said. "Please anyone here who voted nay, correct me if I misspeak. Greg, we aren't going to do *nothing*. Rest assured, we'll certainly pass the information along to the local Dwarven sect there in New Orleans, like we do with all reports of Elven activity in other areas of the world. But that's all we can do. The local branch will have to take the rest from there. Frankly, we can't really help *any* of them at the moment, even if we wanted to. We're simply stretched too thin as it is, as you well know."

I slowly nodded and then sat back down.

Dunmor was right. Besides, I was being sort of selfish. I knew for me this was more about my dad than about Stoney's claims that the Elves were planning something evil, and so to expect the Council to use invaluable resources (and risk their lives) investigating something a thousand miles away so my dad would get back to normal wasn't really all that reasonable, considering the other issues we were up against. Namely: all the mythical monsters showing up with each new day, with each new burst of Galdervatn.

However, that didn't mean *I* was simply going to do nothing. I knew Stoney was telling the truth. And that meant I had to do *something*.

Herein was the real problem: What exactly could *I* do?

How could I face a whole army of Elves a thousand miles away all by myself?

But then I allowed myself to smile as the reality of my new life in the Underground hit me in the best way. I wasn't alone. I already knew a trained army of Dwarves (if you wanted to call us that) who would back me up no matter what I was facing.

CHAPTER 17

Yep, That's Me Just Stuffing a Bunch of Poop into My Pockets

STONEY LIBERATED!" Stoney squealed delightfully in his booming, gravelly voice.

I had just broken the news to him: that his chambers would no longer be locked. I made sure he understood the other conditions and he nodded excitedly.

"GRATITUDE," he said, moving toward me.

"No, no," I said quickly, taking a step back, not wanting another painful, crushing hug of appreciation. "That's okay, Stoney. You're welcome!"

Stoney grinned his lopsided rock grin.

"This is amazing," Ari said. "How did Eagan pull that off?"

"He's a Mooncharm!" I said.

She laughed and nodded.

"Oh, yeah."

Despite Stoney's abundant elation, I was finding it increasingly difficult to stand there and focus on anything else but his bathroom trough. In it were two huge piles of glittering diamonds, sparkling brilliantly even in the dim light of the stone chamber. There were thousands of them, and they ranged in size from tiny pebbles all the way up to golf balls. There were literally hundreds and hundreds of billions of dollars' worth of Troll poop sitting right there in front of me.

I smirked.

In part because it truly exposed just how little that stuff mattered anymore. Growing up, money had never really been important to me or my dad to begin with. But soon the New Magical Age would change everything for everyone. *Money* and *valuables* as we knew them would soon be completely useless. Once the Dawn of Magic finally arrived, concepts like *luxury* would cease to exist. At least in the way they did now.

But even so . . .

I walked over to the trough and dug my hand into the pile of diamonds.

"GREG!" Stoney bellowed in horror. "REPULSIVE!"

And I suppose from his perspective it was pretty gross: I'd just dug my hand into a heap of his poop. Seeing the gems up close, I noticed that they didn't look like diamonds from jewelry store commercials.

They sparkled, but were also rough and uneven—not symmetrical at all. Much more like rocks you'd find lying on the ground. Except much glitzier. Ari must have noticed the way I was looking at them.

"They're uncut," she said. "That's why they look like that. Diamonds don't just come out of the earth in perfect, polished shapes. Jewelers cut them down and shape them."

I nodded and then stuffed a huge handful into my pocket.

Stoney shook his head in horror as I lined my pockets with his waste. Ari shot me a confused look.

"I think these may come in handy," I said, putting another handful into my pocket. "I've got some big news. And big plans. I'll tell you about it later. You'll see."

Ari smiled slyly and nodded.

She knew I had something in mind. Some sort of plan. And she was always on board. Though I loved all my new Dwarven friends, I had to admit that over the past few months my relationship with Ari was the only one that had come close to being like the friendship I'd had with Edwin. I didn't yet feel like I could tell her *anything in the world* like I could have with Edwin, but there wasn't much that I'd leave out.*

I also trusted Ari completely, and she trusted me. Which is a vital element to any close friendship. I knew this because she would always back me up when I had a crazy plan. Like, for instance, the time she helped talk the rest of our friends into infiltrating a secret Elven base to rescue my dad even though we had barely any training and no idea what sort of resistance we might run into. Or, less dramatically, the time a few weeks ago when I suggested we ditch our History of Dwarven Political Theory class to go get ice cream. And instead of talking me out of it, her face lit up excitedly. We had a ton of fun that day eating ice cream and then walking through the Garfield Park Conservatory (a tree-lover's paradise). It was well worth the three days of tunneling duty (the Underground was undergoing a massive expansion project—in part to help make room for new MPM allies) we'd gotten as punishment for skipping class.

---

* Perhaps just how much I loved her laugh.

"Okay, Stoney," I said, turning to face him. He looked like he was still having a hard time getting over watching me stuff his poop into my pockets. "We have to go now. But you'll be okay here? They won't lock the doors."

"AFFIRMATIVE."

"You're going to be fine," I said. "I'll come by and see you again later tonight. But after that I may be going away for a little bit. And you will be starting daily meetings with an MPM committee to evaluate your loyalty and stuff. But my really good friend Eagan will always be present. He promised me."

"EAGAN UNSCRUPULOUS?"

"No, not at all," I assured him. "You trust me, right?" Stoney nodded. "Good. Well, you trust me, and I trust Eagan, and so therefore you can trust Eagan."

Stoney hesitated.

"It's okay," Ari chimed in. "Eagan is the nicest person I know. I trust him more than anyone in the world. Even Greg!"

I tried to pretend I wasn't a little offended. Stoney looked aghast, as if I were the Patron Saint of Honesty and there could be no others more honest. Which of course wasn't true. In fact, Eagan was probably the most honorable person I'd ever met.

"I'll be back tonight to say goodbye," I said.

Stoney nodded as he picked up a hunk of talc from a massive pile in the corner. He crunched down on it with his teeth, taking a huge, crumbling bite. Even though talc was often called the softest rock in the world, and thus was very common Rock Troll food, my own teeth ached just from watching as Stoney calmly chewed it like bread.

"Is that good?" I asked.

Stoney shrugged.

"SILICATE TALC TOLERABLE."

"Well, I'll see if I can't trade some of these diamonds for some gold for you," I said from the doorway.

Stoney looked skeptical as to why anyone would trade the most delicious mineral of all for a handful of Troll dung. But he shrugged and nodded.

Ari and I waved goodbye and then stepped out into the hallway. The armed guard closed the door behind us but did not lock it. He glared at me like he was an on-duty cop and I'd just taken away his bulletproof vest.

Once we were down the hall a ways, Ari grabbed my arm and stopped me.

"So what's going on?" she whispered. "What was all that stuff about going away for a while? And why did you take those diamonds? Dwarves don't care about material wealth. Besides, it's only a matter of time before that stuff will be worthless outside of its use in crafting weapons."

"All good questions," I said. "I'll explain soon. Gather the gang and meet me in the Arena in exactly thirty minutes—we don't have any time to waste."

CHAPTER 18

Of Course the Best Pieces of Turkey Are at the Bottom!

I'm proud of you, Greg," my dad said as I sat down across from him at our small dinner table just a few minutes after parting ways with Ari.

I'd come right home and found a huge feast set out on the table: three pounds of spareribs, braised oxtail with sautéed onions and apple-beef gravy, fried pig ears with a spicy mustard dipping sauce, grilled pork jowls with a reduced duck sauce, and one carrot. And as much as I was in a hurry to meet up with my friends (I'd only really stopped by for a snack and to grab my old backpack), it was hard to turn down sitting for a quick dinner with my dad. Especially since he appeared to be momentarily lucid. Plus, he'd clearly gone to a lot of work preparing all this food and was still an awesome cook. The Elven poison and/or antidote hadn't changed that at least.

I figured I could eat hastily and still be just a few minutes late to the Arena.

"You stood up to the Council, stood up for what you believe in," he continued. "A sign of a true Stormbelly."

"Thanks, Dad," I said, afraid to say much more lest it set off another bizarre rambling episode of strange advice.

He nodded and stuffed a handful of crispy sliced pig ears into his mouth. We ate in silence for a while.

I desperately wanted to ask him more, ask for his *real advice*. Was what I was planning right or wrong? It was likely to be dangerous, poorly planned, and would once again put the lives of my friends at risk. Would it all be worth it? In that moment I just wanted my old dad back, someone I could go to for guidance.

Well, there's your answer, Greggdroule, the Bloodletter said from under my bed. *This is the only way you can have that again. Together, we can make the Elves fix it.*

Of course my ax was correct. The answer to whether this was worth going through with was right there in front of me in the form of the very reason I was agonizing over it all: my dad. All I wanted in the whole world was for him to be back to normal. And my plans (however dangerous they might be) could potentially lead to that. That was worth not only the risk of death and personal injury, but also the wrath likely to be caused by my once again directly ignoring the Council's wishes.

Part of me, as I was sitting there staring at my dad, afraid to speak to him, felt guilty and ungrateful. Just a few months ago, I thought I would never see him again at all. Having him back, even with a weird condition, was still better than losing a dad forever like Edwin had. And despite what everyone else thought of Locien Aldaron, I knew that Edwin had idolized him. He hadn't been able to see the bad in him.

Don't get distracted, Greggdroule, the Bloodletter chimed in.

What happened to your friend doesn't matter anymore. Let me remind you that Locien is the reason your dad has become this shell of a man. Isn't having this version of him around almost kind of worse than losing him forever? Edwin's dad might be gone, but at least Edwin's memories of him are untarnished. Whereas yours are being corrupted by the reality of what Trevor is now. No, you must go on with this plan. We must get to New Orleans and capture a high-ranking Elf. The Elves must either fix this or pay the price for what they've done.

I still don't know, I thought. *I mean, maybe I should just be happy with what I have? Isn't always wanting more than you already have Elven thinking?*

Go on, ask your dad what he thinks, then, the ax replied. *See what he says.*

I knew this was a trick or test of some sort, but I also so badly wanted to ask my dad for his advice that I played along anyway.

"I don't know how far to take it, though," I said to my dad.

"Hmm?" he asked through a mouthful of meat.

"What I believe in," I said. "I stood my ground today, sure, but the Council still said no. I mean, I feel like there's more I should do. I believe Stoney. I believe something terrible is happening in New Orleans, among *other reasons* to go. Can I really just do nothing about it?"

My dad leaned back. His eyes began to glaze over and I almost groaned in despair knowing what was coming next. But to my surprise, he seemed to fight it off this time.

"Greg, you know how I feel," he said, as a rare moment of clarity pierced his eyes. "I've always supported doing what you believe is right. No matter what. As long as it's for the benefit of more than just yourself."

See? the Bloodletter said smugly. *He agrees with me.*

I nodded, equal parts relieved and terrified. My dad had essentially just given me his blessing. Which meant a lot of danger was potentially ahead of my friends and me—even though it was for the greater good.

"Then again, there's always this little *Kernel of Truth*," my dad declared suddenly, losing his struggle to hold it off and going into full-gone mode. "Sometimes the best pieces of turkey are the ones at the bottom! Like that catfish! What was his name? Oh, yes, General Sherman. Don't try to catch General Sherman when everything else you care about is on the line! I mean, forget about those weirdos in the bait shop . . ."

Another reason to go, Greggdroule, the Bloodletter interjected, twisting a knife in my guts. *This can't keep happening. You need your real dad back. Plus, you're forgetting about possibly finding Edwin. About foiling a nefarious and devastating Elven plot. It's basically like your dad said before he lost his marbles again: This is what's right and it's for the benefit of everyone, not just for you.*

The Bloodletter was right, of course. He usually was. (At least in the times when he wasn't suggesting that I cleave someone or something in two just for giggles.)

"Okay, Dad," I said as he continued to ramble on about a giant catfish named General Sherman. "Okay." I stood up from the table. "Look, I have to go meet my friends in the Arena. Thank you for dinner."

I gave his shoulder a pat, but he barely noticed. He'd already moved on to advice about how to appropriately summon someone called Mr. Meeseeks.

But there was no doubt he'd held it off just long enough to give me some real advice: to keep fighting for what I knew was right. No matter how crazy and dangerous that was going to be. And stopping the Elves' plans, finding Edwin, and, most important of all, finding a cure for my dad was right.

I just hoped my friends would view it the same way.

—•I•—

"Of course we're in!" Ari said.

"Yeah, what'd you think?" Glam added. "That we'd pass up a chance to tangle with a bunch of scheming Elves?!"

"Thy wouldst be'est rendered a clotpole lest thy join!" Lake said.

Froggy nodded at me silently, but I noticed his eyes were elsewhere.

"I can't go, of course," Eagan said, before I could ask Froggy if anything was wrong. "But I will do everything I can to help from here, including making sure they keep treating Stoney well. And I'll try to help cover your tracks once the Council finds out you're gone. But . . . I can't lie to them, you all know that, so they will figure it out eventually. Which means once you're there, you'll likely have a limited time to find these Elves and figure out what they're up to."

I nodded.

I'd just finished telling them all about what Stoney had told me. How the Elves were planning *universal annihilation* and how the Council had basically dismissed it as dumb Troll ramblings.

Of course, I'd mostly left out the part about my dad. Or the fact that their leader might be Edwin (though I still hoped not, since it would mean his conscience was totally gone). I wasn't even entirely sure myself why I omitted these factors from what

127

I told my friends, but the Bloodletter had insisted it'd be better that way. That it would be more pure to the cause to focus on what was more important to the world and not on what was important to me.

Don't use your own inner turmoil to manipulate them, he'd said. *Focus on the larger issues, the things that will help everyone. Like preventing these dastardly Elves from initiating their cruel plans, whatever they may be. You and I alone, once there, will deal with finding a fix for your dad.*

To be honest, I never really doubted that my friends would join. Not after the way they'd all jumped in and risked their lives to help me save my dad a few months ago. Back then we hadn't even known each other that well, and they'd still come along without hesitation.

"How will we get there?" Glam asked. "Isn't New Orleans, like, really far away? I've never been on a plane before."

"Me neither," Ari said.

"None of us have," Eagan said.

"We can't fly," I said.

"Wherefore not?" Lake asked, looking disappointed.

"Because the TSA probably won't allow a bunch of kids traveling alone to check several hockey bags stuffed with swords and axes and other weapons on a plane," I said. "So we will take the train. I took the train to Seattle once with my dad when I was eight and they didn't even glance at our bags or wonder what was in them."

"There's still a money issue, though," Eagan said. "I assume that five round-trip train tickets from here to New Orleans are going to cost a lot."

"Don't worry about that," I said with a grin. "I've got it covered."

CHAPTER 19

Grootock Shatterbuckle's Tuitions of Article Impermanence

S o, on Monday, I sold some poop to get the tickets.

Of course, to the guy working at the shady pawnshop around the corner from the Cronenberg's Offal Delicatessen and Rotary Telephone Repair Shop storefront (aka the Underground's secret front entrance), it wasn't Troll poop I was selling, but a handful of uncut diamonds. At first he didn't think they were real. And once he realized they were, he became extremely suspicious, asking all sorts of questions about where I got them.

But there's a reason I chose a seedy pawnshop. Well, two reasons, actually:

1. It was *literally* around the corner (less than a block) from the Underground's entrance.
2. I'd watched a lot of movies in my life growing up in the modern world, and in pretty much every crime movie ever made you could say something

like this at a seedy pawnshop and they won't call
the cops:

"Look, guy," I said. "What do you care where I got them?
They're uncut, which means unregistered. And all I'm asking
for is ten grand in cash money. I don't know a lot about jewelry, but I know these diamonds are worth a *lot* more than
that. So if you want to ask so many questions that I have to
walk away and take this deal with me, then by all means keep
asking."

At that point the shopkeep opened his safe without another
word and placed one neatly bundled stack of hundred-dollar
bills on the counter. I pulled the cash toward me as he scooped
the small pile of diamonds into a black velvet pouch.

We exchanged a single nod and then I was out the door.

My friends were anxiously waiting for me in an alley down
the street.

Glam had her arms folded across her chest (she'd been convinced this wouldn't work—then again, she hadn't even known
what a pawnshop was). Lake looked nervous but excited, his
feet shuffling constantly on the rough alley pavement. Froggy
was leaning against the wall with his earbuds in, looking down,
silently mouthing the words to a song. Ari grinned as soon as
she saw me—she could read me that well now.

"It actually worked?" she asked.

"Of course it did," I said, trying to play it like I had always
thought it would work.

I held up the thick stack of cash.

"Holy Gnarlarg's Horn, that's a lot of cringleback!" Glam
shouted, drawing the interest of several pedestrians across the
street. "What are we going to do with all that kablingy?"

I quickly put the cash into my backpack and motioned for them to follow me quietly.

"Well, for one, let's try not to draw attention to the fact that we're carrying that much money," I whispered as we walked.

"Sorry," Glam said sheepishly.

"It's okay," I said. "But now we just need to get back to the Underground to get our gear. We have a train to catch!"

——✦I✦——

The five of us shared three adjacent sleeper cars on an Amtrak train bound for New Orleans.

I could tell you all about how we made it happen, but to be honest it's not that exciting. So I'll keep it short:

1. We packed up our weapons.
2. We told our parents we were going to the Arena, then all sleeping over at Eagan's.
3. By the time they realized we were gone it'd be too late to catch us.
4. Eagan would anonymously deliver a note to our parents that revealed we were safe, but on a world-saving mission, and would be fully ready to deal with the consequences when we got back.
5. I paid for the tickets in cash at Union Station.

We didn't get the sleeper cars because we liked to travel in style or anything (they're apparently like the first class of train travel), but rather because the extra privacy meant we could talk about Dwarf- and magic- and Monster- and Elf-related stuff during the nineteen-hour train ride without turning too many heads.

Somewhere around the Kentucky-Tennessee border, at close to three in the morning, Lake, Ari, and Froggy were fast asleep in the other two cars, leaving just Glam and myself awake in the third. She was sitting up on the top bunk with a reading light on and an ancient tome spread out across her lap. I lounged on a built-in chair next to the bottom bunk, trying to keep my mind off how insane and dangerous this whole sneaking-off-to-New-Orleans-to-face-off-against-a-mysterious-Elven-army thing was.

Would it be a whole army, or just a few Elves? Would they have monsters on their side, like what we Dwarves were trying to do with our MPMs? They'd almost certainly have more Yysterious (what the Elves called Galdervatn) than they did the last time we'd faced them—which meant we'd no longer have the magic advantage. Or maybe they wouldn't even be there at all? Maybe Stoney was wrong, or perhaps they'd already moved on in the weeks since his escape? And even if it was just a small faction, we'd almost certainly be outnumbered, outgunned, and outmatched. But at a certain point, thinking about it any further might have scared me into calling the whole thing off, so I decided to look for a distraction.

"What are you reading?" I eventually asked Glam, shifting on my bed so I could see her.

Honestly, Glam never struck me as the type who liked to read in her spare time. I sort of figured she spent her recreational hours smashing apart antique wardrobes. Or crushing small animal bones in her palms.

She looked up and grinned.

"Wouldn't you like to know?" she said.

"Well, *yeah*, that's why I asked."

Glam kept smiling.

"It's a second-edition Separate Earth Dwarven textbook recently found deep inside the Lion Cavern mines in Eswatini, formerly Swaziland," she said. "It's called *Grootock Shatterbuckle's Tuitions of Article Impermanence.*"

"What's it about?"

"Basically, different techniques for efficiently destroying all manner of items."

"Why am I not surprised?" I said.

Glam frowned. For a second I was worried I'd actually offended her. But then she shook her head casually.

"I mean, if you must know, I'm reading this to prepare for our upcoming mission, since we have no idea what obstacles might lie ahead," she said. "Not reading it for fun. *That* is what I brought for pleasure reading." She nodded toward the small storage bin on the wall to her right.

Stuffed inside the compartment was another old book. The title was etched in gold on the cover and practically shone right through the mesh netting holding it in place.

Ten Romantic Tales of Fairy Love, Adoringly Lost and Dreamily Found
By Sugarfancy Snowflake

"Sugarfancy Snowflake?" I asked.

That didn't sound like any Dwarven name I'd ever heard.

"She was a Fairy," Glam said. "And we think she was one of the very best romance writers of Separate Earth's second late Romanticism Era."

"You're into Fairy-romance books?" I asked, my voice cracking with outright astonishment. "*Really?!*"

"Yeah, so?" Glam said with a defensive sneer. "Can't a girl

be into both smashing things *and* sweet, heartbreaking tales of Fairies falling in love?"

"I—well—I mean—of course!"

Glam laughed. "You're especially cute when you get embarrassed."

I felt my face flushing.

"So, um, why *do* you like smashing things anyway?" I asked, trying to change the subject. "Since we brought it up."

"I don't know, why do you like chess so much?"

"Because I like games that make me think. Games that don't involve luck. When playing chess, I can completely control my own destiny, win or lose. I'd rather lose by my own hand than win because I got lucky."

"Oh, wow, um, okay," Glam said, seeming flustered. It was an odd look for her and I found it sort of sweet and charming. "I didn't expect you to have such an eloquent answer all ready to go."

"I just spoke honestly and from the heart," I said. "Like always."

"Okay, then I'll do the same," Glam said. "I like smashing because . . . well, because it makes me feel good. But not because I merely like pointless destruction. Smashing relieves me. It's beautiful and simple. There's no guesswork. Something was there in front of us. Whole. Then you smash it and now it's not. It's in pieces on the ground. It's not complicated. I don't like complicated. And there's a splendor to that simplicity. To the way things shatter and crumble. And then there's what comes next."

"What do you mean?" I asked, my voice so hoarse it sounded like a whisper.

"I mean everything always comes back better than it was

before," Glam said, smiling now. Excited. "When something is destroyed, people build it back up, even stronger than it was. Buildings, whole cities, societies, everything. There's almost always progress after destruction. Plus, well, you know, my family is really into smashing, too. And so it was also sort of easy to just follow in their footsteps."

"Why are they into smashing?"

Glam shrugged, but answered anyway.

"It started with Elves," she said. "A pledge made long ago by my ancestors to live every day for smashing Elves and Elven things. It's obviously evolved some since then, you know, with the peace treaty and all. Now we can't just run around the world randomly destroying things without getting into trouble."

"Why would your family even make such a pledge in the first place?"

"Because of what Elves did to my ancestors," Glam said. "It's a long story, one that's been passed down in the Shadowpike family for tens of thousands of years. There was once a time when the Shadowpikes were simple cattle ranchers back in Separate Earth. One day, a young Elven girl named Alinor Dadi showed up at their small cottage and said she'd been cast out by her family, shamed for chopping off her hair and wearing it too short—which is just the sort of superficial thing Elves would throw a fit over. She wondered if they had a bed for her, just for a night. She'd be happy to work for it, she said. Mind you, this was very early on in the world, before the natural tensions had grown to war between Elves and Dwarves. And so they brought the girl in, fed her, and gave her their youngest child's bed for the evening.

"As often happens in stories like these, she ended up staying longer than expected. In fact, she almost became a part of the family. But then a few months later, Alinor discovered that the vast field of quartz deposits on the Shadowpikes' farmland was rich with veins of gold. My ancestors brushed it off. Said they already knew and didn't care. Money and gold were of no use to the Shadowpikes—they did not care for wealth beyond things they needed to merely be happy and content. But Alinor couldn't understand this. Why wouldn't they want more money? It was unfathomable to her. So instead she began to see this as a chance to get back into her parents' good graces. She returned to her old home and told her Elven family about the farm and its hidden riches.

"Naturally, Alinor's family attempted to buy the land from the Shadowpikes and were summarily rejected. They then used their natural Elven charm to convince the Shadowpikes to sell them the land for a hefty sum, but with an enticing perk: the Shadowpikes could stay on the land and farm it and live as they had lived for decades. They wouldn't own the land in name, but would essentially be leasing it for free. The Elves promised to let the Shadowpikes stay on the land as long as they wished, an indefinite lease. And the Shadowpikes, accustomed to dealing primarily with other Dwarves, who almost always said what they meant, took their word for it.

"Of course, as I'm sure you're already predicting, Alinor's family did not keep their promise. Three days after the documents were signed, they used a hidden loophole in the contract's fine print to promptly and legally evict the Shadowpikes, leaving them homeless. While the Elves used the land and its gold deposits to become even richer, the Shadowpikes had to move to an unfarmable, rocky hillside. Inches from starvation, they were forced to become stone harvesters at a nearby quarry. Within months, a few of them fell ill and the youngest eventually died.

They lost all they cared for, the land and livestock that they had found so humbly rewarding, all because of the generosity they showed to an inherently greedy and selfish Elven girl. Plus, the real gut punch is the ending."

"Oh no," I said warily, not seeing how it could get worse.

"Yeah, exactly," Glam said. "Roughly a decade later, gold was found in the quarry as well, part of the Shadowpikes' new land. And sure enough the Elves, who had become very prominent in this region of Separate Earth, found a way to tax the Shadowpikes' new gold deposits so heavily that the family couldn't afford to stay there either. The Elves forced them off their new land and managed to steal everything they had a second time!

"So," Glam said at the end, her fists balled so tightly that her knuckles were white and shaking, "hearing this story, among so many others, all throughout my childhood, it was hard to grow up *not* hating Elves. I mean, how can people put financial gain over the well-being of others? Or lie to someone to make money? It's baffling to me that *any* living creature could be so heartless, let alone people who claim to be morally civilized, superior even."

It was hard to argue with her points. But then again, this was just an isolated story in history. It didn't mean that *all* Elves would have acted the same way.

"I could argue that perhaps it wasn't because Alinor's family were Elves, but just greedy, terrible people in general?" I suggested. "We shouldn't define people based on things their ancient ancestors did. We make our own destiny. Our legacy is what we as individuals do, not what our parents or grandparents did."

"Fine, I get that. But let me ask you this: How many greedy, self-serving *Dwarves* have you met?" Glam challenged. "Dwarves who would put their own needs above the well-being of others in such a vicious way? I may live Underground, but that doesn't mean I'm not aware of what modern Elves are doing. Shareholders and board members and executives always find ways to reap personal benefits, even when the actual workers are penalized. Rich people excel at finding ways to expand their already absurd wealth at the expense of the poor. It's the way of the modern world, dominated by Elves. How many Dwarves do you know doing things like that?"

I was shocked, having assumed that living Underground her whole life would have made her entirely ambivalent to the world above. But even separatist, traditional Dwarves like Glam's family apparently always kept one eye on the Elves and what they were doing.

"Well," I started. "I mean—that's a complicated question."

"No, it's not. The answer can come in the form of a basic whole number. Zero? One? Maybe five at most?"

"That's not what I mean," I said, thinking about how much I was risking by even being here on this train in an effort to cure my dad—which could definitely be perceived as a semi-selfish pursuit. "First you'd have to be sure that everything you think you see when you meet a person is what they actually are. Which is almost impossible. Then you'd need to define what *greedy* means. Because if you're including anyone who simply wants a better life, that's pretty broad. Then you have to dissect the nuances of how and why people view the world the way they do and reconcile that with your own values and—"

"Okay, okay!" Glam held up her palms. "Forget I asked! Morgor's Beard, Greg! You're a pretty unusual guy, you know that? You seem so easygoing all the time, almost dopey. You're so . . . *earnest*. Even for a Dwarf. And quiet. But then I ask you a simple question about Elves and Dwarves and you turn into a freaking philosopher on me."

I grinned, trying to pretend my face wasn't turning red again.

"Okay, I'll let you get back to your Smashing Instruction Manual," I said. "I really should try to sleep before we get there. I mean, Eagan gave Ari a lead to follow when we arrive, but she said it wasn't much to go on. We may end up spending a whole day just aimlessly wandering the city. So you should get some sleep, too. I've read that New Orleans heat makes Chicago feel like the Arctic."

"Don't tell me what to do," Glam said playfully. "Only my mustache gets that right."

I laughed as I climbed into the lower bunk and switched off the reading light in the cubby. The thin mattress was lumpy and hard, but still undoubtedly better than a regular train seat. Glam's reading light above me clicked off a short time later and then there was only darkness and the sounds of the train clanking and clunking as it rattled across the tracks.

She's right about Elves, you know. The Bloodletter's voice filled my head.

It was just outside our sleeper car, wrapped up in blankets inside a hockey bag on the luggage rack.

I'm not surprised you'd say that, I thought back.

If I keep saying it, maybe you'll believe me eventually, the Bloodletter challenged. *Elves are not good for this world. I know. I've been around longer than you can even picture in your head. The things I've seen would make the story she just told feel like a fairy tale* with a sappy ending where a unicorn barfs a rainbow of joy all over a bunch of well-behaved kids.

Yeah, you keep saying that, I thought. But the world is different now.

But soon it won't be. It will go right back to what it was all those years ago. Magic is coming back more rapidly now. I can feel it, and I'm sure you can, too. That's why the Council is so overworked. They can't keep up. This world is on its last legs. Its time is short. In fact, you could say it's already passed.

Shhh, you're scaring me, I thought, only half kidding. I'll have nightmares.

You should. It will prepare you for what's ahead. In many ways, the new world will BE a nightmare.

CHAPTER 20

Moss-Covered Logs, Traffic Jams, and an Outlaw with No Name

When I woke at just after one in the afternoon, Glam was snoring loudly, her Fairy-romance book lying open across her chest.

We were scheduled to arrive in New Orleans around 5:00 p.m. The other two sleeper cars were empty, and I figured Lake, Ari, and Froggy might have gone to the dining car for lunch. I headed that way through the narrow, jostling aisles of the half-empty train cars.

But I stopped when I got to the observation deck—a train car made mostly of windows so people could take in the passing scenery. It was empty except for a young couple in the corner sitting side by side, sharing a sandwich and giggling about something; an old man near the center of the car, looking out at the trees and farm fields as they whipped by; and a few tables behind him, Froggy sitting quietly.

He was alone and surprisingly not wearing his earbuds. Instead, he just sat there staring at the window. Not through it at the scenery outside, but at the glass itself, like he was look-ing at his own reflection, or perhaps at nothing at all. His face rested on one hand cupping his cheek.

"Can I join you?" I asked.

He looked up, startled. After a few seconds, during which I worried I shouldn't be there interrupting him, he finally nodded.

I sat down across from him.

"Everything okay?" I asked. "You know, you didn't have to come with us just because everyone else did. I wouldn't have held it against you."

Froggy shrugged.

"I wanted to help a friend," he said. "But I am conflicted about it all."

I waited for him to say more—which with Froggy was cer-tainly no guarantee.

After a healthy pause, he did finally continue.

"I have doubts about this mission," he said. I was about to once again plead my case about stopping the Elves' sinister plans, but Froggy held up his hand to stop me. "Not the point behind the mission. Whether it's to stop an evil plan or save your dad doesn't even matter—I agreed to come because I sim-ply wanted to help you. It's the *other* specifics of the mission that worry me."

"I don't . . . I don't really follow . . ." I said, realizing this might already be the most I'd ever heard Froggy say in one sitting—and we were clearly just getting started with the conversation.

"I'm half Elf, remember?" he said quietly. "But I really don't even think that's the reason I'm so torn. The Battle of Hancock Tower really messed me up. To me, that night, I wasn't fighting—and potentially harming—*Elves*. I was fighting, simply, other people. Other living beings. And I didn't like it."

"Well, I mean, if it makes you feel better, I don't think any of us took pleasure in battling Elves—aside from maybe Glam. And even for her, I'm not sure how much she really enjoyed it or just pretended to because that's how she was raised to be— she's just living up to a family image. But the point is: I think that night was traumatic for all of us."

"I don't think you understand," Froggy said. I nodded, but he shook his head emphatically. "You may think you do, but you don't. To you, and to most Dwarves, *Elf* is a loaded word. *Troll* is a loaded word. *Goblin. Werewolf.* Etcetera. Even if you're willing to judge each Elf or Troll or Goblin individually, you still start with an idea based on something else. You see them as a member of a race and not merely a member of society. It makes me uncomfortable when Dwarves view the world this way, which they frequently do. As someone who grew up in both worlds, it's hard for me to see things from either a purely Dwarven or a purely Elven perspective. And I *like* that I don't have to feel obligated to, even if it does make me feel abnormal most of the time."

I nodded slowly.

He was right. And I knew he was right because I felt that way, too. Ever since I found out I was a Dwarf, although I fit in with them immediately, I'd still always grappled with their somewhat singular vision of the world and of Elves in particular. And I'd been struggling to not let Dwarven biases get to me. It'd been a difficult thing to do, considering the fact that Elves had, in fact, taken my dad prisoner, tortured him, and then tried to kill us when we went to rescue him. Elven behavior so far had mostly only confirmed some of those biases.

But then on the flip side, of course, was Edwin.

"Don't forget my best friend was an Elf," I said. "And, sure, after I found out, it complicated things. Because you're right: Dwarves can't let go of the past and it's clouding their view on things now that magic is returning. But Elves do the same thing. So do Humans. And dogs and cats. And all species who naturally don't understand each other, exceptions aside. Every creature on this earth is prone to this type of thing—rushing to judgments, letting stereotypes or instincts influence their thinking. You're the outlier, Froggy, one of the rare people able to totally and authentically rise above it somehow. It's a good thing, though. I mean, I wish *more* Dwarves thought that way."

"It doesn't always feel like a good thing," Froggy said. "It makes me dangerous for this mission, for example. For every mission of all kinds going forward."

"What do you mean?"

"I mean, I'm not sure I can fight Elves again, even if they are up to no good," Froggy said, looking up at me, making direct eye contact for what felt like the first time since we'd started talking. "But what if they're hurting you, or Ari, or any of my friends? Or even innocent bystanders? Is violence toward Elves, or anyone, justified in that kind of case? The easy answer is *yes, of course.* But I don't find violence against living beings *easy*, ever. No matter the circumstances. I don't know the right answer to that question. Maybe there isn't one? Maybe this is just the way life is supposed to be? A series of enigmas and struggles and contradictions that all end in all of us dying eventually anyway?"

I didn't know what to say. In Froggy's mind, the world was a bleak place. And was he wrong? Especially considering where I knew the world was heading. Where we were headed at that very moment: to New Orleans to face off in battle with a group of Elves planning a "universal annihilation." But to Froggy's point, was our potentially also doing something bad in an effort to stop them really worth it? Was fighting these Elves the right solution or would it just add more fuel to the larger fire?

Tell him if he's not ready for this to stay on the train, the Bloodletter interjected from several train cars away. *He doesn't have to help. But you can't let him get in our way. You can't let him stop us from doing what we KNOW is right.*

So I did as the Bloodletter suggested, because he did make a good point. I was the reason my friends were doing this, and I didn't want anyone along who might compromise the safety of the group. Someone we couldn't rely on to fight back when we needed them most.

Froggy listened and nodded and for a few seconds actually seemed close to accepting the offer. But then he finally shook his head as the train began slowing for its next stop.

"No, I agreed to help and I meant it," he said. "I can deal with all these thoughts later. For now, we need to find out if what Stoney said was true. And if so, we need to stop the Elves by any means necessary."

Good. Good, the Bloodletter nearly whispered in my ear. *He may be useful to us, after all.*

Then Froggy smirked at me knowingly.

"And, hopefully, we can find a way to cure your dad while we're at it," he said.

"Thank you, Froggy," I said. "By the way, how in the world did you get that nickname? I've been meaning to ask."

"That," he said, still smiling, "is a story for another time, probably. I think I've already met my quota of spoken words for the week. Probably even for the whole month."

I laughed.

Ah, drat! the Bloodletter complained, sounding less amused. *I've been wondering that myself all this time!*

"But," Froggy continued, "I can tell you it involves moss-covered logs, a traffic jam, and a gun-toting Old West outlaw with no name."

I shook my head in wonder, knowing he couldn't possibly be making that up.

He may be weak willed, the Bloodletter said. *But I'll give the kid this: he definitely knows how to build drama.*

CHAPTER 21

Yoley Jumps Face-First into a Pile of Rocks

Before we knew it, we were standing outside the Union Passenger Terminal near downtown New Orleans, hockey bags full of Dwarven weapons at our feet, looking at one another and wondering what exactly we'd gotten ourselves into.

"Well, now what?" Glam asked.

"Eagan said we should contact the local Dwarven sect after we arrived," Ari said. "He gave me this."

She held out a small slip of parchment. Glam snatched it and glanced at the writing. Then she tossed it toward me dismissively.

"Some help that is."

I fumbled with the parchment for a few seconds, but finally managed to corral it to my chest. There were only a few perplexing words scratched across the thick paper in Eagan's handwriting:

River Walk Under River

"*This* is the lead he gave you?" I asked, hopelessness (aka Dwarviness) creeping in. "Oh man . . ."

"Yeah," Ari said. "He also told me to warn you guys."

"Wherefore ye leitmotif of ye gents' heed to caution?" Lake asked.

"He said this local sect, who call themselves the NOLA Swamp Dwarves, are rather . . ." Ari paused as if mulling over a secret. "Well, they're a bit—*notorious*—is the word he used. For being somewhat strange."

"Strange how?" I asked.

Ari shrugged. "That's all he said. He had to run off to a Council meeting—he was acting pretty harried about all of this. I think he's really nervous about being complicit in anything sneaky now that he's the newest and youngest member of the Council."

"Well, though, aren't we all a little strange?" Froggy asked from the background, as he reached out toward me amid our muffled laughs. "Let me see that parchment, Greg."

I handed it to him. He took one look at it and then nodded.

"I know where we need to go," he said.

"How?" Glam demanded. "From that note? It's utter nonsense!"

"Because I've been here before," Froggy said. "To New Orleans, I mean."

I sometimes forgot that he spent a lot of his childhood with his Elven mom and his super-rich Elven stepdad. Which I'm sure meant a lot of family vacations to cool places. Well, at least until he came to live with his real dad, our Dwarven combat instructor: Thufir Stonequarry Noblebeard, aka Buck. Not that Froggy seemed to mind. While Buck was generally gruff and rude to the rest of us, he and Froggy were like best pals. Over the past few months I'd noticed they'd developed a close father-and-son bond that's hard to replicate. Plus, it didn't hurt that both of them rarely spoke. The rest of us suspected that Froggy and his dad spent most evenings at home simply enjoying each other's company in total silence. Which, if you really think about it, is a pretty special relationship.

"We need to go toward the French Quarter," Froggy said, pointing at a string of cabs lined up on the curb.

—•I•—

The guys on the radio talk show in the minivan taxi were discussing ghosts.

And it wasn't one of those kooky shows where all they talk about is conspiracy theories and alien abductions. It was actually supposed to be a local sports show. But instead of debating the start of the New Orleans Saints training camp, they spent the whole fifteen minutes talking about the sudden explosion of recent ghost sightings all around the city. The great majority of them had occurred in St. Louis Cemetery #2, near the French Quarter.

"I mean," one of the radio guys was saying, "this city has always been known to be *haunted*. But like most of the skeptics out there, I always thought it was mostly a joke. However, what's been seen lately around town has—well, I'm just going to go ahead and say this, Speegs, but I'm scared to go out alone at night!"

This was followed by strangely bellowing yet uneasy laughter from the two co-hosts.

We all glanced nervously at one another inside the cab,

knowing full well that the recent ghost sightings were almost certainly real. There were a number of fantastical Separate Earth beasts that either were, or could be mistaken for, ghosts: Specters, Wraiths, Shrieks, Foglets, Aureras, and Fart Clouds,* to name just a few.

"Yeah," Speegs finally said. "I guess people living nearby have been hearing horrible shrieking coming from the cemetery every night for the past few days. Cops are baffled."

"Oh, you mean they actually looked into something for once?" the other guy quipped.

"Yeah, at least until they realized ghosts can't offer bribes . . ."

The taxi pulled up near a huge strip mall on the other side of the downtown area as the radio guys exploded with laughter.

The combination mall was flanked to the left by a green-and-gray statue of some guy on horseback and an archway with massive blue letters that announced we were at the RIVERWALK. We piled out of the van and retrieved our hockey bags full of Dwarven armaments.**

"Sounds like there may be a lot of fantastical creatures returning around here," Ari said as the taxi pulled away.

"Really?" Glam asked. "You think ghosts are one of the creatures magic is bringing back?"

---

* Yes, a real Separate Earth creature, believe it or not. They're essentially sentient vapor particles that operate as a colony, kind of like ants. The technical name for these beasts is Xeneroykwolk, but long ago everyone just started calling them Fart Clouds because they manifest in swarms that look like puffs of green smoke and smell vaguely of sulfur.

** You should have seen the look the cabdriver shot us as he loaded the trunk with our bags, the contents clanking loudly.

"Forsooth be'est ye apparition common," Lake said. "Th're art ye sundry stable of creatures yond howl 'neath ye moon and dwell amongst ye deceased."

"Yeah," Ari agreed with her brother. "There are many creatures that shriek in the night and live among the dead."

Lake nodded solemnly.

"Either way, never mind that for now," I said, trying to keep them all on track. "We've got our own mission to deal with. Finding the local Dwarven sect so they can, hopefully, point us in the right direction of the Elves who once imprisoned Stoney."

The Riverwalk area was clearly pretty touristy. Like Navy Pier in Chicago, it was teeming with people: families with shopping bags, teens taking selfies in front of the river, and various vagrants asking anybody who would even glance their way for spare change.

I handed one such dude, who was wearing what appeared to be old newspapers around his legs like pants, a handful of leftover cash from the sale of Stoney's poop. He gaped at the ball of twenties I put into his open palms, too stunned to say anything as we passed.

We followed Froggy up a small set of stairs toward a red-brick, concrete, and grass boardwalk that spanned a long length of the river. We stepped to the river's edge and peered down at the brackish, green-brown water. It looked thick enough to walk on.

"Well, now what?" I asked Froggy.

He shrugged and then handed Eagan's note back to Ari.

"*River walk*," Ari said, looking down at the parchment. "Well, we're here. Next is *Under River*."

Our stares lolled gloomily back toward the seeping "river."

"No way am I getting into that stream of sewage," Glam said defiantly.

"I mean, I hate to be a Pyxeesprite* about it, but . . ." Ari started, gulping down a gag. "I don't really like the idea either."

"Are we sure we're even interpreting the note correctly?" I asked.

"Aye, y'all most certainly find thee in ye location thee seek," a voice behind us said.

It was a teenager. Short and skinny with long black hair and a complexion like coffee. She grinned at our confused expressions.

"Lest *I be* incorrect," she added.

Her deeply Southern accent sounded even more bizarre combined with the odd, almost Lake-like way she spoke.

"Be'est thee expressions of ye traditional linguistics," Lake said, looking equally baffled and excited. "Yet, thy dialect, nay recognizeth."

"Hear tell, y'all's tongue echoes mighty peculiar to me, eke," she said in her half-Southern, half-Dwarven slang. "But at least I knoweth yond y'alls' folk be my folk and I wasn't indecorously assuming such."

"How did you know we were Dwarves?" Ari asked.

"Y'all kidding me?" the strange girl said with a smile. "I knoweth a horde of Dwarves at which hour they past crost my vision. Coequal though we're scarce as a hen's teeth in yonder proximity. So I figure y'alls searching for ye NOLA Underground?"

We all nodded dumbly.

---

* A type of Fairy notorious for being finicky neat freaks and positively terrified of germs to the point that they are said to travel around in magical, airtight bubbles.

"Come on, then, proceed on thyne heels," she said, not waiting around for agreement.

She glanced back a few times as we followed her along the Riverwalk, away from downtown. We introduced ourselves to her as we walked. She weaved easily through the thinning crowd of tourists and evening joggers. We struggled to keep up, what with our huge hockey bags full of armaments and our backpacks of clothes.

After we'd gone maybe a hundred yards, and the people around us had dwindled considerably, she looked back again.

"Mine own nameth be Yolebena Ashbender, by the way," she said with a toothy smile. "But folks 'round here calleth me Yoley."

Yoley led us past all the commercial tents, stores, and marketplaces. Past a huge, weedy parking lot flanking the Riverwalk mall. She led us farther down the river, where there were no tourists aside from a few joggers off in the distance, looping around back toward downtown. Finally, we stopped at a small inlet on the riverbank, where the slimy water lapped against a cluster of large stones piled against the pier.

"Down yonder," she said, and then hopped onto the narrow riverbank next to the rocks.

The gooey water lapped at her feet.

We all hesitated, looking at the polluted and muddy river with apprehension. This close you could make out actual objects floating in the muck: old candy wrappers, a fast food soda cup from some place called Krystal, a dead fish, a suspicious-looking latex glove (like the kind killers wore in movies), cigarette butts, and a general layer of indistinguishable goop.

Don't be a Pricklebink, Greggdroule, the Bloodletter taunted. *Come on, dive in! I would.*

Whatever, I thought back. *You complain when I use the wrong polish to clean your blade. If I threw you in this river, you'd be crying like a baby.*

You'd better not ever throw me in ANY body of water! the Bloodletter joked. *I can't swim. I'd sink like a hunk of heavy metal.*

"Cometh on, then." Yoley beckoned while looking up at us. "Y'all ain't truly afraid of a dram of muck and grime, art thee?"

In addition to the ghastly sight of the water, it also smelled like a combination of Troll feet and rotting pepperoni. Sure, the water in the Chicago River wasn't exactly potable, but in a lot of ways the bizarre, glowing aqua green of all the chemicals in it was more comforting than this, which looked to be composed of at least 20 percent Human feces. But at the same time, we were Dwarves, weren't we? Not squeamish Elves who were too good for dirty work.

So I hopped down next to Yoley.

"Come on, guys," I said.

Froggy and Glam finally got over the smell and climbed down next to me. Lake and Ari followed. Once we had assembled in a line behind Yoley on the narrow bank next to the rock pile, she turned and smirked back at us.

"Don't think," she said. "Just jump."

Without waiting for a response, she dove face-first right into the huge pile of stones. My heart leaped up into my throat as I turned quickly away so I didn't have to see her face smash into the boulders. But instead of a sick THWACK and cries of pain, there was a brief, nearly inaudible *creak* and then just the sounds of the waves lapping at our feet and the distant chatter of the tourists at the other end of the Riverwalk.

When I looked back, I didn't find Yoley crumpled on the rocks with a bloody, broken face. There was nothing. It was as if she'd simply vanished. I was stunned for a moment, but then Glam snapped me out of it.

"Come on, Greg!" she said. "What are you waiting for?"

I looked back at the impatient faces of my friends. Of course, they'd spent their whole lives around such displays of Dwarven engineering ingenuity. So watching a teenager dive face-first into a pile of rocks only to disappear a second later was somewhat commonplace. Even after months of witnessing similarly impossible-looking feats, it still caught me off guard. That said, I knew I could trust Dwarven construction.

So I took a deep breath—and after a few false starts, which garnered some impatient groans from my friends—finally dove into the rock pile on the shore of the Mississippi River.

CHAPTER 22

Jazz Legends and Fried Alligator Glands

Part of me still expected my face to crash painfully into the rocks.

But of course that's not what happened. As I neared almost-certain bodily harm, a secret trapdoor that looked remarkably like rocks gave way on incredibly smooth hinges beneath me. And in less than a second I was plunged into a dark chute, sliding headfirst down a smooth tunnel. It turned sharply to the right and got steeper, bending this way and that. Somewhere along the twists and turns I'd spun around so I was going feetfirst. Eventually it leveled off gradually and deposited me onto a stone floor in a dimly lit cavern not altogether dissimilar from Chicago's Dwarven Underground.

Yoley grinned at me as I stood from the crouch I'd landed in and quickly stepped out of the way of the chute and joined her near an entrance to a narrow tunnel.

"What taketh so long?" she asked.

I shrugged as Glam, clutching a hockey bag of weapons to

her chest, came flying from the end of the chute and landed easily on her feet.

That was sort of fun, the Bloodletter said from the bag in Glam's arms. *But not nearly as fun as this one time I decapitated an Orc lord named Gnarg. Did I ever tell you about that one, Greggdroule? The time I beheaded Lord Gnarg?*

Only seven or eight times, I thought back.

Well, you don't have to be snide about it. A simple yes would have sufficed.

Once the rest of the group was in the chamber, Yoley led us into the tunnel across from the chute. Their Underground was somewhat similar to ours in that it was skillfully carved from bedrock and reinforced in some areas with neat stone blocks, dimly lit, and smelled very distinctly of Dwarven body odor. But it was also different in a lot of ways that reminded us we were far from home and at the beginning of a potentially dangerous mission.

For instance, the walls and ceilings of the passageways of this Underground were a lot narrower and damper. A bizarre and striking mixture of purple and green mosses covered nearly half of the exposed surfaces around us. The tunnels had a vaguely sour, bitter, but strangely pleasant odor (on top of the very distinct aforementioned smell of Dwarves).

"So are we under the river right now?" Ari asked as we walked.

"Aye, ma'am," Yoley said. "Thirty-seven Lachters 'neath ye riverbed."

"Lachter?" I asked.

"Tis ye traditional Dwarven standard for interval dimensions whence per Separate Earth," Lake explained.

Yoley nodded in agreement.

As we walked, the tunnels eventually expanded and widened to something closer in size to the Chicago Underground and the weird multicolored moss coverage also diminished. We passed a few Dwarves on the way to wherever Yoley was leading us. They glanced at us, but said nothing, offering only jovially silent gestures of greeting.

"So do all Dwarven sects exist Underground, then?" I asked.

Yoley was suddenly laughing so hard she had to stop walking to catch her breath.

"Thy adorable gent," she said, patting me on the shoulder between desperate sobs of laughter. "Wilt just hath newly become privy to his sooth pedigree, huh?"

"Yeah, just like three months ago," Glam chimed in quickly, seeming anxious to defend my apparent ignorance.

"Aye, aye," Yoley finally said with a grin. "Y'all newbie folks can be very much comical oft sometimes. Come on, then."

She continued forward through the damp maze of tunnels.

"Was the question really that funny?" I whispered to Ari as we walked.

"No, not really," Ari assured me, shaking her head. "I think this is part of what Eagan meant when he said this sect is a little odd. *But*, to be totally honest, you asking that question was a bit like if you'd asked whether fire was hot."

"Oh. Well . . ."

"I know, Greg," Ari whispered. "There's no way you could have known."

"Why wasn't it mentioned in any of our classes?"

"Because I guess our instructors didn't think there was a need," Ari said. "I mean, would they teach teenagers that fire is hot in a Human Chemistry class?"

I was about to tell her that it wasn't really same thing, but I figured there was no point to dragging this on. Now I knew better and that was that.

"Is there a reason we all live Underground?" I asked instead. "Besides just that we're hiding out like rats hoping to avoid capture or something?"

This time Ari chuckled and shook her head.

"It's not like that at all, Greg," Ari said. "Quite the opposite. We live Underground because we *want* to. In fact, it's considered an honor. Dwarves came from the earth, remember? Brought into existence before Separate Earth was Separate Earth. Back when it was just another rock in the cosmos. Supposedly, anyway . . . I mean, our whole origin story should probably be considered with a shank of lamb.* But the point is, since we're of this earth, then it's only natural for us to feel comforted the closer we get to its core. It's like our collective heart, as cheesy as that sounds. I mean, why do Humans like sunshine so much? Or swimming in lakes? There aren't really logical answers to those questions either. For Dwarves, the earth and its elements are like our sun and our swimming."

I nodded slowly, suddenly realizing that I knew she was right even if I hadn't known it before now. I had always felt better, calmer, during the times I was in the Underground—much in the same way being outside in sunny eighty-degree weather just naturally made most Humans happy.

"Where are you taking us, anyway?" Glam asked, clearly getting impatient with Yoley's mostly silent wandering.

"To see Kimmy," Yoley said.

---

* The old Dwarven version of the saying "Should probably be taken with a grain of salt."

"Kimmy?" Glam asked like she'd just taken a bite of a rotten apple. "Who's Kimmy?"

"Kimmuren Bitterspine," Yoley said. "Ye elected chief of ye NOLA Dwarven Committee. Ye lady's going to be right tickled that ye Council in Chicago hath finally sent us some reinforcements. We've been asking for comfort for nearly a fortnight now past."

"Well, we're actually here to—" Ari started, attempting to explain that we hadn't actually been sent by the Council, and that we were there on our own mission, and not to help them specifically.

But Yoley cut her off excitedly.

"I knoweth, I knoweth," Yoley said. "Y'alls be mighty youthful. But we sure do needeth all ye help we can receiveth, nonetheless. What with all them monsters running to and fro all about these surroundings and whatnot. I desire thee art all ready for some serious fighting!"

—◆I◆—

Kimmuren "Kimmy" Bitterspine was unlike any Dwarf I'd ever met.

Okay, so yeah, most of the "known" Dwarves in my life thus far (including me) had all been a bit short and round. But only slightly—still well within the realm of most Humans' body types. Some Dwarves, including Eagan, Yoley, and Froggy, were actually pretty thin.

Kimmy, however, filled a room. She engulfed a massive chair, like a throne, at the center of a large chamber. Except that her "throne" was actually a huge leather recliner with the retractable footrest lodged in the Up position.

I was instantly struck by the grandness of her presence,

both physically and psychologically. Seeing her almost made me want to literally drop to my knees and kneel before her like she was a king or queen. She was quite simply *imposing*. Almost enviable in some strange way. And it extended all the way to her puffy yet regal feet, which dangled bare off the end of the recliner's footrest like two huge marshmallows.

Part of her power came from looking ageless. She was definitely an adult, in the sense that she was at least eighteen. But beyond that, it was nearly impossible to tell how old she was. Kimmy might have been nineteen years old, but she just as easily could have been sixty. Her skin was smooth and shiny, with a luster not unlike gold. Her movements were quick and youthful, despite the impressive size of her limbs, but her eyes looked like they belonged to someone who'd lived close to a century.

The best part was how she greeted our arrival: with thunderous laughter that filled the chamber like laughing gas.

"Blessed be, blessed be!" she cried through tears of joy. "I sure am happy to see the lot of y'all. Even if you are a bit scrawny for Dwarves!"

Next to me, Glam puffed up her chest trying to look every bit as imposing as she normally was. *Scrawny* was the last word anyone would usually use to describe Glam. But I had to admit, in the presence of Kimmy, Glamenhilda Shadowpike looked about as imposing as a lone dandelion swaying in the wind.

"Thanks for welcoming us so kindly," Ari said. "But we must say that—"

"Nonsense!" Kimmy declared. "Nothing at all must be said at the moment, darlin'. First let us celebrate your arrival with a *feast!*"

"But we really must—" Ari tried again.

"*Eat?*" Kimmy thundered joyously. "I know! The Lords

know I know! You read my mind, sweetie. So that's what we're fixin' to do! Let's feast like we're all gonna die someday!"

We could tell that she was the sort of Dwarf for whom, when she decreed something, it happened whether you liked it or not. It didn't matter that you were in a rush to find Elves that could save your dad (and might possibly be planning to destroy the world). You simply could not argue with Kimmy Bitterspine, that much was clear.

And so we barely managed to sputter half a protest as we were suddenly whisked into a room just a short way down the hall. A pair of wooden doors opened right on our arrival, as if they'd been expecting us for dinner all along.

The room within was less a room and more one of the grandest dining halls I'd ever seen (Underground or otherwise). At least in size—it still wasn't exactly what I would call *fancy*. That's not Dwarves' style. The room was nearly the size of a football field and lined with tables and cooking stations. Our Underground had a cafeteria for government workers, but mostly we all just ate by ourselves in our apartments. Clearly the NOLA Dwarves, however, ate almost every meal together as a massive group.

The dining hall was filled with smaller tables that surrounded a giant polished-maple forty-seater in the center. The entire room probably sat close to three or four hundred at full capacity, but at the moment only the grand table in the middle was set with utensils. Somehow Kimmy was already there sitting in the middle seat along one of the broad sides of the long rectangle. In addition to already being set up with plates and silverware, the table was also covered with massive platters of food.

Suddenly the urgency to find the Elves *right this second*

diminished as our perpetually hungry Dwarven stomachs took over. We quickly sat down in five empty seats across from Kimmy and dug in.*

We feasted on Dwarven-smithed metal trays filled with all sorts of local delicacies: battered and fried alligator sweetbreads, shrimp étouffée, sausage gumbo, at least twenty pounds of crawfish, piles of chicken gizzards, a cauldron of jambalaya with no less than six kinds of proteins in it, dozens and dozens of fresh oysters—so many that the empty shells could have filled two barrels—at least six pans of corn bread, and several massive, colorful king cakes, among many other foods.

Kimmy allowed no *business* talk at the table. After stuffing my face with two full plates of food, I had finally taken a breath so I could bring up why we were there. But she stopped me with a simple hand gesture before I even got a word out.

"I know what you're about to say, darlin'," she said. "Let me stop you. We don't talk shop while eating. We don't disrespect our chefs like that—we focus on the food. Now, we can converse and chitchat about all manner of unimportant things, but only such that is deemed fun and polite and not more significant than this here spread of delectable treats."

I wanted to argue, especially now that my stomach had shifted from *starving* to *only slightly hungry*. But I knew she would be valuable in finding the Elves, and I didn't want to insult her, especially after such welcoming hospitality so far. Besides, Dwarves were notoriously fast eaters and so at this rate

---

* I know what you're thinking: *You just helped yourselves!? That's a little rude.* And a few months ago, I'd have agreed. But in Dwarven culture it's considered rude to *not* just start eating right away, no matter where you are or who is serving you.

the whole dinner would be over in less than thirty minutes, start to finish.

"Yes, ma'am," I said instead, and then shoved another andouille sausage link into my mouth.

Instead of business talk, in between bites, the NOLA Dwarves regaled us with all sorts of colorful tales about local Dwarven history. For example, one of Kimmy's closest advisers, a young Dwarf named Doddgogg Hornheart was named after his great-great-great-grandpappy Johnny Dodds. Who was supposedly one of the legendary founders of American jazz (and whose real Dwarven name was Jonkdodd Hornheart).

Less than an hour later, we were back in the, uh, throne room, I guess you could call it, barely standing, with our hands on our stomachs as if holding it all together. As Dwarves, it was normally hard to feel full. Our two basic states were either *starving* or *just kinda hungry*. But after feasting with Kimmy and her inner circle of advisers for close to forty-five minutes (which, as I said, is a pretty long meal for Dwarves), we were weak in the knees and about to explode.

But at least Kimmy was finally ready to talk about important matters.

"I guess what surprises me most," Kimmy started, more reserved now as she leaned back in her huge recliner chair, but still as animated as an actual cartoon character, "is that the Council would send a party down here and not inform us. That's almost lower than a snake's belly in a wagon rut!"

"That's what we've been trying to tell you," Ari said. "We weren't—"

"Trying to tell me what? That you're here to help? I know it, dear girl, I know it," Kimmy said, shaking her head. "That really just dills my pickle! But then there's only five of you. We need many more than that. At least thirty! I mean, I don't suppose there's any chance y'all could ask your Council for more troops, is there? Maybe some who are fittin' to legally drink while they're at it! I mean, look at you, y'alls is barely older than my son, Giggles!"

"We can't do that," Ari said, speaking rapidly. "Because the Council didn't send us here to help you."

"They didn't?" Kimmy asked. "Well, then wHy in tarnation *did* they send you?"

"They didn't send us at all," Ari said. "We came on our own for a different sort of mission."

"Hah! Color me red and call me a barn!" Kimmy said with surprisingly good humor. "Why didn't you just say so from the start?"

She filled the hall with more explosive laughter. Ari looked as if she was going to lose her mind for a second. But then she glanced at me and Glam and merely shrugged at Kimmy.

"Well, shoot!" Kimmy yelled, switching from laughter to frustration in an instant. Even her angry state had a kind of infectiously optimistic energy to it. "Darn! Darn, darn, darn, dagnabbit, son of a butcher! Shoot. I mean, shucks to heck in a handbasket! I'm about to have a dying-duck fit with a burr in my saddle! Pardon me, folks. Didn't mean to cuss quite so offensively. But I'm right upset, you see. We have ourselves quite a situation seeing as we're as busy as a one-legged cat in a sandbox. And I thought y'all was here to aid and assist us. And now, well, I'm rightly disappointed that ain't the case."

We looked around uncomfortably. It certainly didn't feel good to be welcomed as saviors and then to so ruthlessly disappoint your hosts. Even I was starting to feel disappointed in myself and I hadn't even done anything wrong, technically!

"Fact is," Kimmy continued, speaking as quietly as I'd heard her be since we arrived. "We got a problem. You see, nobody 'cept some legendary cleric named Trevorthunn Stormbelly ever expected magic to come back! And so we—well, to be right frank with y'all, we really kind of let our standards for Separate Earth combat training fall by the wayside. As did many other local Committees around the globe. Sounds like there in the Dwarven Capital City of Chicago is one of the few places in the world that still has an active Dwarven Sentry.

"So now the whole Dwarven community worldwide is stretched thin for instructors and weapons for proper training! We're woefully ill-suited to deal with all these monsters at the moment. That's not even mentioning magic! I mean, now that Fenmir Mystmossman has trained himself a few underling teachers, that still only leaves a dozen for the whole global community. And NOLA apparently ain't high on the list of priorities 'cause not one of them magic instructors has been here even once! So every time there's a burst of naturally occurring Galdervatn nearby, we got several Dwarves around here with the Ability doing all sorts of strange magical stuff they don't fully understand. But anyway, I'm sorry for talking your ears off with *our* problems. What about y'all, then? If you're not here on the orders of the Council, then why are you here? What's this mission you spoke of?"

Ari and I proceeded to explain to Kimmy and her advisers how we had befriended Stoney and what he had told us about the things he saw and heard as a prisoner in New Orleans.

"Yeah," Kimmy said at the end of our story. "Oh, yeah. Yeah, we got Elves around here. Sure, we got Elves. And by

George's Great Gander, they're definitely up to something. 'Course, we don't rightly know what. Because, frankly, we got bigger problems. Like the monsters and what-have-you."

"Wait!" Glam demanded. "You mean you knew Elves were around here, up to no good, and you did nothing?"

Kimmy looked at Glam for several seconds, but it felt like minutes in the rare silence.

"Girl, you got yourself a mighty fine stache for such a youngling," Kimmy finally said. "Which maybe explains why you assume everything you say is correct and right. I bet your whole life, people have been bending over backward for you."

"Hey now—" I started.

But Kimmy held up a meaty paw, cutting me off without a word.

"Because had you developed the ability to listen to others," Kimmy explained to Glam, "then you would have heard what I've been saying this whole time. We *did* do something. We told the Council in Chicago about these Elves many times. We asked for help investigating matters further. We were dismissed out of hand. Same as with the help we requested for MPMs. 'Not enough resources,' they said. 'Deal with it yourselves,' they said. Remember: we don't have a single Dwarf here who has any training whatsoever on how to control Dwarven magic or cast spells and such."

Glam breathed out her frustration in a long and slow sigh. Then she nodded. And what else could she do? We'd been on two MPMs, after all, and there was no way we would have stood a chance in either of them without our training. And MPMs were probably like playing dolls compared with taking on a whole faction of Elves.

"Y'all see our predicament now?" Kimmy asked.

Glam nodded again. But her fists were still clenched at her sides.

"But can you at least tell us where the Elves are?" Glam said. "If you can't stop them, *we will*. Or at least die trying."

Kimmy sighed. Then laughed. Then shook her head sadly. It was like watching someone spin a wheel of emotions.

"I can," she finally said. "But, dear children, it really pains me to see y'all go. I really, truly thought y'all was here to help us. Lords know we need it. Something bad, we need it. But if you must . . ."

"Wait," I said, speaking before really thinking through what I was about to say.

The room was silent, all eyes were on me.

There was no backing out now. That was not what Dwarves or any good people did.

"I'd like to offer a deal," I said. "We will help you with one or two MPMs. We'll take some of your most promising warriors with us and teach them what we know during the missions—about magic and about fighting monsters and using ancient Dwarven weapons. Then you show us where the Elves are. And if any of your newly trained warriors, and hopefully a newly allied monster or two, want to help us, then we'd certainly welcome it. And when we get back to Chicago, we'll do our best to get the Council to send reinforcements your way. But no promises on that. You know how Dwarves can be about taking action . . ."

Kimmy burst out laughing and nodded.

"Yes, sir, I do," she bellowed. "I like you. You've got fire in your guts. And you're cute." She turned toward one of her advisers. "He's cute." Then she addressed me again. "That's a mightily generous offer you make. And we'll gladly accept.

There are dozens of reported monsters in the area in the past week alone. But there's one in particular that's a real doozy. A Moonwraith has been terrorizing people in St. Louis Cemetery #2 for going on a week now."

"Oh dear," Ari said quietly.

Lake exhaled suddenly, like he'd just been punched in the lungs.

I didn't remember learning much about Wraiths in any of our classes yet, but I got the sense everyone else did. Even the normally overconfident Glam shook her head miserably. The Bloodletter, from where it was stowed in an adjacent room, confirmed just how dire this was.

Oh man, that's bad, Greggdroule, he said. *Wraiths are undead spectral entities. They have only a partial presence in the realm of the living.*

So? I thought back. *What does that mean?*

It means that all your Dwarven swords and axes and weapons will be darn near useless against it. Including me.

CHAPTER 23

I Discover My True Language Is ζφλξφιδθψω

We got to know our new NOLA companions a little while hanging out in their Underground, planning, and waiting for midnight (which we were told was the hour at which Moonwraiths first appear) to roll around.

It was hard for me to sit there and make small talk when I knew the answer to fixing my dad might be somewhere in that very city. Might even be as close as a few blocks away. And also that Edwin, my former best friend, could also be there in New Orleans, nearby. But I knew the path to finding out these things (and the right thing to do) was to help the NOLA Dwarves with some of their local monster sightings and MPMs first.

They had an area that was sort of like our Arena back home. A place where all the kids hung out and had fun and did Dwarfy things. But their version of the Arena was a lot smaller and less traditional. There were supplies for more modern activities. Stuff like baseball gloves, footballs, old video arcade games, and board games.

The weirdly familiar *newness* of the place helped put my dad, and Edwin, and facing off against an army of Elves out of my mind. At least enough so that I could focus on getting to know the locals who were going to come along with us on the Moonwraith hunt:

- Yoley Ashbender: As one of the few NOLA Dwarves obsessed with ancient Dwarven culture, she refused to be left out of this. She and Lake had a blast that evening discussing various Separate Earth Dwarven dialects they'd studied as they played an old video arcade fantasy game called *Golden Axe III*. I didn't catch much of their conversation, but it turns out that many of the world's "modern" languages (including English) are derived from an ancient Dwarven dialect called ζφλξφιδθψω. If I tried to pronounce it for you, I might choke on my own tongue.
- Giggles Bitterspine: He didn't actually giggle very much. In fact, Kimmy's son didn't talk much at all. Which is perhaps why it was weird when he and Froggy seemed to hit it off. How do two people who basically don't talk become friends? Giggles was the total opposite of his mom: small and skinny and very quiet. Instead of filling a room with his presence, it seemed more like he was perpetually trying to melt into the cracks in the stone floor. While he and Froggy played an old Dwarven card game, they exchanged more looks than actual words.
- Boozy Alemaul: At twenty-two he was the oldest of the group. Boozy was from a legendary family

of partiers, which helped explain why he lived in a city famous for its parties. He laughed a lot when we all shared what we knew about Moonwraiths, and didn't seem concerned that we would soon be facing off against one. Which was especially troublesome when we collectively discovered that nobody really knew how to defeat a Moonwraith. As the oldest of the group, he probably should have been taking this the *most* seriously. But just the same, there was something about his never-ending smile and carefree attitude that was hard not to like.

- Tiki Woodjaw: At eleven years old, she was the youngest in the group. And she could easily have passed for eight. But don't let that fool you. The fiery and fierce little girl, with straight black hair that covered her face, cursed more than anyone I'd ever met. Though I'd never even heard of most of the swear words she used. Hanklebump, anyone? Or like when she called Boozy *a plorping kunk with a smidgy oppo for a murm*. I didn't know if those were exclusively Dwarven curse words, or what they meant, but they drew some offended gasps from other NOLA Dwarves playing games nearby. Anyway, as long as you're not easily offended, Tiki was pretty fun to be around.

Overall, they seemed like a fun bunch. But they were also clearly determined to learn as much as they could (Boozy's nonchalant demeanor aside) about MPMs and magic. They were really eager to show us they could help—that with some training they could be Dwarven warriors as well.

They asked a lot of questions about our past MPMs and how much Galdervatn we had access to back in the Chicago Underground and what it was like to actually fight Elves.

"It's awesome!" Glam said before anyone could respond. "Just like all the stories you've been told growing up!"

"Well, honestly," Tiki said, "based on the stories I've read it doesn't sound very fun to me. I think it sounds pretty purbogging scary."

"It is," Ari said. "And it's *not* awesome or fun. It's horrible."

"Well, okay," Glam said, looking flustered. "Maybe I exaggerated a bit. But the Elves we faced were trying to hurt us. And it felt really good to be able to save my friends by smashing things. Elven things."

"That part is true," Ari admitted reluctantly.

And I agreed.

When you worked so hard to train for something, practicing for hours, it did feel satisfying to finally use those new skills in a real way to help save family and friends from danger. Even if the other parts of battle were scary and gut-wrenching and nightmarish.

"Mayhap lest we'll all find out yonder," Yoley said.

"In fact, really soon," Boozy said, standing up. "It's already eleven, which means it's time to head out and finally take down this Moonwraith!"

CHAPTER 24

The Most Boring and Normal Team of Ghost Hunters Ever Assembled

We were just a normal group of ghost-hunting kids with plain old names like: Thoggus "Froggy" Stonequarry, Lakeland "Lake" Brightsmasher, Ariyna "Ari" Brightsmasher, Glamenhilda "Glam" Shadowpike, Yolebena "Yoley" Ashbender, Giggulir "Giggles" Bitterspine, Boozzoid "Boozy" Alemaul, Masticha "Tiki" Woodjaw, and me, Greggdroule "Greg" Stormbelly.

So yeah, just your standard Dwarven gang hanging out in a haunted cemetery at midnight, looking for trouble.

Well, we weren't looking for trouble specifically, of course. But when your primary goals are to

1. find a violent and dangerous Specter and
2. start a conflict with said ghost,

then, well, trouble was probably in your future. I wished we had a better plan, but since none of us had ever faced (let alone even seen) a Moonwraith before, we honestly didn't quite know what to expect outside of the limited details we'd read in our ancient history books. And so we arrived at the cemetery with a general plan to wander around until we found the monster. From there, we'd wing it, kind of like we always did.

St. Louis Cemetery #2 was deserted at midnight. After breaking in through a locked gate, we walked among the maze of tightly packed impressive mausoleums, our eyes peeled open. It was like walking through a small city of miniature brown-and-gray buildings, broken up only by the occasional palm tree.

When I die, Greggdroule, the Bloodletter said as we pushed forward into the silent cemetery, *can you bury me in one of these cool tombs?*

Like I could afford one.

Need I remind you about that trough of Rock Troll poop worth probably billions of dollars in the modern world?

Yeah, but for how long? I thought. *Once the Dawn of a New Magical Age plunges the world into chaos, diamonds will be nothing more than just another mineral.*

Diamonds can be very useful for making weapons—they'll never completely lose their value.

Okay, fine, I thought. *But it likely won't matter since I assume you can't actually die, can you? And thus will never need a tombstone?*

The Bloodletter didn't answer me.

Up ahead, a strange blue glow lit up the surrounding mausoleums. The nine of us tensed, crouching instinctively as we huddled behind a huge marble tomb. Glam passed around a flask of Galdervatn. Though Tiki and Giggles both had the Ability, we decided it wasn't a good idea for them to drink any of the swirling essence of magic. Without proper training, it was possible they'd do more harm than good.

"So what now?" Boozy asked, finally looking at least a little nervous.

"Now that we're all hopped up on magic, I say we just go in there and destroy the thing," Glam said.

"Do you even know how to do that?" Ari asked pointedly.

"Well, I assume Moonwraiths can be smashed like anything else," Glam said, momentarily sounding a lot younger than fourteen years old.

"Thy erstwhile discourses gainsaid such avenues of combat," Lake said.

"Lake is right, we've already been over this," I said. "And we decided that simply taking it by force probably won't work."

We had talked about Wraiths back at the Underground as we were preparing for the mission, pooling our collective knowledge on these mysterious, long-dormant creatures.

What we knew: Wraiths were like ghosts, but with more of an actual presence in this world, stuck somewhere between the now, the physical reality, and the spectral plain of the dead. They were deceased people whose spiritual existence was tortured—it wasn't known whether by something that had happened in their life or that was happening now in their otherworldly present time and place. Moonwraiths in particular only appeared in the waxing gibbous phase of the moon, with the zenith of their power occurring during the first night of a full moon—at which time they became powerful enough to actually kill. The full moon was just a week away, so it was imperative we stop this thing now—tonight. Lastly, it was suspected that Wraiths existed primarily for one reason: to show the rest of the world the pain they carried. To make everyone feel the agony they suffered. Of course, as we'd all discussed these things, the Bloodletter couldn't help but crack another lame joke in my head: *You want to feel my suffering? Imagine being left out in the corner of a room, forced to watch your old owner make out with a hairy Gnarlaak for half an hour.*

What we didn't know: A lot. Turned out old Dwarven texts were pretty light on Wraiths. You see, Dwarves don't believe in burying our dead (which is admittedly odd considering how much we revere the earth). But regardless, it meant that Dwarves historically didn't spend much time in or near cemeteries. And since Wraiths only appear near graveyards or burial sites, they've never been much of a concern for Dwarves, even back in Separate Earth, when they were relatively common-place. So what we collectively didn't know about Wraiths could fill a book. Or two. Or a few dozen. And last and probably most important: We still had no idea how to kill one. Or if they could be killed at all. Maybe they merely needed to be banished back into the spectral plane (whatever that even was)? We really had no idea—which was, needless to say, a major problem.

"Well, maybe we start where we always do," Ari suggested. "We walk out there and try to reason with it?"

We looked at one another with uncertainty. It definitely didn't sound like a rock-solid plan that was sure to end well. But at the same time, it was probably our best option until we could figure out more about this particular Wraith and what it wanted.

"After you, then," Glam said.

Ari rolled her eyes but led the way as we crept forward, toward the glowing blue light up ahead.

A dreadful, tortured shriek suddenly ripped into the night. The pure agony behind it was almost as chilling as the ethereal, inhuman reverberation that ran up my spine. Everyone drew their weapons instinctively.

I grabbed the Bloodletter, pulling it free from the sheath on my back.

I already told you I'm useless against a Moonwraith, it said. *And so are your companions' weapons. You may as well just leave us all here. We'll only slow you down.*

I passed this information along to the group.

"Wait, your what told you what now?" Giggles asked, looking confused.

"His ax talks to him," Glam said proudly.

The NOLA Dwarves' expressions changed to awe and admiration, even under the layer of obvious anxiety and fear.

"By gods," Yoley whispered. "You're Trevorthunn Stormbelly's kin? The legendary *Greggdroule Stormbelly*?"

"I am?" I said, shocked they would have heard of me.

"We've heard stories about you," Tiki said. "About how the greatest bloggurgin weapon ever made chose you to rise up and restore our greatness."

She's pretty bloggurgin right about that! the Bloodletter boasted to me. *At least the part about me being the greatest weapon. It remains to be seen if you've got the plorbies to fulfill your destiny and restore Dwarven supremacy.*

"And about how you and your father single-handedly defeated the Elf Lord and his whole army!" Boozy added.

"Well, I mean, my friends were there, too," I said, gesturing at Lake, Ari, Glam, and Froggy. "And we didn't really defeat them. It was . . . well, more complicated than that."

"Ah, he's as modest as the tales foretold!" the normally quiet Giggles exclaimed.

Suddenly they didn't seem nearly as nervous. Knowing I was the *legendary* Greggdroule Stormbelly seemed to have given them a burst of assured confidence. Like, if this was a sport, they now knew they had the best player on their team and so they'd win no matter how poorly everyone else played.

But they didn't know the full truth.

That I never could have done anything *great* on my own. In fact, you could argue that all I'd ever done so far was manage to make things worse and just happened to have survived by dumb luck. Anything good I'd accomplished was mostly the result of help from my friends as opposed to anything I personally had done.

I opened my mouth to tell them this, but their excited chatter over the fact that they were looking at *the* Bloodletter, right now, in my hands, cut me off. I'd forgotten that the weapon was famed and revered among kids who grew up learning about Dwarven culture their whole lives. It was basically the Dwarven mythical equivalent of Excalibur. But greater, since most Dwarves never questioned whether the Bloodletter was actually real.

"Guys, this is great and all," Ari said. "But can I remind you about the Moonwraith just past these mausoleums? Like, twenty feet away?"

"She's right, y'all," Yoley said, still staring at my ax in awe. "Thyne company of warriors still hath a mission to attend to."

"So the Bloodletter really told you our weapons were useless?" Glam asked.

I nodded.

Everyone looked down at their own weapons warily. Though they trusted the legend of the Bloodletter, they also likely couldn't deny feeling at least somewhat comforted, even if falsely, by holding on to their swords and axes and maces. Nobody made a move to leave their weapon behind as the Bloodletter suggested.

"Okay, then, let's keep moving," Ari said, her own battle-ax still gripped in her right hand.

We continued on toward the blue glow, weapons drawn. Toward the terrible screeching that seemed to make my knee joints rattle together like chattering teeth. The mausoleums to our sides were so tall now that it felt like we were in a slaughterhouse being forced through a chute toward the killing floor.

The glow was coming from a small clearing near the center of the cemetery. We stepped into the light.

And there it was: the Moonwraith.

A shimmering blue Specter hovering off the ground, she circled a plain mausoleum no larger than a small shed. It was covered in dozens, perhaps hundreds of sets of XXX in various shapes, sizes, and colors, drawn on by markers and spray paint, some etched right into the concrete. The glowing phantom howled and shrieked with agony and wrath as she floated back and forth in front of the vandalized tomb. We gathered around her in a half circle.

She finally noticed our presence and stopped in midair, turning to face us. I got a look at her up close and the image would now be seared into my brain forever, unfortunately.

I swore I even heard the Bloodletter gasp at the sight of her (telepathically, of course, since, you know, an ax can't actually gasp).

The Moonwraith was nothing more than a semi-translucent skeleton covered in a thin layer of withering skin, draped in rotting flesh and shreds of a filthy greenish-gray nightgown that likely used to be as white as fresh snow. Her curly black-and-gray hair waved wildly around her head almost like tiny snakes on a Medusa. Her face was gaunt and ghoulish, her teeth surprisingly white under the rotting flesh. Her eyes were gone and the empty sockets flickered with blue-and-orange flames that swirled inside the skull like fog. She opened her mouth to shriek again and a green snake with red stripes poked its head out and flicked its tongue.

"Oh my gods," Boozy said solemnly. "I think it's Marie Laveau."

"Who?" Ari asked.

"The Voodoo Queen of New Orleans," Tiki said in an awed whisper.

"Did she die in some horrible, tragic way?" I asked through another of the Moonwraith's awful wails.

"Nay," Yoley said. "She passed on right peacefully amidst a slumber just beyond eighty years fusty."

"Well, something is torturing her soul enough to bring her back as a Wraith," Ari said. "We need to figure out what it is—"

She didn't get to finish. Because just then the wraith swooped in, charging at her with flames licking from her eye sockets. Ari dove out of the way as blue light and swirls of smoke spewed over us.

Lake quickly leaped up and swung a short sword at the Moonwraith as she floated by. His blade passed right through the glowing Specter.

See what I mean? the Bloodletter said. *Useless.*

Ari rolled into a crouch and placed her hand on the ground. She closed her eyes and I knew she was attempting to summon a spell. The ground rumbled and shook and the earth split open beneath the Moonwraith. Vines and roots unfurled from the newly formed crevice and twisted up toward Marie Laveau's tortured apparition. The Wraith casually glanced down at the magical vines and roots and they suddenly incinerated out of existence, leaving behind only trails of sour-smelling gray smoke.

We scrambled as the Moonwraith shrieked again.

"How do we stop this thing?" Glam shouted.

Nobody had an answer as the Moonwraith raged around us. We all crouched behind separate mausoleums, dumbly staring across the ethereally lit cemetery at one another with helpless expressions. But then I realized something: Everyone else *wasn't* just staring at one another in a wild panic. They were all staring directly at *me* (in a wild panic).

The NOLA Dwarves in particular seemed to think I would just be able to come up with an easy solution to defeat this thing. And suddenly I hated the idea that I was famous among Dwarves. It felt like my heart was being crushed right inside my chest—like I didn't have a magical talking ax or amazing friends to help, like all I had was me, myself, and I. And the crushing pressure of being expected to rise up and become a great warrior, a great leader, like my family name supposedly portended.

I remembered what my friends had told me about my *destiny* all those months ago, the very night I first met them and found out I was a Dwarf. They'd said: *You come from one of the most courageous Dwarven families ever known to exist.* And then they'd regaled me with a tale of how extraordinary my ancestor Maddog Stormbelly was for leading his troops into battles where he was far outmatched.

I wish I could say that was what pushed me into doing what I did next. That I was feeling the courage, the power of my bloodline to fulfill my destiny to be a hero. That I thought I could save everyone and be the great warrior everyone assumed I already was.

But the reality was, I did it out of pure fear. Fear that I had led my friends here and gotten them into this situation just so I could find out how to fix my dad. And now I'd have to watch them suffer for it. The thought that my friends might be harmed (or worse) trying to help me was scarier than anything the Wraith might have been able to do to me.

So it wasn't courage that led to what I did next, it was fear.

I put the Bloodletter back in its sheath and then stood up and stepped into the clearing in front of the Wraith's mausoleum.

What are you doing, Greggdroule? the Bloodletter asked.

The concerned panic in his voice was a little touching.

"Marie Laveau!" I shouted at the Wraith.

She stopped swirling and turned her gaze on me.

"Let us help you set right whatever is causing you so much pain!" I cried, willing myself not to turn away in disgust or run in terror as she zoomed toward me, her horrific face twisted into a furious snarl. "We can help! We can make things right!"

She pulled up in front of me, her glowing face just inches from my own. Spirit or not, she definitely smelled like a decaying corpse that I could actually reach out and touch.

Heat unfurled from her flaming eye sockets and my own eyes began to burn.

The Wraith opened her mouth. The snake I'd seen before was gone. Instead, a strange green fog spewed from her rotting face. It blasted over me, oddly sweet and intoxicating. I gasped and reluctantly breathed in a lungful of the strange Wraith mist.

And then I dropped to my knees and screamed—the pain so unimaginable words could never do it justice.

CHAPTER 25

My Battle-Ax Is Also My Therapist

The pain wasn't entirely physical.

It was much worse than that. I mean, yeah, it definitely hurt in that way, too. My lungs burned as if I'd just breathed in fire. My bones shook within me like they were trying to break free. I writhed in physical pain. But the worst was how I felt in the depths of my heart.

It was nothing but dread and sorrow, like the whole thing— eating, breathing, *living*—was all utterly pointless. As a Dwarf, I was accustomed to feeling generally pessimistic. But that was different, because as Dwarves we'd learned to channel that worldview into happiness, to use it to see the good in everything, even in events that most people would see as bad. But this new feeling the Wraith poured into me was something altogether different. It was as if for the first time ever, I truly knew what real *hopelessness* was. What it truly felt like to simply want to die—a feeling I hope you never know.

First I saw visions of my dad and me when I was younger,

going to Chinatown, where he'd shop for hard-to-find tea ingredients. Then I saw him now, babbling, spouting off nonsensical advice to nobody. Next I saw myself yelling at him inside our old store, just before a Mountain Troll destroyed the place, wiping it clean off the map. Then I saw Edwin, the time he gave me his old bike after someone stole everything off mine but the frame. All the times we played chess and talked about space exploration. How we laughed at everyone's reactions at the PEE that one time I came to school with my pockets stuffed full of bacon.

Then his pain hit me and it was even worse than anything I could imagine. It was the betrayal he had felt when I didn't listen to him and attacked his parents' office building. The pain he felt when he found out his parents had died in the battle I initiated. Edwin still thought it was entirely my fault and feeling his agony now doubled me over there in St. Louis Cemetery #2, screaming as a decade of all my past miseries squeezed my whole being into pure hopelessness.

Last, the Wraith's fog showed me a vision of my friends dying here in New Orleans. All of them. One at a time, I had to watch them each perish, knowing that it was my fault. That they were there because of me. And the images in my head were so vivid that I began to think they might be real, that these weren't hallucinations at all but that my friends were actually dying right now in front of me while I rolled around on the ground in my own selfish misery and did nothing to help them.

But it was this last thought that finally brought me back to my feet.

That forced me back into the now.

Back to reality.

And I saw that there was indeed a battle raging all around

me. My friends threw spells and launched attacks at the Wraith as she floated past, unaffected by their futile efforts, spewing even more of her pain onto them in the form of that horrible green fog.

Snap out of it, Greggdroule. The Bloodletter's voice cut through the chaos in my head. *All those things are done and over with now. Hurting won't change what happened. You've got to help your friends, or else the last vision you saw will become a reality.*

I shook my head and stood tall. My ax was right, whatever spell the Wraith had cast over me, I needed make it go away. Now. There wasn't time to wallow in my past. I held up the Bloodletter. The Wraith's back was to me as she descended on Ari, covering her in that strange pain smoke.

That's when the Bloodletter started glowing bright blue. I felt the Galdervatn I had drunk surge into the ax. I wasn't sure what was happening to it, or me, but suddenly I realized I could do anything. Like I could even end the world, if I wanted to.

Reveling in my newfound strength, I lifted the glowing blade of the ax and charged at the Moonwraith.

But before I reached her, something clanged into the Bloodletter with enough force to knock it from my grip. It went pinwheeling across the rough concrete as an arrow clattered to the ground near a huge marble mausoleum behind me.

THWACK!

Another arrow appeared with a soft *whoosh*, lodging into the trunk of a Canary Island date palm tree behind me, missing my face by inches. The fletching was made from gold-and-green feathers and the arrow shaft was conditioned Port Orford cedar. Instantly, I knew it was Elven.

All at once, Elves were rushing into the cemetery, at least a dozen, armed to the nines with swords and bows.

"Protect the Wraith!" one of them shouted. "Form a perimeter and bring me the Sprythe Crystal. We can trap her spirit inside it."

"What of the Dwarves?" an Elven voice asked.

"Kill them all."

The order was given like someone might order a coffee.

I spun around in an effort to find the Elf who'd just issued an order to kill nine kids as easily as asking for no pickles on their cheeseburger. Though I was now unarmed, I still had a very strongly worded insult all ready to go for him.

But as I turned, the very next thing I saw was a blade flying toward my face.

I dropped to the ground like deadweight just in time, actually feeling the sharp edge of the sword graze my hair. I rolled and another sword descended, thumping into the ground where my neck had been half a second before.

The Elf standing above me had two small swords and he spun around with them, twirling like an acrobat. I realized I couldn't dodge his next attack fast enough, and so instead I summoned magic to conjure the most basic Dwarven defense spell.

By the time his swords reached me, they clanged harmlessly off my now-stone midsection.

Greggdroule, you need me!

I quickly shifted back to flesh and blood and lunged toward the Bloodletter, which was close to thirty feet away near the base of a small brick tomb. The Elf followed, spinning his swords at my back like a windmill. They clinked and jangled on the concrete just behind my heels, sending up a spray of sparks.

As I neared the Bloodletter, I passed another Elf, engaged in an epic sword fight with Tiki Woodjaw. As Tiki stepped backward she tripped over the heavy ax, stumbled, and then landed on her back with a *thud*. Her Dwarven shortsword fell from her hand as she gasped for air, now completely defenseless.

I almost had a chance to grab the Bloodletter, but there wasn't time. Instead, I threw myself at the Elf standing over Tiki as she swung her sword down in a sharp arc. My shoulder slammed into the Elf's midsection and she flew backward into a mausoleum with a grunt.

I rolled to my feet, my eyes searching the ground for the Bloodletter. It was no longer in sight. Tiki was catching her breath and desperately reaching for her sword as the double-bladed Elf who had been pursuing me now spun his blades at her instead. Just beyond them I saw three Elves battling the Moonwraith. One was holding up an orange crystal like an offering.

The Moonwraith shrieked as she tried to get away.

But I couldn't worry about that now—Tiki was still in danger. I charged forward, pulling my dagger, Blackout, from its scabbard. I thrust it in between Tiki and the Elven blades just in time. The force of the blow easily knocked Blackout from my hand, but it bought Tiki just enough time to retrieve her sword and climb back to her feet.

Greggdroule, where are you? the Bloodletter called out.

I didn't have time to answer as Tiki engaged in battle with the two-sworded Elf. Her lack of training was clear right away as she desperately struggled to fend off the Elf's quick and efficient attacks. I dove to the ground and picked up Blackout, springing back up to help.

The Elf stunned Tiki with an attack, sending her to the ground. I intervened again, managing to deflect one of the Elf's swords with Blackout, painful reverberations shooting through my hand. The Elf's other sword was suddenly tangled in some vines I had magically summoned to life from a nearby mausoleum.

But the Elf simply let the sword go, freeing himself. He placed two hands on his remaining sword and grinned at me, looking more cold and heartless than even the Moonwraith had up close. I rolled away from the Elf's next attack and then lunged at his legs with Blackout.

He easily jumped over my counterattack and landed softly behind me, like he was made of air. Then he swung his sword down in a quick arc, the blade now in flames from Elven magic.

But I surprised him by charging forward, into the attack instead of away from it. My shoulder collided with his midsection and he flew backward and landed on the ground with a breathless OOOMPH. The Elf rolled slowly to his side, groaning and dazed.

I helped Tiki back to her feet and then spun around to assess the rest of the battle.

It was utter madness.

On one side of the cemetery, Ari, Boozy, and Lake worked to fend off five Elven attackers. On the other, Glam took on three Elves by herself. Arrows were sticking out from her back and thigh, but she fought on fiercely as if they were mere mosquito bites.

But in that quick glance, I saw how outnumbered we were.

"Run!" I yelled at my friends. "We need to get out of here, we can't beat them!"

Tiki ran over to help Yoley, and I started toward a fray in which Froggy was desperately fighting off an Elf and a huge green monster with armor made from bones. It had thick, muscular arms and a hunched back. An Orc, clearly allied with the Elves. Froggy held two small axes and stood bravely in front of an unconscious Giggles in an effort to protect him.

But before I could get there to help, something else caught my eye. Something shocking and confusing that I didn't fully understand. Behind Froggy, back near a huge palm tree, was another portion of the battle. It looked like there were Elves fighting against *other Elves*.

I stood there for a second, trying to make sense of what I was seeing.

But then something slammed into the back of my head and everything went dark.

CHAPTER 26

An Old Friend Calls Me a Cockroach

When I opened my eyes and saw Edwin's face, I assumed I was dreaming.

So I closed them again and tried to melt back into the sort of sleep that didn't come with dreams. Or a pounding head-ache. But as I lay there, I realized that my bed was hard and lumpy. And that there was a smell about me that was musty and unpleasant. And that Edwin's face had been behind rusty iron bars.

Was he in a prison cell? Had we captured him? What had happened back at the cemetery? Were my friends okay?

I didn't want to reopen my eyes—I still felt too groggy to actually believe anything I would see was real.

Where are you? I called out to the Bloodletter in my mind. *What happened?*

My magical ax didn't reply. Of course the one time I actu-ally wanted the ax that wouldn't shut up to speak, he stayed quiet. There was only silence in my head and the faint noise of shuffling feet on concrete in the real world.

I wasn't asleep and couldn't pretend that I was anymore.

So I finally reopened my eyes.

And there was Edwin's smiling face, still behind bars.

"Hello, Greg," he said. "It's actually good to see you again."

If it weren't for my headache I'd have been slapping my own face to see if I were dreaming. Was it really possible I was here, now, looking at my old best friend? And had he really just said it was *good* to see me? It sounded like he meant it. But how could he be so bright and chipper inside a prison? I slowly sat up and looked around, only to realize Edwin wasn't in prison.

I was.

My cell was tiny, with dirty walls that had been mostly stripped of their cream-colored and green paint long ago. For furnishings, there was only a small, hard cot on which I was lying, an old toilet in the corner, and a little wall-mounted table next to the cot. Water dripped slowly somewhere nearby.

Sunlight painted the floor in a huge hallway behind Edwin's smiling face.

Large birds cawed somewhere close by.

So I wasn't Underground.

My mind was spinning. Did this mean that Edwin was the leader of the group of Elves in New Orleans, after all? It had to—my brain couldn't find any other reasonable conclusion. Then again, my pounding head and foggy memory were indicators that my brain wasn't exactly functioning at full capacity either.

"Not going to say anything?" he asked. "Maybe you're still

reeling from the blow you took to the back of your head? I was told it was pretty bad. Nothing a Human could have survived. But you Dwarves have stubborn bones. You're like bugs with hard shells."

"My friends?" I finally said, my voice hoarse.

Edwin gestured toward a glass of water on the small table next to my creaky cot. I reached over and drained it all in one drink.

"You were out for nearly twenty-four hours," Edwin said, ignoring my question. "You must be hungry. And groggy. I'll have some food brought and then once you gather your wits about you we can talk, Greg. This might surprise you, but I really do miss you. You were my best friend once, whether you want to believe it or not. Anyway . . ."

He turned and stalked away quickly, as if staying any longer would have been dangerous.

"Wait . . ." I tried to call out, still having so many questions, but my voice was only a hoarse croak, barely above a whisper.

He was already gone either way.

I closed my eyes and lay back down, my head thumping with pain. The back of it throbbed where I'd been struck by something. I ran my fingertips across my skull. Dried, crusty blood matted my hair.

Bloodletter? I tried again. *Carl? Where are you?*

Silence.

Distance had never been much of an issue in our telepathic communications. But I'd also never been farther than five or six miles from my ax from the moment I first saw it. So how far away was I now? Where was I? Where was it? Was the Bloodletter okay? It felt absurd to be worrying about an ax's well-being. Especially since I still didn't know what had happened to my friends. What had happened at all, really.

Carl, tell me everyone is okay. What happened? Why won't you respond?

I lay there in my cell and waited for an answer.

But there was only silence.

CHAPTER 27

Al Capone and I Now Have One More Thing in Common

I'm not sure when I fell back asleep, but it was likely within seconds.

Otherwise, my many spinning thoughts and questions would have taken over, even in spite of a likely concussion, and made sleep impossible. I awoke sometime later with all my panic and worry and questions rushing back in like a mental dam had just burst. I didn't know how much later it was. It might have been two hours or two days for all I knew. But that didn't concern me much just then. As I sat up, a few realizations hit me (some surprising, others more obvious):

1. I was almost in a can't-breathe panic attack worrying about the fates of my friends. After all, the Moonwraith had already shown me what it would feel like to lose them on this mission.

2. Not knowing where I was or what was happening

was nearly as excruciating as the physical pain hammering inside my skull.

3. Part of me was relieved, almost elated, that I now knew Edwin was alive and seemingly quite well.

4. But the relief was almost overtaken by worries that Edwin was indeed the mysterious leader of the Elves who had imprisoned Stoney, tortured his fellow inmates, and was rumored to be planning something horrible and destructive. The part of me that wasn't relieved thought it might be easier to handle news that he had died a good person, rather than discover he was even more evil than I ever thought possible.

One thing I did know was that I was being watched. Because within minutes of me waking, a middle-aged Elf in jeans and a hoodie brought me food, just as Edwin had promised. He set the tray on the floor and then slid it under the narrow gap below the cell door.

He sneered at me like I was a pile of mud, then turned and left without saying anything, his footsteps echoing down a massive hallway.

There were no other voices or sounds around me. Whatever prison this was, I may very well have been its only inmate.

The plastic food tray held a pile of lukewarm SpaghettiOs, a few pieces of plain white bread, and a Snickers candy bar. I ate the food hastily, not caring that there wasn't any meat. Of course, without meat, it hadn't really felt like much of a meal at all, but beggars can't be choosers. Especially when you're a prisoner.

After eating, I spent my quiet isolation trying to ignore my growling stomach and growing concern for my friends and ax. What if they hadn't made it out of the cemetery alive? Maybe Edwin had captured them as well, but had not spared their lives? Maybe I had it all wrong and this wasn't as bad as it looked? Maybe this was all a dream and I was still lying in the cemetery unconscious or worse?

The maybes were enough to nearly drive me mad.

⊹

Edwin eventually came back like he said he would.

It might have been twenty minutes or two hours after I ate. One thing I was finding out was that being alone in a small cell warped your sense of time.

Edwin arrived flanked by two armed guards.

"If I let you out and we go for a walk, can I assume you won't try anything?" he asked. "Or do I need to get the shackles?"

His blue eyes were like sparkling gems as they stared at me.

I was surprised I wasn't more upset that my friend had just suggested putting me in restraints like some kind of violent criminal. But then again, it was hard to blame him. In his mind I was probably still the rogue Dwarf willing to stop at nothing to help his friends and family, even to the point that it might cause injury (or in the case of his parents: death) to anyone who got in my way.

If I were him, I'd be wary of not using restraints, too.

I shook my head to say that I wouldn't try anything, and I meant it. I still didn't even know where I was. Plus, I was unarmed and groggy, with a massive headache and having eaten no meat for the past day, at least. I was in no shape or condition to take on four armed Elven guards (at a minimum).

Edwin must have sensed my sincerity because he nodded

and motioned for the cell to be opened. There was an echoing electronic buzz off in the distance and the lock opened with a metallic *clang*. The cell door slid open, grinding and creaking on old metal hinges.

"Come on, then," Edwin said.

I followed him down a cellblock filled with empty cells that were likely at least a hundred years old. We went up a metal staircase, Edwin still not saying anything. The guards stayed behind us at least ten or fifteen feet, but they were always there, watching me.

Finally we emerged onto a concrete patio (of sorts), bright with sunlight. I instantly smelled the briny salt water of an ocean or sea as my eyes adjusted to the light. Across a large, sparkling body of water, the skyline of a city loomed on the opposite shore, built along sprawling hills with a modern, shiny downtown at the tip of a peninsula. It looked vaguely familiar, but I couldn't place it right away. I looked around us at the prison complex, every bit as ancient looking on the outside as it was on the inside. Below us, a rocky shore was being bombarded by frothy waves. To my right loomed a massive reddish-orange bridge with a limitless ocean behind it. I instantly recognized it from photos.

The Golden Gate Bridge.

Which meant the city across the bay was San Francisco.

And that I was on Alcatraz Island.

I'd never been here before, but it was probably America's most famous prison. Plus, it had been featured in several action movies I'd seen alone in my living room on the many weekends my dad had been out of town hunting for magic. I didn't know a whole lot about the prison, except that it was old, at least a hundred years, and also that it hadn't been used as a prison in a long time—probably since the 1980s at least, and maybe even before that. My understanding was that it was now more like a museum, a tourist attraction. Edwin had once told me about it in sixth grade after his parents took him to some fancy, invite-only art exhibition that was held here.

"Like my new fortress?" Edwin asked with a smirk.

"How did you pull this off?" I asked, my mind reeling.

How could anyone, let alone a kid, gain total control of a huge prison and one of the country's most famous historical landmarks?

"As you know, I was the sole inheritor of my parents' vast fortune," Edwin said. "And *everything* has a price. Especially with the world slowly descending into chaos. The seams of organized society are barely holding together anymore, Greg. It's really quite frightening."

I nodded. On that much we still very much agreed.

But the real question remained: Was Edwin partially responsible for that? Was he really planning something to accelerate the destruction of the modern world? Or was there still hope that we could team up (like we once would have) to try to fix all of this? I desperately wanted to ask him these questions, but figured I might get more out of him if I didn't immediately initiate an interrogation. After all, I was his prisoner and so he technically had all the power. If he really was that evil, then I was perhaps lucky to be alive at all. Especially if he still was bitter and vengeful about what happened the last time I saw him.

We both leaned against a railing and looked out across the bay at the sprawling city that was the heart of the modern technological age. A heart that would very soon stop beating entirely—when magic came all the way back. The rolling blackouts happening more frequently around the world had pretty much proven that one of the Dwarves' theories about the effects of magic was correct: It would end technology as we knew it. All electronics, all machines, anything with moving parts powered by a battery or by fuel would cease to function in the New Magical Age.

"You seem . . ." I started, but then stopped. Edwin looked at me out of the corner of one eye. "I'm surprised you're still not angry with me is all."

I remembered the look he'd given me back on Navy Pier several months ago. That searing look of hatred. Betrayal. In his mind, I had ruined his whole life. And in a way, I supposed that was true. Every time I thought about what had happened back then, my stomach burned like it was on fire.

"Time helps," Edwin said. "When things threaten to tear your world down you can sit back and let them, or get up and rebuild it. We have to move on from tragedy, not wallow in it."

"You always did have the heart of a poet," I joked.

"Shut up, you Gwint," Edwin said, but he was smirking. "Or, I guess I'm not allowed to call you that anymore, am I? Not if we're to keep things civil. Which is very much what I want. After all, I never did know it was as insulting a term as it is."

And in that moment, I believed him. Looking at his playful smile, it even almost felt like old times again. Like I wasn't his prisoner. Like we were still best friends. But then his smile faded and the emptiness in his expression made me wonder if it had ever really been there at all.

"I'm still plenty angry, though, Greg," he admitted. "We're not even yet. But I realize now that you never *wanted* that to happen. You didn't *want* my parents to die. Of course, that still doesn't change the fact that they did. Even so, I'm not such a vile creature, as many Dwarves believe, that I mean to harm you. In fact, quite the opposite. Elves are misunderstood. Well, most of us, anyway. And I want you to realize this, to see the truth, before I go forward with my plan to save the world. Because from a certain point of view, it will seem like we're the bad guys. But that's not the case. And it will be easier for you to recognize that here and now, before the chaos really hits."

"What are you talking about?" I asked, the sunlight pounding into my throbbing head like a hammer. "What plan to *save the world*?"

Edwin smiled and shook his head.

"I've said too much already," he said. "For now. But I just wanted you to know that I don't intend to harm you. Your . . . *imprisonment* has more to do with your safety than with wanting to inflict any undue unpleasantness on you. Not that you don't actually deserve *some*. But I'm not a vindictive person, Greg. You know that."

I sighed and looked down at the green-blue waves crashing into the rocks below me. He was right, he wasn't. Edwin had never been the sort to hold a grudge. In fact, he'd been maybe the most forgiving person I had met until everything went sideways.

"Can you tell me what happened back in New Orleans?" I asked. "How did I get here? Are my friends okay? Why were Elves trying to capture the Moonwraith? What were you doing there?"

I had so many questions.

Aside from worrying about my friends and wondering why I had seen Elves fighting one another, I was still concerned about my dad. And now that I'd found Edwin, I hoped he might actually know how to help me. But I decided to hold back on that one for now. After all, it might be better to show Edwin that I could play along before I started asking for favors. Besides, I was technically still in captivity, so there wasn't really much I could even *do* to help my dad at that moment anyway.

"All good questions," Edwin admitted, facing me. "Some are more complicated to answer. And I don't have great answers to all of them. At least not yet. But I will tell you I'm afraid I don't know what happened to your friends. I wasn't actually in New Orleans myself. But my highest-ranking officer was, and he has been fully debriefed. I can only share with you what he saw: Your Dwarven companions were trying to retreat, but stayed behind looking for you. The last he saw them, they were still engaged in battle. But I must be off now—the rest we will discuss another time. I assume you'll find your way back to the cell?"

His eyes flicked toward the armed guards flanking the metal staircase. I looked at them and their swords, which were ready for anything.

"You're really just going to leave?" I asked, growing frustrated. "You can't tell me where you've been or why I'm your prisoner? You really have better things to do?"

"Actually, yes, I do," Edwin said somewhat coldly. "I wouldn't expect you to understand that right now. But once I can share more, you'll realize just how dire a situation we're all in. And you'll know exactly why I have so much more to do than catch up with my *former* best friend. Now I'll ask you again: Can you find your own way back to the cell? I don't need to have you dragged there kicking and screaming, do I?"

I shook my head slowly, stuck somewhere between anger and frustration. I couldn't help it, but a small part of me wished I could just spend more time with him, that we could just hang out like old times. Back before I learned we were destined to be enemies.

"Good," Edwin said, then he slapped me on the shoulder. "This is all rather complicated for me, but I'm surprised how good it is to see you again. I look forward to talking more soon."

He spun on his heels and clanked down the stairs before I could answer. The guards looked at me, waiting patiently, apparently okay with me taking a few extra minutes outside in the fresh Bay air. This certainly wasn't what I would have expected being an Elven prisoner to be like.

As I looked back across the water toward the city, I found myself feeling oddly . . . happy. In spite of everything that was going on. And there really was only one explanation: Edwin was right—it was, though certainly complicated, truly good to see each other again. It felt like a tremendous weight had suddenly been lifted off me. Like I could finally breathe properly again for the first time in months.

I hated that I felt that way.

I wanted to be angrier with him. Between what happened back in Chicago and now, the reasons were endless. But none of that changed how nice it was to see him in person again, rather than just in my nightmares, where I repeatedly saw him drowning or dying, feeling betrayed and abandoned and hating his former best friend with all his soul.

And despite being a Dwarf, despite being practically allergic to optimism, the happiness I reluctantly felt actually gave me real hope.

CHAPTER 28

———— ◆—◈—◆ ————

If Only This Was a Generic Superhero Movie

The next day, Edwin surprised me by showing up at my cell with lunch and a chess set.

"For old times' sake?" he asked.

The guards brought in a small folding table and two chairs. As Edwin set up the game, I ate my lunch: three greasy hamburgers from a local fast food chain called In-N-Out. They were no Chicago burgers (Chicago was quietly the best at hamburgers), but I had to admit they were pretty darn good. Though, to be fair, probably the only way to make a hamburger that didn't taste good would be to use fake meat.

"It's been a while," I said, looking over the game board, struggling to make my first move, "since I played someone good."

I was black, and his first move had caught me off guard. It was an opening he'd never used before, and was not one of the four standard openers that almost all good players used as white.

"Yeah, me too," Edwin said. "I haven't played at all since our last game. There hasn't exactly been a lot of time for chess. It's not easy trying to reassemble an entire Elven society."

I nodded and quietly made my first move. I wanted to forget about what had happened and pretend that we were still just friends, but it seemed like everything we said connected back to his parents' deaths in one way or another. It didn't help when he brought it up directly like he did several moves into the game.

"They never found their bodies, you know," he said. "My parents. We never found their bodies in the rubble."

My heart skipped a few beats. I think he knew I didn't want to talk about them and was only doing it to make me uncomfortable. To make me feel some of his pain. But then again, I already did. Seeing him the day before had cemented just how bad I still felt about what had happened. I never actually wanted to do anything to harm Edwin. Even now.

"How can you be sure they died, then?" I asked.

"You think they would just disappear voluntarily and leave their whole empire, everything they worked their whole lives for, in utter chaos and ruin?" Edwin asked. "You know them better than that. There was nothing my parents loved more than their Elven and business empires. Maybe not even me, as hard as that is to admit now."

I nodded.

Edwin was right: His parents cared more about their money and power than anyone or anything. Running off and giving it all up wouldn't make any sense.

"I called off the search early," Edwin admitted. "For one thing, there was too much to do to devote that many resources to finding them. Keeping the whole thing covered up from the Human public was difficult enough. But I think, deep down, part of me also didn't want them to be found. It would have made me have to face the truth."

It struck me then that Edwin suddenly seemed a lot older than fourteen. It was almost as if he had aged a decade in the three months since I'd seen him, even though just one birthday had passed. Perhaps losing your parents and having a whole race of people (not just any people, but rich, important, and influential people) suddenly thrust under your reign had a way of making you grow up quickly. After all, even though my friends and I still liked to spend our free time playing games and joking around, once you start getting assigned missions to confront literal monsters, you have to leave at least some of that carefree fun behind you forever.

There was nothing I could say back to Edwin's revelation about his parents and so we just played chess in silence for a while. He was definitely playing differently than he ever had before, making bold, seemingly illogical moves that didn't follow the book lines at all. For one thing, Edwin had moved his king out to the middle of the board by the tenth move, which is usually suicide in chess (not just suicide but basically universally unheard-of—even among total amateurs). But despite this apparent blunder, I was only up by two pawns by the time his king was tucked safely behind a rook and a bishop clear on the other side of the board.

"What are you up to, Edwin?" I asked.

"Hey, just because I haven't played in a while doesn't mean I'm going to give away my strategy!" he said.

"No, I mean out here, on Alcatraz," I said. "Dwarves . . . I mean, all we're doing is spending every waking minute trying to protect Humans and the earth from the coming chaos, from the monsters that have already come back. What have you been up to here? You said yesterday you wanted to save the world, but—"

"I do," he cut me off. "And I will."

"Then help us," I pleaded, finally feeling comfortable enough to extend my version of an olive branch. "Let's join forces and work together to pacify the returning creatures of magic. To keep them from causing too much harm."

Edwin shook his head dismissively.

"No, it would never work," he said confidently. "The natural conflict that would arise while trying to work together would only distract all of us from the end goal. Besides, what you guys are doing, your so-called Monster Pacification Missions, are shortsighted solutions to a much-larger problem. It's like trying to fix a leaky roof with a bucket. Sure you'll keep the floor dry for a while, but it won't fix the actual hole the water is leaking through—a hole that will only get worse in time. When magic finally fully bursts forth, no number of trained Dwarves or Elves in the world will be able to stop the monsters from wreaking havoc. Pacifying monsters now is all well and good in small doses, but it's ultimately doing nothing to solve the larger problem. I want to actually fix the roof. Replace it altogether— make it even better than it was before."

"Oh, so you have some genius plan that will just make everything all better?" I asked.

"I do, actually," Edwin said. "And *that's* what I'm working on out here. And I'm close. Very close. There's just a—well, a few complications we need to take care of first."

"So what's this plan?" I asked.

"Easy: I'm going to strip the world of all magic once again,"

Edwin said. "Just like the Fairies did long ago. Things will go back to how they were before your dad found the leaking Yysterious—or Galdervatn, as you guys call it."

"But that's not even possible," I nearly shouted in disbelief. "It's coming back, we see more signs of that every day. It's seeping up through cracks in the earth like natural gas or something. It can't be stopped."

"How can you be so sure?" he challenged.

"Well, because . . . I mean, stopping a vapor, a gas, from coming back all over the globe all at once is—well, impossible."

"Just like how people turning into Mountain Trolls was thought to be impossible before you saw it with your own eyes?"

I shook my head, thinking he couldn't actually be right.

"But this is different," I said. "I mean, Dunmor told me how the Fairies banished magic."

"Oh, did he?"

"Don't be condescending, dude."

"Okay, then, just tell me about it," Edwin said. "What did Dunmor say?"

"He said they used some special amulet or something," I said. "But it's gone now, the Fairies either destroyed it or hid it in some magical forest that can't even be accessed until magic comes back, by which time you'd obviously be too late to stop it."

Edwin seemed to consider all of this and his expression was hard to read. But then he smiled and made another chess move, putting me into check in a way I hadn't seen coming. His board was so chaotic it had been hard to keep track of all the moving parts. And that was probably his plan all along: to distract me with unusually bold moves while he developed a real attack strategy right under my nose.

"Okay, fine," I said, forgetting about the game—it hardly mattered just then. "Let's say, theoretically, there's another way to strip the world of magic again that nobody knows about except you. How? How are you going to do it? I mean, such an absurd plan requires an explanation."

"This isn't one of those cheesy superhero movies," Edwin said with a grin, "where I reveal everything to you before I've actually pulled it off, giving you a chance to stop me. You'll just have to trust me: I know a way. And I don't *trust you* enough to say what it is."

I wanted to be hurt and offended. But deep down I didn't blame him. Why should he trust me? I wouldn't if things were the other way around. After all, suppose Edwin did tell me his whole plan and I somehow escaped. Would I really go back to Chicago and not tell the Council, or anyone, about what Edwin was planning?

Of course I would tell them, especially if it was the same plan Stoney had talked about. Because the truth was I didn't fully trust Edwin anymore either—at least not like I used to. He claimed he wanted to save the world, but could I truly know that was the case? And even if his motivations were pure, would banishing magic once again really be better? Or could it some-how only make things worse now that it had already started?

"You know, Edwin," I said, "my dad told me the return of magic was the *only* way to bring the world to peace. Let's say you actually stop it from coming back. How can you be so sure it's the right thing to do? He was, let me remind you, one of the only people who correctly predicted its return in the first place.

Are you positive he's wrong about it also bringing peace and not destruction?"

"Definitely," Edwin said so confidently that I almost believed him right then and there.

He made his next move and I realized the chess game was now out of reach. So I laid my king down in defeat. Edwin grinned, but it faded seconds later.

"What has the return of magic actually brought us so far?" he asked.

"Well, I mean, there's bound to be some growing pains until we figure out how to use it for the greater good."

My own words didn't sound very convincing, even to me.

"Now you're talking like an Elf, Greg," Edwin said sharply. "At least, like my parents. Always willing to overlook *little cases of misery* for some greater cause. But I'll tell you what magic is really bringing: death and destruction. So far it has led to the death of, in no particular order: my parents, our friendship, an eons-old peace treaty, who knows how many unsuspecting Humans who have crossed paths unwittingly with a dangerous fantastical creature, *and* it's in the process of turning the earth into a violent, postapocalyptic hellscape populated by even more magical monsters."

It was hard for me to argue against any of that. So I didn't.

"Magic has to go," Edwin reasoned. "For the sake of all living creatures. Banishing it once again will save the world, whether you want to admit it or not. Your dad is a brilliant, kind, and amazing person, Greg. I always liked him, even for a Dwarf. Or maybe even more so because of it. But that doesn't mean he can't be wrong about some things. He's not perfect. Nobody is."

I nodded.

Edwin was right again. But at the same time, I still truly believed in my dad's vision. That magic could unite the world and lead to peace. But me thinking he was right didn't mean *he actually was right*. He very well could be wrong. And my nearly blind faith in my dad would be exposed for a son's simple admiration of his own father.

It made it even worse that I couldn't ask him about it. I'd tried no less than a dozen times, and each time had resulted in an increasingly absurd *Kernel of Truth*, the last one being: *Peace is a tricky thing. I mean, they're small and green and can turn to mush in an instant. But I really like my peas best covered in cheese. And when I'm wearing boots with red laces. Cowboy boots with laces.*

"Speaking of my dad," I said, figuring this was as good a time as any to finally ask the question that had landed me here in the first place. "He's . . . well, I found the antidote to the poison. Right where you said it'd be."

"I noticed that stuff was all gone when I finally went back to my parents' house," Edwin said. "You're welcome."

I wasn't sure if he was being sarcastic or not, and it probably didn't matter either way.

"Anyway," I said. "It, or the poison, or *something* had a side effect. He's not the same anymore. He's gone a little mad. For real this time. And I was hoping that . . . well . . ."

"You want me to help you?" Edwin finished mercifully, sparing me the hard part. "Give you access to ancient Elven books on potions and poisons and such? Help you figure out what's wrong with him? Is that it?"

I nodded.

"It might be the key to unlocking the truth behind magic,"

I said. "If he could get his mind fully back, he might be able to tell us why he thought magic would bring peace and not destruction like you say it will."

"Why should I help you?" he asked. "You still have your dad. Don't you think it's better to have a crazy one than no dad at all?"

The obvious answer was yes, but I didn't think he'd listen to me if I tried to explain how curing my own dad wasn't even related to his parents anymore, so that shouldn't be a reason *not* to help.

"If not for me, then for him," I finally said.

Edwin shrugged.

"I doubt there's anything I could do," he said. "I've got bigger problems on my hands. I don't really have time to be sitting around reading old books about even older potions."

"So you really don't know what's happening to him?" I asked.

"No, why would I?" Edwin said. "I never meddled with my parents' stuff. And I have no interest in ancient poisons that were only meant to hurt people."

He stood up now and motioned at the guards to take the table and game away. He headed toward the open cell door.

"Maybe there's an Elven doctor or alchemist here, or back in New Orleans, who might know—" I started, but he pivoted back toward me at the entrance to my prison cell and cut me off with a wave of the hand.

"I'm not going to devote any resources away from my main goal, Greg, I'm sorry," he said. "Look, I enjoyed our chat, but I'll be away for the next little while now. At least a few days, probably longer. I'll be sure you're fed and watered. And I'll send someone to take you outside to see the sun and breathe fresh air every once in a while. Don't say I never showed you any mercy."

He turned and left as the guards collected the chess game and table and took them away. I sat there feeling dejected, yet torn. On one hand, any hopes of working together with Edwin to save the world seemed farther away than ever, especially since his plan involved something that by all accounts was impossible—and directly contradicted what my dad had been working toward (before he'd lost his mind). But at the same time, I'd seen a glimmer of the old Edwin I knew back at the PEE. Even though he'd said he couldn't help me with my dad, there was still an undeniable humanity and kindness underneath his new bitter and cynical exterior. He was definitely different, darker, since his parents' deaths, but he was still a good person. I didn't think he could or would fake his sincere desire to keep the world from collapsing into magical chaos.

And for the first time, maybe ever, a Dwarf's optimism actually grew.

CHAPTER 29

--- ❖ ---

Ways to Make a Dwarf Smell Even Worse

For almost two days I had nothing but my own thoughts for company.

The guards brought me three meals a day, but always dropped them off and then picked up the empty trays without a word. I wasn't sure what had happened to Edwin's promise to let me get outside once in a while, but for those two days I lay in my cell without reprieve. Dwarves were already known for their fairly potent body odor, but after nearly four days of lying in bed with no showers or changes of clothes, I was starting to suffocate in my own musk.

Two days is also a long time without someone to talk to. Without even a book. I spent as much of it sleeping as I could. But that had its limits, especially on the small, uncomfortable cot built for making criminals miserable.

I constantly tried calling out to the Bloodletter. But there was only mental radio silence. Less surprising now that I knew just how far away I was from both Chicago and New Orleans. I wasn't sure how our magically telepathic link worked, but distance probably played at least some role.

The alternative wasn't something I wanted to consider.

I missed my ax. Almost as much as I missed my real Dwarven friends. Which really surprised me. I hadn't realized just how used to his relentless chatter I'd become. But at the same time, there was something sort of liberating about his absence. Constantly being reminded that an ultimate conflict lay in your future, that it was your destiny to defeat enemies in battle, was stressful to say the least. Having a voice in your head that craved violence in the name of justice and revenge was a dark thing to carry around with you. Of course I knew a confrontation was still probably in my future, but without the Bloodletter reminding me of it several times a day, my mind could actually pretend otherwise for a few rare, fleeting moments.

It felt nice to hope for peace rather than be preparing for conflict—even if the latter was still the more likely outcome.

But most of my waking hours were filled with concern for my friends. Had they made it out of New Orleans alive? Were they back in Chicago? Had they gotten themselves captured or injured or worse by sticking around trying to find me? Could I end up being responsible for their deaths as well (like the Moonwraith's green fog had showed me)? Should I officially change my name to Grimsley Reaper, Master of Death?

But in the better moments, I distracted myself from those worries by thinking about what Edwin had said.

I pondered the possibility that he might be right. Maybe we all would be better off returning to the way things had been before the discovery of Galdervatn. Sure, Dwarves had been relegated to relative poverty (not that we really cared), while the Elves used their powers of persuasion and manipulation to amass most of the world's wealth. But at least the planet wasn't about to be besieged by monsters and magical wars that would kill who knew how many people.

Perhaps the magical drive of the vengeance of the Bloodletter had blinded me somewhat to the reality of what was actually going on? Without the ax by my side, things seemed a lot murkier. I wasn't really sure what was right or wrong anymore. Whereas before, the Bloodletter usually convinced me he was right no matter what. Which had made things simpler, in a way, but maybe not always *correct*. For instance, the Bloodletter had convinced me that the return of magic was a good thing. That it would help Dwarves finally put the Elves back in their place. Or something like that. Which wasn't too different from what my dad had preached before he lost his mind. But in my dad's version, magic would unite everyone and bring about world peace for the first time since . . . well, pretty much ever.

Either way you looked at it, I'd been convinced that the return of magic was ultimately good.

Now all I could wonder was whether that was actually true. Would magic coming back, bringing with it monsters and possibly a new magical war, really be worth it? Would it truly be good for the world?

After all, Trevor Stormbelly wasn't the same Trevor Stormbelly anymore. So he couldn't tell anyone how magic could possibly create peace rather than obliterate it. Every time I had tried to ask him, the question automatically set off another spell of lunacy without fail. Like it was a trigger.

But deep down I still trusted my old dad, and his vision for the world. And if I fought for that in the end (assuming

I ever got out of here), what would happen if he turned out to be wrong? If *peace through magic* was impossible, as Edwin claimed, then I would be fighting for a future that involved battling horrible monsters until the end of time (or until magic brought about the end of all life on earth the way the Fairies once predicted).

Could I really take that chance?

CHAPTER 30

I Get Taken for a Walk Like a Dog (Except Without the Leash)

Sometime during my third (or fourth?) day of captivity, an Elven girl around my age arrived outside my prison cell.

"I'm here to take you out for a . . . well, a walk, I guess," she said awkwardly. "Not that you're a pet or anything . . ."

I actually laughed. Not so much because her referencing taking me for a walk like a dog was funny, but more out of pure elation that another living thing was talking to me for the first time in days.

"Please," I said, standing up from the bed, moving toward the prison bars. "I'd love to get out of here. Even if it's on a leash, I don't care."

She didn't laugh at my joke, but instead took several steps back and held her sleeve to her face.

"Um, maybe I'll have the guards take you to the shower room first," she said, her voice muffled by a sweatshirt sleeve.

After I'd showered (in a positively ancient and creepy prison shower room), I was brought fresh clothes. I put on a pair of jeans and a purple *Star Wars* sweatshirt with a vintage design on the front that made it look like it'd come from the 1970s.

The Elven girl came back a short time later. She had long dark hair that was pulled back into a haphazard bun with several wild strands escaping like tentacles. She had light brown skin and was tall, taller than me anyway, and wore green skinny pants and an oversize gray sweatshirt that draped off her like a dress. I thought she looked vaguely familiar but I couldn't quite figure out why.

"Ready?" she asked.

"Do I smell better?" I asked.

"Slightly."

I laughed although I wasn't sure if she was actually kidding or not. The cell door clicked open and she motioned for me to follow her. I almost felt giddy with excitement at finally getting out of my cell. In fact, I might even have been skipping as I followed her through the empty hallways of the prison.

"No guards?" I asked, when I first noticed that we were alone.

"You don't think I can take care of myself?"

"I didn't say that . . ."

"You implied it," she said with a sly grin. "Besides, let's say you did attack me, manage to defeat me, and get away. Where are you going to go? We're on an island."

I shrugged. She had a point.

We kept walking, passing a few Elves in another room who were tightening the strings on their bows. They glanced up as we passed then did a double take at the sight of me. They looked more surprised than disgusted or angry.

Eventually we were outside, on the ground level of the prison island. Podiums with placards dotted the concrete walkways, containing all sorts of historical information for tourists, who, it seemed, were no longer allowed out to the landmark island.

"So where to now?" I asked.

"You tell me," the girl said. "This is *your* recess."

I looked around. Several Elven guards were posted on the old prison's roof. A few other Elves walked the grounds with purpose, appearing to be on their way to or from a meeting, as if they were all working on something important. And according to what Edwin had said, they *were* working on something important: banishing magic from the earth.

Several of the passing Elves stared at me. Some sneered or made faces. But most walked by without anything more than a curious glance.

"So what's your name?" I finally asked. "Or am I not allowed to ask that?"

She laughed. It sounded musical, almost like it was coming from a strange instrument that hadn't yet been invented.

"Why wouldn't you be able to?" she said.

"Well, I guess because I thought I was a prisoner or something."

"That doesn't mean common decency has to stop," she said. "Lixiss Lurora."

"Huh?"

"That's my name," she said. "My friends call me Lixi. But you can call me Your Elven Highness the Great and Lustrous Princess Lurora. For now."

Everything she said had a mischievous subtext—like she was always poking fun at herself (and me). As if nothing should be taken at face value. It was so different from what I was used to, having interacted almost exclusively with Dwarves the past few months—Dwarves, who were virtually incapable of subtlety or misdirection of any kind, for better or worse.

"Um, okay. You know my name?"

"Why, do you think you're famous or something?" she asked, but again she was nearly grinning, having fun at my expense rather than actually annoyed or offended.

"Well, yeah, sort of," I played along, since I had recently discovered that I was actually famous (at least among Dwarves). "As the only actual prisoner in this massive prison, it makes me *one of a kind*."

"Come on, Greg," Lixi said dryly. "You only have an hour, so you better get walking if you want to stretch your legs out."

I took her advice and kept walking. Since I'd never been to Alcatraz (or the West Coast at all for that matter), I didn't really know where to go. So basically I sort of just aimlessly wandered the exterior grounds. Taking in the sun and the view of the Bay and the fresh, briny sea breeze. I just enjoyed getting to walk around an area larger than a broom closet.

Lixi let me relish the first part of my walk in silence, aside from the sounds of birds and waves.

"So, Your Elven Highness the Great and Lustrous Princess Lurora," I eventually said, turning to face her as we walked out into the prison's old exercise yard. She laughed at me using her "full name," but she also didn't correct me. "How did you end up with babysitting duty anyway?"

"What if I volunteered?" she asked.

My cheeks grew hot and I looked away.

"Of course I didn't," she added, and I instantly felt foolish for feeling even slightly flattered. "Edwin asked me as a favor. Said I was the best one because of my background with you."

"What does that mean?" I asked.

"You still don't remember, do you?" Lixi said, shaking her head. "You really can be as thickheaded as Edwin described."

I shook my head, feeling terrible for not having any idea what she was talking about.

"I don't get it, do I know you?" I asked. "I mean, I guess you look sort of familiar . . ."

"Edwin always said you were bummed about nobody at the PEE liking you," she said. "He said you never complained about it, that it wasn't your style, but he knew that it bothered you. Except he always added that you could have had way more friends if you'd actually tried. Instead of assuming we all hated you, if you'd just once or twice talked to a classmate who smiled at you, or didn't look away when you made eye contact . . . Maybe if you'd not been such a self-defeating Dwarf about it, you could have been nearly as popular as Edwin."

I stared at her in stunned silence. He had said those things to me in one fashion or another all the time. But surely he'd seen what had happened the few times I did try. I just wasn't as naturally likable as Edwin—and I was fine with that. We can't all be that charismatic; the world would be insufferable. I'd always assumed he kept saying those things to be nice and encouraging and not because he actually believed them.

"Greg, you saw me every day for a whole school year," Lixi finally elaborated. "I was in your sixth-grade English class at the PEE. Hot Sauce was our teacher, remember? He really disliked you and your *witty* comments. But I used to laugh at *all* of your lame jokes. I was the only one that did."

It hit me then.

"Oh man," I said. "You went by Alexis there, didn't you?"

Lixi smiled and framed her face with her hands sarcastically.

"I always thought you were laughing *at me*," I said. "Not at my jokes. I thought you hated me. That you thought I was just a fat, goofy nerd who tried too hard."

"You were all of those things," Lixi said. "But I *liked* that about you. It was funny. Your heartfelt, awkward inability to even *try* to be cool in any way was sort of . . . well, cute. More of us felt that way than you probably realize."

I sighed.

Could that really be true? Or was this a simple trick of Elven manipulation? Make someone feel liked, open them up, then move in for the kill? Lixi seemed genuine, but if she was right, then that meant that everything I'd thought had made up my whole existence at the PEE might not have been true. It would mean the entirety of my two and half years there was suddenly uncertain. It would make my memories totally unreliable.

And she *could* have been right.

My memories of the PEE very easily could be misleading. Maybe if I had framed my experiences differently back then, as someone slightly less cynical, as someone hopeful about making friends rather than as someone who was sure that everyone hated him (or at the very least thought he was a total dork), then I could have seen a different reality? The real one. Maybe I could have had a lot more friends all along?

I'd gone into the PEE thinking like a typical Dwarf.

Had I gone in thinking more like Edwin or my dad . . .

"Man," I said.

"This is a real mind-bender for you, huh?" Lixi said with a smile somehow displaying equal parts sympathy and triumph. "I knew a lot of kids who would have liked to hang out with you and Edwin. And do the weird things you guys did. Even play chess with you. In fact, one of them tried to get a Chess Club started, hoping you guys would join."

"Really? I had no idea."

Lixi nodded. "That's because they were too afraid to ask you directly. They thought *you thought* they were too . . . like, basic, or something for you guys. You two *brilliant nerds*. That just because you were smart enough to get into the PEE on a scholarship, it put you above them. That their accomplishments weren't *earned*, but rather they were only there because of Mommy and Daddy's money."

"I . . ."

But I was speechless. Had I really come off that way at the PEE? Had a few isolated instances of getting bullied, and my own Dwarfy tendencies, really made me come off as standoffish and superior? Had my bitterness over seeing them only as spoiled rich kids blinded me from the reality of who they were as people? Edwin had always tried to include me more with his other friends. And I'd almost always declined. The few times I did go along, I bailed at the first sign of his pals laughing at me. But what if they were laughing *with* me the way Edwin did?

Or, again, maybe this was just some sort of Elven mind game. Maybe I had it right all along and Lixi was using her Elven mind tricks on me? If so, they were clearly working.

If I could be uncertain about something as simple as going to middle school, then how could I trust anything I believed anymore? I'd never doubted myself quite like this before, and it was terrifying. Because if what Lixi said about me at the PEE was completely true, then it opened up a very frightening possibility:

What if I was wrong about *everything*?

CHAPTER 31

Never Touch a Kiwi Fruit Unless You're Prepared to Taste a Rainbow

The next morning, before even a glint of sunlight had filtered into the prison, a guard clanged a sword on the iron bars of my cell.

I sat up and looked groggily toward the dark hallway. A middle-aged woman in a business suit was standing just outside my "room."

"Sorry to be so early," she said. "But it was the only time I could fit into my schedule."

I mumbled something incoherent back—not even sure myself what I said or was trying to say.

"So let's make this quick, then," she insisted, ignoring my half-asleep rambling. "I have a lot to do."

"Make what quick?" I managed, still trying to push away the lingering fog of a surprisingly (and rare) deep sleep.

"Elf Lord Aldaron said you had a somewhat urgent need for me."

Elf Lord Aldaron? He was dead, wasn't he? What was going

on? But once I fully sat up and put my feet on the cold concrete floor, everything clicked into place. She was referring to *Edwin* Aldaron, not his dad, Locien.

"Who are you?" I asked.

The woman sighed as if she was one more dumb question away from bailing on this assignment.

"I'm Dr. Zaleria Yelwarin," she said stiffly. "Chief of Internal Medicine at UCSF Health and part-time professor at Tulane University School of Medicine in the Human world. But also the Chief Alchemy Adviser to the Elf Lord."

For a few seconds I was at a total loss. But then I realized why Edwin had sent her. A pang of guilt stabbed my chest. Guilt and something close to relief. If Edwin had sent Dr. Yelwarin to help me figure out what was wrong with my dad, then maybe deep down he was still the same person who'd once been my best friend. And why would he do this at all if he didn't plan on letting me go eventually? If he didn't truly want my dad to be alive and well someday?

"My dad has been acting funny lately," I started. "Not funny ha-ha but funny strange. And scary."

She started to turn away, rolling her eyes.

"Wait!" I said, resisting the urge to leap to my feet. "It was an Elven poison. Or the antidote did it. We don't know what caused it or how to cure him."

She faced me again, cautiously.

"And you expect me to help out a Dwarf after what you did to our former Elf Lord and his queen?"

"Well, I mean . . ."

I stopped and considered the complications of trying to explain the nuances of everything that had happened. But I figured that such a lengthy clarification might outlast her clearly thinning patience. So I tried a different angle instead.

"Didn't you take an oath of some sort?" I asked. "As a doctor? To not let anyone die if you can help them?"

"*Acting funny strange and scary* doesn't sound very life-threatening to me," she said coldly.

"Why would Edwin have sent you here if he didn't want you to help me?" I asked.

Dr. Yelwarin stared at me, her sharp blue eyes not seeming to blink. Ever. They burned like white flame and she finally nodded ever so slightly. Almost as if her neck had simply gotten tired for a second rather than it being an intentional gesture.

"What happened to him?" she asked.

I started explaining how he'd been poisoned and then how I'd found maybe the antidote but a bunch of other potions, too. And how our own doctor didn't know much about Elven potions so we just gave him all of them. And now we weren't sure which substance might have caused it, but—

The doctor cut me off somewhere in the middle of my babbling.

"Just tell me his exact symptoms," she said.

I explained what had been happening lately. The random fits of wacky advice (such as this gem: *Never touch a kiwi fruit unless you're prepared to taste a rainbow*) and the hauntingly empty reveries and whatnot, expecting her to scoff at the bizarre nature of it all and then actually walk away for real this time.

But instead she nodded.

"Yes, I know what caused this," she said.

"You do?!"

"It was a rare Elven concoction that I personally brewed for the former Elf Lord some time ago," she said. "Though I only made a very small amount since I wasn't even sure I could do it without full use of magical herbs and ingredients. Only he and I had any. It's a variation of an ancient Elven Separate Earth potion called *Shawara Marar Yarda*. It contains a neurotoxin that seeps into various parts of the brain and remains there forever, severely altering the person's behavior in ways identical or similar to what you're describing with your father."

"*Forever?*" I asked, my heart crashing into a dark ocean of dread.

"Yes," she said. "Without treatment."

I kept my breath in, not wanting to get hopeful all over again for nothing. She seemed to understand this and continued quickly without prompt.

"It is, however, theoretically curable with proper treatment. It would involve finding a few potion ingredients that haven't been known to exist since the times of Separate Earth."

"What are they?"

"They're very rare. You won't be able to find them," she said. "Especially not if we undo the return of magic the way the new Elf Lord claims we will . . ."

"Well, then, there's certainly no harm in telling me anyway," I argued.

Dr. Yelwarin hesitated, but finally relented.

"The potion requires many ingredients, most of which can still be found today," she said. "But the three items that would be most troublesome to find, since they haven't been seen in tens of thousands of years, are three finger-lengths of *tafroogmash* root, a single wing from an Asrai Fairy, and seven petals from an extinct, toxic flower called *nidiocory*."

"A Fairy wing?!"

"They grow back," Dr. Yelwarin said. "Besides, the Fairies banished themselves forever to bring us all these years of peace. I doubt even this New Magical Age could bring them back. I'm sorry."

She didn't sound sorry, but I did think she was. At least a little bit. Nobody who wasn't a total monster would have enjoyed telling a kid (Dwarf or not) that his dad was likely going to be messed up forever. As if to confirm this, before leaving she told me about a book I could find in most Elven libraries that contained the full recipe for the antidote.

As she stalked away down the dark hallway, I sank back into my cot. Though there was certainly no way I'd be able to get back to sleep now. At least not without incurring more nightmares.

It was weird: I'd finally gotten what I went to New Orleans for in the first place: finding out what exactly what was wrong with my dad and how to fix it.

So why wasn't I happier?

I mean, this was what I'd risked my life (and let my friends risk theirs) over. And now I had it. But instead of relief, the pit of despair in my stomach only seemed to deepen. And it wasn't just because she'd said it would be virtually impossible to cure him, though that was definitely also a problem. Because if Edwin succeeded and magic was vanquished once again, then the doctor was definitely right: there'd be no way to find those three elusive, enchanted ingredients.

But that wasn't the main reason I felt so sick inside.

It had more to do with still not knowing if my friends were okay. Now that I had obtained what I'd been seeking all along, I finally realized that if they weren't okay, *it wasn't worth it.* I'd rather have a kooky dad forever and all my friends alive than be able to cure him and lose even one of them. That seemed so obvious now—why had I been so clouded before? Why had I been so convinced it'd be worth it just a few days ago, but now the very thought sounded horrible and selfish? What else could have possibly changed in just a few days to shift my thinking so dramatically?

And then the answer hit me all at once:

The Bloodletter.

CHAPTER 32

I Tell an Elf I'm a Dipstick

I'm ashamed to admit that I sort of enjoyed my next four days of captivity.

And Lixi was the main reason.

It started the very day the doctor had come to visit me and delivered the crushing news about my dad. After she left, I basically just lay there and stared up at the ceiling trying not to cry about it all (though the *Dwarves never cry* rule hardly seemed to matter anymore). I did what I could to push my friends, my dad, and our future from my thoughts, and tried to focus on my breakfast, which I attempted to nibble on, mostly unsuccessfully.

And then, just before lunch, Lixi showed up again for a daily recess.

Her initial presence alone wasn't enough to pull me from my funk, but after we started walking, it didn't take long for me to start legitimately smiling. I mean, for one thing: Lixi was funny. At least, *I* found her funny. Our walk started out with this:

"Greg, can I ask you something serious?" she said, after we'd gotten just a few dozen feet down the hall from my cell.

"Um, okay?" I'd replied, my mind still on other things (aside from my dad and my friends, I now had the corrupting powers of the Bloodletter to worry about, too).

"I mean, I hate to get all dark on you right away this afternoon," she said. "But it's important I know the truth."

"Uhh . . ." I managed, not sure I could handle any more darkness in my head.

"When you ate Fun Dip, were you the sort of kid who ate the sugar and threw away the Lik-a-Stix afterward?" she asked, her expression grim, as if she were asking me what I wanted my own funeral to be like. "Or were you the kid who threw away all the sugar uneaten and just ate the dipstick plain?"

I was so caught off guard by the inanity of the question and the deadpan way she'd asked it that all I could do for a few seconds was stare at her and stammer like I had no tongue. But then I burst out laughing. Which really shocked me, because I didn't think I was even capable of smiling in my current mood, let alone giggling like I was eight again.

And that, I would quickly discover, was the power of Lixi.

No matter how down or depressed I was feeling, she could find a way to get me to smile or laugh. I mean, even if my life depended on staying grumpy and frowny, Lixi could probably still get me to break in less than a minute.

"Thanks," I said, when I'd managed to calm down. "I needed that."

"Greg," she said, still not cracking a smile. "You still haven't answered my question."

I let out a final guffaw and then considered her question, ridiculous or not.

"I guess I was a dipstick guy," I said. "I rarely ate the sugar at all, unless it was grape. I usually just ate the stick and gave away the sugar packets. It wasn't as sweet."

"That's what I figured," Lixi said, sounding disappointed. "I guess we can't be friends, after all, since I'm also a Dipsticker. We'd be constantly fighting over who gets it. You know, a very famous psychiatrist once did a study on the psychology of Fun Dip. Her name was Dr. Maeve Shula and she was actually able to accurately predict psychosis and mental illness in her patients based solely on whether they were a Sugarhead or Dipsticker."

"*Really?*" I asked, momentarily wondering if she'd been kidding, after all.

Lixi stared back at me evenly for a few seconds, her face blank. Then finally her lips parted into a smile and she laughed.

"No, of course not!" she said, then paused. "I mean, okay, all of that is actually true. Just not the part about me being a Dipsticker. I'm definitely a Sugarhead."

I laughed again as we stepped outside into a cool afternoon sea breeze.

But all of that isn't to say it was just silly non sequiturs and jokes between us, although I made her laugh just as much—she really did think I was funny for some inexplicable reason, just like she said she had back in sixth grade. We also talked about other stuff, too.

For instance, after joking around about Fun Dip and the ability to predict serial killers for a few more minutes, she brought up something more serious.

"I know you guys think Elves have this charmed life in the modern world," she said. "That because most of us are rich, we have no cares in the world. But being a *rich kid* isn't as great as it sounds."

It was a sudden shift, but I got the feeling that she'd had an agenda to bring it up from the start. And I guess it was hard to blame her. I mean, nobody likes feeling misunderstood—like other people think they're something they're not. In many ways, it's the worst feeling in the world. So I decided to dive headfirst into this conversation, skeptical or not.

"Oh, yeah?" I said. "How so?"

"There's a lot of pressure, for one thing," she said. "Pressure to *become something*. To outdo and outperform the other kids, not just at school, but in life. And then there's the built-in guilt. There with you, every day, like a shadow. I mean, not all rich kids felt that way, but I did."

"What do you mean?"

"It's hard to explain," Lixi said, sitting down on an old bench on the roof of a guard tower with a particularly nice view of the San Francisco skyline.

"Try," I said. "I've got nothing better to do but sit around inside an old prison cell and try to think of creative things to do with my toenails."

"Gross!" Lixi said, but she was also laughing. Then it faded quickly and she raised her eyebrows. "You know we all sleep in old prison cells here, right? Even me."

"Really?" I asked over the sound of the crashing waves against the rocks below—a sound that had become somewhat comforting to me over the past few days.

"Yeah," she said. "Well, our doors don't get closed and locked every night, but almost all of us sleep in cells not much different from yours. We're in the newer wing, though, so the beds are more comfortable and we've got the ability to come and go as we please, but still . . ."

"Spoiled," I said.

Lixi laughed that almost musical laugh of hers again.

I felt a pang of guilt every time I heard it. Talking with her reminded me of Ari—they were different in a lot of ways, but I loved their laughs and they both made me feel so relaxed. It was hard not to feel guilty thinking about Ari, because here I was laughing and joking with a new friend and I didn't know if Ari was even okay.

"Anyway," Lixi said. "To answer your question about Rich Kids' Guilt, it happened every time I got something expensive. Or got to do things most kids didn't. Every time. Like, when we went to the West Side in Chicago to sit in my dad's luxury suite at Blackhawks and Bulls games, I always felt more guilt than joy. I didn't ask to get to do those types of things, I certainly didn't do anything to *deserve them*. I was just born into a wealthy family. So why did I get to live such a charmed life when tens of thousands of kids all around the city struggled to get three basic meals each day? I mean, I could never get over how unfair it all was. How little sense it made."

"I never even considered you guys might feel that way," I said.

"Nobody does," she said. "And you can't really tell anyone because then all they see is a spoiled kid complaining that they have it *too good*. It's a no-win situation unless you're able to just accept that you're a Lucky Chosen One and simply sit back and *enjoy the ride*. Something I failed to do. Not that I'm complaining, I mean, I still wouldn't have traded with other kids. And I think that fact alone makes me more ashamed than anything else. I tried to convince my parents to give more to charity, to be more generous and less frivolous with all our wealth. And they did give a lot to charity, but not nearly enough, still just a fraction of their discretionary money. They were obsessed with building what they called *generational wealth*. For me. They withheld and hoarded money for *me* and my kids and their kids, all of whom don't even exist and maybe never will!"

She stopped, taking a few deep breaths. It was as if she'd been waiting a long time for someone outside her circle, someone who wasn't an Elf, to come along so she could finally unload all this and not be judged. And not be told to stop being ungrateful.

"I understand," I said. "That really doesn't sound all that great."

And I meant it. Growing up relatively poor wasn't exactly a blast—having to work a near full-time job at my dad's store ever since I was eleven while also going to school wasn't the sort of life kids dreamed of. But at least I truly felt like I had earned most of what I had. And I still enjoyed life in all the small ways that weren't luxury seats at sporting events and concerts and lavish trips to cool Caribbean islands. I'm not sure I would have wanted to trade places with her, all things considered.

"It's weird," Lixi said with a humorless laugh. "Somehow, getting everything I ever wanted all the time left me feeling weirdly empty. In fact, my therapist once told me I was *depressed*. You'd think that would have worried my parents, but it only disappointed them."

"Really?" I said, hardly able to imagine that. Even though he was sometimes aloof, my dad was always so caring and kind—even now, "episodes" and all.

"Yeah, they're not really the *affectionate* type," she said.

"Which is common among Elves. Very few of us at the PEE, including me, get encouraging words from our parents. Most of us spent more time when we were kids with our nannies than we did our own moms or dads. My dad has never given me a hug, or even once said the words *I love you*."

"Want a hug?"

I opened my arms, hoping that this wasn't making light of her clearly unhappy childhood. To my relief, her face lit up with a smile and then she laughed again.

"It's a little too early in the day for hugs from a Dwarf," she said.

"Well, then, offer rescinded," I said, pretending to be offended.

"Besides, it wasn't all doom and gloom," Lixi insisted. "There were a lot of good things about growing up an Elf, too."

"Name one," I joked.

"Elves *love* music," she said, prompting me to wonder if this was partially why Froggy was so obsessed with it. "I mean, we practically invented modern pop music. Three of the four Beatles were Elves. And also about half the artists currently atop the Billboard charts. Elves have won over 75 percent of all Grammys ever awarded."

"Okay, okay, quit bragging," I said. "Elvis was a Dwarf, so take that!"

"Do you even know one of his songs?"

"Well, um, no," I admitted—I only knew he was a Dwarf because I overheard Ari and Froggy talking about it once. "But that doesn't mean he wasn't good! Back in the day and whatnot."

"And what day was that?" she asked with that sly grin on her face.

"Uhh . . . the . . . 1940s?"

Lixi just laughed and didn't reveal if I'd guessed correctly or not.

"We love our ancient music, too," she continued. "At all the traditional Elven festivals, like Qitris, a band plays famous Elven folk songs by an ancient Separate Earth band called Method of Valor. There's even a really good cover band of them called Modus Virtuti. The bands play all night and we dance until our feet and legs are sore. We also love playing games—I mean, just laughing and having fun in general."

It sounded like a weird statement to me at first, but then I realized something.

"You know, Dwarves actually don't really laugh that much," I said. "And our version of fun usually involves more serious things like blowing glass, making weapons, mining, eating, and telling stories from Separate Earth. And not even fun ones."

"Whereas," Lixi said theatrically, "Elves like games so much that we were the ones who invented baseball. It's a variation of an ancient Elven game called pyre pitch. The best team back then, and still the most popular in our inner circles even though they're well over 100,000 years extinct, was the Felselian United Krakens. They were like the New York Yankees of pyre pitch."

We sat outside on a bench and talked about sports for a bit longer, even though the main thread of the conversation was about how neither of us really liked sports. But eventually we started heading back toward my cell.

At one point during the walk back, magic came up. Lixi seemed genuinely impressed when I said I had the Ability.

"Won't you miss magic?" I asked.

"What do you mean?"

"Like, if Edwin succeeds in banishing it forever," I said. "Won't part of you miss magic? All the cool things it can do. Even if you don't have the Ability, just seeing your friends do magic is really neat."

Lixi frowned deeply and looked at her feet as she walked, almost as if there was something she wanted to say but couldn't because I wouldn't like it. She remained silent for longer than what would be considered a normal pause.

"What's wrong?" I asked. "Do you not have the Ability?"

"I don't," she admitted. "But it's not that . . . It's, well, never mind. Magic is complicated for me to talk about, Greg."

"Okay . . ." I said, waiting for her to elaborate.

She didn't, and we just walked in silence for a bit longer. It was the first time there had been even a hint of tension that day, and that's probably what prompted her next question.

"What's your favorite Marvel movie?" she asked suddenly. "Mine was *Thor: Ragnarok*. Or are you one of those Dwarves who rejects all things modern?"

"Uhhh," I started, not really wanting to admit that I was the only kid alive who didn't really care for the Marvel movies. "My favorite is the one, like, with the big ship that explodes?"

"Which one?" Lixi asked with a smirk. "That happens in twenty-one of the twenty-four movies."

"Um, I forget the name of it, but it's also the one where, you know, two of the good guys argue and actually fight *each other* instead of just the bad guys."

This time Lixi laughed.

"Greg, that still leaves, like, thirteen of the movies it could be," she said as we arrived at my cell. "It's okay if you're a DC nerd. No shame in that."

I didn't have the heart to tell her I wasn't really into *any* superhero movies, DC or Marvel. So I just grinned and shrugged helplessly.

"You're funny, Greg," she said as I stepped back into my cell. "That definitely hasn't changed."

I kept smiling as the iron bars of my prison door slammed closed between us.

CHAPTER 33

Turns Out I've Been Eating Quail Supplies

As the days went on, I really started looking forward to my walks with Lixi.

In fact, for the next three days, Lixi started showing up two or three times for walks around the old prison instead of just once. Honestly, with the way things were going, it was getting harder to keep seeing Elves as my natural-born enemies. Especially once she started introducing me to some of the other Elves working at the base. If it weren't for the locked cell, I'd be less a prisoner and more like a guest.

Take, for instance, the day she introduced me to Elven food.

It turned out that Elves loved good food every bit as much as Dwarves, even though their idea of a full meal was more what I'd consider a light snack. They believed in *quality over quantity.* Which sounded insane to me—why not just have both? But some old Elven favorites were dishes like pea tendrils with crispy rice and fermented cucumbers with lavender mustard.

Or beet petals with smoked pistachios and black garlic foam. And I had to admit they tasted pretty good, even if the portions were tiny and light on meat.

I knew all of this because one day we stopped by the kitchen and I met the head chef and her two assistants, who did all the cooking for the complex.

"Merethyl Umelar," she introduced herself. "And these are my sous chefs, Tolthe and Tlannatar."

They were young, probably just out of college, and had tons of tattoos. We hung out with them for nearly an hour and I could tell right away that they had a blast cooking all day. They laughed and joked around a lot and it didn't even feel like any of them were actually "working."

Chef Umelar even taught me the proper way to chop an onion. Before, during the few times my dad had asked me to help him cook, I'd just hack away at it until it was in smallish pieces. After all, my dad had always said, "Greg, the size and shape of things won't affect how they taste."

But apparently that wasn't quite the case.

"Slice it in half first," Chef Umelar said, showing me how to chop—which partially meant entrusting me with a very sharp Elven cooking knife.

As I cut the onion in half, I realized it was the first time I'd held a weapon, any weapon, since I lost the Bloodletter. It once again sort of made me miss him, even after the realization of how much he'd been pushing me to endanger my friends for a cause that wasn't ultimately worth it.

But even more than that, I was shocked that these Elves would entrust a prisoner with a weapon. A prisoner who, depending on how much Galdervatn might be seeping up through the earth naturally on this very spot, could potentially also perform magic. Which, in some ways, made me a prisoner who could escape right now if I got lucky and tried hard enough.

Honestly, though, I never even gave escape a thought. They trusted me enough to give me a knife to teach me something out of kindness (or perhaps boredom?). And Dwarves *never* betrayed a person's trust. No matter what. Some would call that a fault, but it was something I was personally quite proud of. Which was why I used the knife to cut the onion and nothing more.

"Good," the chef said. "Now cut one half into strips to the core but not all the way through."

She did one half first to show me and then handed the knife back. None of the Elves present even seemed to bat an eye that they'd given a weapon to a Dwarven prisoner. It made me feel guilty for even mentally making a thing out of it.

Chef Umelar showed remarkable patience as she guided me through the rest—until I had a pile of decently diced onion in front of me.

"Uniform food size means that everything will be equally seasoned and cook at the same rate," she said.

I found out later that she used to be the head chef at a trendy and successful restaurant in San Francisco called Quail Supplies. That was back before Edwin came calling with a greater purpose in mind.

On another day, Lixi introduced me to the fortress janitor, an older Elf named Ivlisar Torwraek.

"But everyone around here usually just calls me Wrecking Ball," he said.

"Because you're clumsy and break things a lot?" I joked.

He looked at me sideways and laughed.

"Not exactly," he said. "I have this condition, and one of the symptoms for me is that everything needs to be perfectly tidy. Neat and orderly and clean as a whistle. So the name, it's ironic, see?"

I laughed nervously, worried I might have offended him or made light of his condition. Then Wrecking Ball grinned at my obvious discomfort and laughed along with me.

"It makes this a perfect job for me, though," he added as he picked a tiny piece of lint off his impeccably ironed gray uniform. "I'd be walking around cleaning anyway. So I might as well help the cause while I'm at it."*

Perhaps my favorite Elf of all (aside from Lixi), though, was Foxflame Farro (yeah, his real name), the fortress Spiritual Guide of Ancient Elven Mysticism. Basically he was like a priest. His religion was called Alaflusy Celority, which roughly means Communion of Four Gods. Though now a virtually extinct faith, most Elves still practiced it in passing, merely out of respect and habit. Very few believed any of the founding lore.

Foxflame was tall and lanky and very funny. He was almost hopelessly happy, goofy, and charming. Which was of course not at all what the Dwarves thought of when they spoke of Elves. In fact, many of the Elves I'd met so far directly contradicted everything the Dwarves believed about them.

Foxflame was constantly riding around the halls of Alcatraz on a skateboard, often doing cool tricks along the way. Sometimes, when I was alone in my cell in the evenings, I could hear the echoes of his wheels rolling down some distant hallway

---

* That was a common theme among the Elves I met around Alcatraz. All of them seemed fully devoted to Edwin's cause: ending the return of magic for good.

or cellblock. The guard outside my cell would roll his eyes and sigh. Which always made me smirk.

Foxflame and I talked a lot about the difference between Elves and Dwarves. He found Dwarven culture nearly as fascinating as I did theirs. Turned out they had a lot of incorrect (and some totally correct) preconceived notions about us as well. Like, they always assumed that Dwarves slept on stone and not in beds (hilarious). And that we refused eat anything that didn't have meat on it (which wasn't actually *that far* from the truth). He nearly choked on his own tongue when I told him I actually had a Dwarven friend who was a vegetarian.

It was during one of these types of discussions, inside the old prison chapel, that he finally talked about some of the ideas behind the religion he had devoted his life to.

We had already discussed Human religions and how funny it was to both of us that many Humans actually believed in stuff that had only been written down three or four thousand years ago—which is like a micro-fraction of Human existence.

"You know, Greg," Foxflame said. "Elves and Dwarves, actually, are not so dissimilar from one another in our original beliefs."

"Really? But we're so different in almost every other way . . ."

"Are we?" he asked, and then laughed. "I would argue that things like Elves preferring vegetables over meat, or being slightly taller and thinner on average, or even having different values on the whole, are all superficial characteristics, at best. Those aren't the things that really make us who we are. Even major differences in belief systems are meaningless—that's where the Humans have it all wrong. Take my ancient religion after all: Alaflusy Celority. It's virtually identical to the Dwarves' original religion."

"I didn't even know we had a religion," I said.

"Well, in both of our cultures many of these old ideas became lost with time," he said. "In Alaflusy Celority, the fundamental belief is that the universe was created from a single point of light by four gods: Bitrix, Keeper of Death; Onja, Keeper of Hope; Igmir, Keeper of Love; Kymtos, Keeper of Life. These are the four guiding principles of being—the only things that are assured in any form of existence. These deities guided the physics of the cosmos, creating life as part of a chain reaction, a virus that moved from one separating piece of energy to the next, constantly evolving and changing on each one in new and different ways. Life was never meant to worship a higher being, but rather to celebrate its own existence and the joys and happiness that consciousness can bring if experienced with a pure spirit. Life is about a constant search for harmony.

"Your ancient, original religion is called Vapigar drung Struzen. Which means the Followers of Eventuality. The fundamental belief was that all life started with the earth itself. At its core was a single point of energy. The original Dwarven gods, Woohr, God of Elements; Ereus, God of Light; and Xuntar, God of Dark, collectively planted life there, like a seed. And from it bloomed the planet itself, layers upon layers of rock and soil and geothermal forces that were once considered mystical. From there it spread throughout the universe, like a flower blowing pollen across a field with the wind, life following with it. Your religion was also never about worshipping gods, but rather about worshipping the elements, the light, and the dark, and all the things they bring to life. Are you seeing the similarities now? Of course, neither race has much use for these types of fantastic tales anymore."

"Don't you believe in them?"

"In a way," he said. "I mean, whether they happened exactly like this or not doesn't matter. It's the spirit of them that I admire. And wish we all still believed in. But mostly, my new one true god is . . . *ice cream*. Good Lord Univar the Almighty himself do I love ice cream."

He looked at me, his dark youthful eyes so serious. And then we both exploded into fits of laughter. Lixi looked up at us from a nearby pew where she'd been reading and rolled her eyes with a grin.

"The point is, Greg," Foxflame said, "just love as much as you can. Even if it's things like ice cream. If we only celebrated the good rather than dwelled on the bad, everything would be different. It sounds lame, but if this were a universal trait we all shared all the time, it would actually work."

"I agree," I said. "But you can't tell people what to do . . ."

"Of course not!" he said, and laughed. "These aren't realistic hopes of mine. Just fanciful visions of a world with sugar-coated rainbows and cotton-candy clouds, right? But a guy can dream. Anyway, want to see me do a sick plasma spin flip into a salad grind on the front railing over there?"

He held up his skateboard, that flighty grin planted on his face.

I nodded, smiling in spite of everything.

Through it all, though, meeting new Elves, even becoming friends with some of them, I still never forgot about my Dwarven companions. My nights were tortured wondering if they were okay. I had led them to New Orleans on a rogue mission, after all. If they were indeed hurt or worse, it was a simple, undeniable fact that it was my fault. But in the moments I could get past that, and convince myself that they were still alive, I thought a lot about how amazing it would be for my friends and other Dwarves to come and live here for a little while. They would see firsthand that most Elves were not at all inherently bad. In fact, they were just like us in most ways. In the ways that really mattered: they cared about their friends and family and helping one another survive more than anything else.

But I knew that wasn't possible. You could change a Dwarf's or an Elf's mind one at a time. Maybe. But it wouldn't be fast enough. It would take too long, and even then there'd be certain Elves (like Locien Aldaron or Dr. Yelwarin) and certain Dwarves (like Ooj the Leprechaun) who would never fully change. Never let themselves see the truth.

And that was what broke my heart. Knowing that war was still probably inevitable, whether I wanted it or not. Whether I had changed or not.

And that my new Elven friends would one day again (probably sooner than we all expected) be my enemies.

CHAPTER 34

◆ ─ ※◆※ ─ ◆

My Dad's Magical Utopia Gets Even Farther Away

E ventually Edwin was back.

I think it was roughly eleven or twelve days after our first chess game. But like I said, keeping track of time as a prisoner in an old concrete cell was difficult. Before long the days began to bleed together, especially once I started enjoying my time with Lixi and Foxflame and the other Elves.

But it was definitely in the morning when he showed up at my cell again. I know this because he woke me by shaking my shoulder and repeating one of our favorite bad puns (one that was so bad and nonsensical we couldn't help but to laugh every time we heard it) back from the good old days when our friendship was simpler (and still intact).

"Egg morning," he said. "It's a brewtiful sunrise and I like you a waffle lot."

There was humor in his eyes. And for a moment, I almost believed we *were* back in the good old days, in his room having a sleepover, the past four months having all been a bad dream.

But of course that wasn't the case. And the prison bars behind his grinning face reminded me of that right away.

"Not even a pity laugh?" he said.

I managed a grin.

"Okay, good enough," he said. "Come on, let's go get some breakfast."

I followed him to the prison cafeteria, which was empty, either because it was too early for anyone else to be up eating or because he'd wanted it that way. A standard American breakfast of bacon, eggs, toast, and hash browns was already laid out on two plates.

He didn't seem outright friendly, but he was definitely treating me differently than at our last meeting. I wondered if part of him hoped that my time here with the Elves had allowed me to see the truth: that they weren't naturally evil—just as he'd been telling me since the moment I'd found out I was a Dwarf. And now that my mind was clear, maybe he hoped we could begin to rebuild what we once had?

As we ate, I noticed something different about Edwin. Underneath the friendliness, he also seemed worried. Stressed. Perhaps even afraid—of what, I had no clue. I still didn't know where he'd been, or what he'd been doing during his nearly two weeks away, but he looked less confident than when he first told me he would *save the world*.

I could see it in the way he was wringing his hands together between bites of eggs. Or in the way that, every time he wasn't looking at me, his face formed into a deep frown. And most of all by what he said to me after a few silent first bites:

"I think someone is trying to stab me in the back," he said. Then he quickly smiled and shook his head. "No, not you. I mean, whatever damage you caused, I know you didn't mean to. That doesn't mean I'm fully over it, but I know you didn't intend to harm me or my family."

"Oh . . ." I said, completely unsure of how to respond.

This surprisingly made Edwin laugh, but it faded quickly and he wrinkled his forehead again with concern. And in that brief silence, I noticed for the first time that there wasn't a single guard in sight—it was just me and him alone in the cafeteria—surely not by accident.

"I think I have a mole here, a double agent," he said. "And they're trying to sabotage my plan. That's the thing about Elves, Greg. We're not exactly like the Dwarves think we are, but you guys *are* right about one thing: We're good liars. We're masters of deception. I just don't know who I can trust anymore. Except you, oddly enough, as hilarious as that sounds now, given our circumstances. At least with Dwarves, they always say what they mean, for better or worse."

I sat there stunned.

There was so much I wanted to say and ask him, but I didn't. Partly because I didn't want to break this spell. This moment at breakfast was the closest I'd felt to being friends again since it all went wrong back at the former Hancock building. But also because his long, tired sigh sort of told me he didn't really want to talk about it anymore.

He confirmed as much a moment later.

"I just need a half day to relax like old times," he said, his throat tight. "Being a leader is hard, Greg—which is the understatement of the decade, surely. I just want to play chess and joke around for a few hours. Can you do that with me? Even if you're only pretending?"

I nodded slowly, still struggling to find any words.

"Of course," I finally managed to say. "That would be awesome."

During the rest of breakfast I told him that I'd been treated very well in his absence. Our conversation eventually shifted into us laughing fondly over what a character Foxflame was, and how funny Lixi could be—sometimes so subtly that you didn't even realize it until hours later. Edwin called her *undercover funny*.

Afterward, he led to me an office deep inside the prison. A chess game was already set up on the small desk, with two chairs facing each other. We sat down and started playing without saying anything.

I was white this time, since we always alternated. The last time he'd been white and had destroyed me despite using a bizarre new strategy that I never could have envisioned working, regardless of who was using it.

This time around, he played much more like he used to. He followed the book lines and made logical, if not conservative, moves. Then again, Edwin rarely played anything exactly the same way twice. My motto in chess took after my dad's: Master *one* opening before moving on to more. But Edwin always had a different perspective: Keep the enemy guessing and explore all sorts of avenues toward victory—you never know what you might stumble upon.

For most of the game, the conversation was light like Edwin had requested. We talked about old times. Things we had done in the past that had made us laugh.

Like the time we stayed up all night watching this weird, but oddly compelling Korean TV show on Netflix about a female pasta chef and her misogynistic boss, who also happened to be her love interest! It had started out as a joke: Let's watch one episode, just out of pure curiosity. But then before we knew it, we had stayed up all night binge-watching the entire first season. And by episode four we were barely chiming in to make fun of the cheesy production values and melodrama anymore, but rather simply enjoying the story.

Or like the time we rode around the city on our bikes on May 5 wearing Santa costumes that Edwin had bought. We carried huge, red-velvet sacks chock-full of Wendy's hamburgers that we passed out to pretty much anyone who would accept them—which was surprisingly just about everyone we asked. In fact, we emptied our bags so fast that we next hit up a nearby McDonald's to reload, and then a local burger joint called Fatso's Last Stand for the third refill.

After that, it sort of became a tradition—we did the same thing the next two May fifths. Except we changed up our outfit each year. In year two we dressed up as *Mario Kart* characters, complete with fake *Mario* "karts." And in year three Edwin dressed up in a giant foam novelty-burrito-mascot outfit, and I wore a huge panda-bear costume.

Sadly, year four had been just a few weeks away when our friendship imploded. We'd been discussing a few different costume options for that year, including the two burglar villains from *Home Alone*, or Jason from *Friday the 13th* and Michael Myers from *Halloween*.

But our conversation as we played chess wasn't stuck totally in the past. We also talked about all the funny theories we'd read or heard about that Humans were coming up with to try to explain all the weird magic-related stuff happening lately. Some of our favorites involved a race of aliens called the Reptilians, who just happened to look like, you guessed it, giant lizards.

And then there was the one in which it was all a conspiracy orchestrated by the Australian government to bring more attention to some koala crisis.

Edwin even updated me on the state of things at the PEE. A lot of kids had dropped out when his parents died—which made sense since it was a mostly Elven school and many of the associated families went into panic mode and still hadn't fully calmed down.

About thirty minutes into the game, I looked down at the chessboard and realized we were still tied. Which was shocking. I rarely beat him, and even the six or seven times I remembered doing so, I was pretty sure he'd let me win. And I couldn't remember beating him, or even getting a draw, since at least the end of sixth grade, which was hundreds of matches ago. But yet here I was, approaching endgame and still tied in total material.

He must have realized the same thing, because pretty much all conversation ceased at that point and we both just focused on the game. And even though I got to an endgame where I thought I might at least manage a draw (he had his king, three pawns, and a bishop versus my king, three pawns, and a knight), he still managed to eke out a win by slipping a pawn past my pieces to get a new queen.

At that point, I resigned, knowing even a draw would be impossible.

"Well, I'm impressed," Edwin said afterward, almost looking a little shocked he came even that close to a draw. "I thought you said you haven't been playing much."

"I haven't," I said. "Or, well, I've been playing against my friend Lake, but he's honestly pretty terrible. And my dad would still be good if he could ever make it through a whole game without an *episode*."

"Well, you played really well," he said. "And I had a lot of fun. This has been just what I needed. Thank you, Greg. I mean it."

I nodded.

And that's when I ruined it all.

In my defense, I didn't mean to. It all started out innocently enough. I mean there we were, playing chess and joking around like old times. And it was really giving me hope that our friendship was salvageable. For some crazy reason, it gave me the confidence to bring up magic again.

So I did—even quoting my last conversation with Foxflame, sharing with Edwin his belief that we're really not all that different, and how it tied in to his fanciful vision for a better world. I pointed out that it wasn't so far off from what my dad has said about magic.

"I mean, my dad still could be right," I said. "Maybe magic is the way we can get other Elves and Dwarves, and Humans and other creatures for that matter, to see the truth. To realize that we're all more the same than we think. That the specific differences between us all are meaningless when it comes down to what really matters."

"We don't disagree about any of that," Edwin said. "Just on the *how to achieve it* part."

"I think magic could actually do that," I said. "Magic could be, like, the ultimate Hallmark card come to life? I mean, we can't really know because we've never known a fully magical world."

"No way," Edwin said. "Like I said before: so far magic has only brought death and destruction. And it will get worse when it comes back fully. Right now it's only been strong enough to affect small areas for limited moments in time. But what happens when enough magic has returned to start making planes lose power midflight and fall from the sky? Have you thought about that?"

I shook my head.

It was a good point. But I still thought it was a shortsighted way to think of things. After all, Edwin was approaching this from the perspective of the modern world. But the return of magic would mean a global shift away from everything we thought we knew. There wouldn't *be* any planes to fall from the sky soon enough. Especially not if we showed the world what was coming before we got to that point. If we got the planes out of the sky before that could happen.

I explained all of that to Edwin. And then I went even further.

"The world as it is now, without magic, has a *ton* of problems," I said. "Just because Elves have it good as the überwealthy elite doesn't mean war, terrorism, starvation, disease, poverty, etcetera, aren't killing hundreds of thousands of people every year. You've been living in a virtual *wonderland*, but what about everyone else? Are you really going to just accept that you have it good and others don't and be fine with that? As long as number one is covered, then, oh well?"

"Well, unfortunately that's just the reality of the world," Edwin said. "I don't like it, but that's how it's always been. Even back in Separate Earth. You can't please everyone—you would drive yourself insane trying."

"But maybe you can!" I said. "That's my whole point. What's the one thing that we've never tried in history to solve all the world's problems? Because wars and religion and industry certainly haven't done the trick. Not for *all people*."

"Oh geez, I see where this is going already," Edwin said, rolling his eyes.

"Right," I said. "*Magic*. So maybe that's the one thing that will actually work? Who's to say the New Magical Age would actually be worse for most people? There have been plenty of horrible wars and violence over the past so many thousand years without magic, after all. So we don't have that much to lose by trying. I mean, you guys got your mansions and luxury cars and private jets, you could lose all that stuff, but what about the billions living in poverty or in daily violence? They have nothing to lose."

Edwin sighed. He stared off behind me at the bare wall of the small office.

"There's an answer to these concerns," he said. "But you're not going to like it. I've been . . . Well, I've been holding something back. You'll think it's terrible, but I assure you the whole point behind it will be to fix all the things you just said. To ensure that things get better for *everyone*."

"Do I even want to know?" I sighed.

"You said yourself how much you like Foxflame and Lixi and Wrecking Ball and the others," he began. "Hopefully you see that we're every bit as good a people as Dwarves or Humans or anyone. I guess the reason I'm saying all this, Greg, is that not *all* magic will be gone if we succeed with our plan."

"What do you mean?" I asked.

"If my plan works, the Elves will still have magic," he said. "I mean, not all Elves, which is complicated in itself. Just us. Me and my loyal followers. All of us who are committed to peace."

"I don't understand," I said, shaking my head.

This sounded even worse, somehow, than the problems of

the modern world. Not only would an elite group have most of the wealth, but they'd *also* have magic on their side? It sounded insanely one-sided. Selfish. Maybe this Edwin wasn't the same old Edwin deep down, after all, like I'd let myself start to believe. Even if he meant well, which I was pretty sure he did, his plan showed just how warped his mind had gotten.

"Hear me out," Edwin said.

I nodded, because what more could I do? Honestly, I wanted to hear him explain himself. I wanted him to convince me this wasn't as bad as it sounded. Because it sounded pretty bad. In fact, it sounded like Edwin was trying to use the power of magic—his exclusive access to it—to essentially rule the world. Unless there was some twist to this I was missing?

"We'll only keep magic as a way to end all that nonsense you were referring to: wars and poverty and such," Edwin said passionately, his eyes practically glowing with sincerity. "We want to use magic as a way to keep all the other people in line. The Elves, who I would argue are the natural choice as curators of this new world, since we are the most level-headed and historically most successful at implementing societal structure, can police the planet and take care of everyone. Without magic, nobody will be able to oppose us. And thus we can ensure that there will be no wars, no violence, no bloodshed, no poverty, ever again."

"You're talking about a dictatorship," I said, still not believing what I was hearing. "With required obedience. No freedoms. Isn't freedom worth something, too?"

"It's not like that, Greg." Edwin sighed. "There will only be initial obedience, which we can peacefully enforce with magic. And then eventually it will all turn into free will and harmony. Trust me, once everyone sees how peaceful this new world can and will be, they won't even *want* to resist it. It would only lead to pointless violence. Besides, I am not an oppressor, quite the opposite. In the new world, I will be a liberator, an agent of peace. My plan is the only one where potentially *nobody* dies. In a way, maybe your dad was right all along: maybe *through Elves* magic *can* bring a lasting peace?"

I *hated* the idea of him warping my dad's vision. I knew that was not what my dad had in mind when he spoke of a *magical utopia*. Far from it. In the magical world my dad had imagined, there would be no need for *curators* or *peacekeepers* at all.

"So you really think you can trust only Elves with magic?" I asked, the snarling anger in my voice surprising even me. "When you just told me a few hours ago that an Elf could be double-crossing you? And that Elves can't be trusted! How can you now sit there and say they're the only ones who can be trusted?!"

"Well, I mean, that's different," Edwin said, but I could tell his mind was reeling. "I mean, not all Elves would have access to magic. Only those I trust the most."

"Oh, I see, well, it's a good thing you're a perfect judge of people and can't make mistakes," I said. "Like possibly allowing a mole into your base here. Glad we can assume that won't happen again."

"There's no need for sarcasm," he said calmly, but I could tell he knew I was right. Then he sighed and shook his head. "I know it's not perfect yet. But I will figure it out. I mean, *I'll* be the only one with magic if that's what it takes to keep people from dying."

Whether his plan ultimately proved to be right or wrong, one thing was clear: He truly believed it was the best for everyone. Unless he was duping me with his famous Elven powers of persuasion, he hadn't come up with this plan in his own self-interest. But I still couldn't overlook the built-in Elven superiority and elitism of the whole thing.

"You realize this plan means you think Dwarves are inherently lesser than you, right?" I asked. "If some Elves can be trusted with magic, but no Dwarves can?"

"That's not . . . You're warping my words now," he said.

"Am I?" I asked.

"Okay, I know it sounds bad," Edwin admitted reluctantly. "But at least this way people won't be killing one another anymore."

I nodded.

On that point it was hard to argue. If *only Elves* had magic, then it was entirely possible they could somehow force the whole world into a kind of uneasy "peace." But would it really be harmonious without free will? Plus, that was also assuming that all Elves would be on the same page.

Something I *knew* wasn't true.

Because of both his confession to me just an hour ago, and also because of what I saw in St. Louis Cemetery #2 in New Orleans. And so I figured now was as good a time as any to ask him about it, being that this conversation couldn't get much worse.

"Back in New Orleans," I started, "just before I got knocked out, I saw something strange. I saw Elves fighting Elves, Edwin. I'm sure of it now. What was that all about?"

Edwin sat forward in his chair again, his forehead scrunched with worry. For the first time since I'd been there, he looked every bit as young as he was. He looked once again like a kid who had just turned fourteen and still had a lot to learn. His expression grew dark as he debated what to tell me.

"I can't talk about the specifics of that yet," he said. "But we're dealing with it. Speaking of, I think it's best I get back to work. Playtime is over."

He stood from his chair so suddenly that the chess pieces on the table rattled, and I knew that our meeting was finished.

CHAPTER 35

There Will Still Be Time for Bike Rides and Board Games During the Apocalypse

My last-ever walk with Lixi happened the next day.

She came to get me just before lunch, smiling brightly, as always. She even brought me a gift, something wrapped in an old piece of leather. I undid the bindings and beneath the soft animal hide was a green amulet on a gold chain. It was oval, but uneven, a few inches long, consisting of a stone base with a green gemstone in the center with little silver runes carved into it.

It was cool and all, but I didn't quite know what I was looking at.

"Is this like some kind of magical Elven-charm thingy with special powers?" I asked.

"Nah, they gave it away as a promotion at the newest super-hero movie I went to," Lixi said. "I just thought it looked neat."

"Oh . . ."

She burst out laughing. I held the heavy pendant, totally unsure if I should laugh along with her.

"I'm just kidding," Lixi finally said. "You were sort of right the first time. It's a Talisman of Barriers. Elven lore says that they grant you safe passage between spiritual worlds after death. Some people also claim they bring luck. Most think they're just cool-looking trinkets. But who knows? Traditionally, every Elf born under a blue moon gets one on their first birthday. I want you to have mine."

"I can't accept this."

I tried to hand it back, but she shook her head and put her hands behind her back.

"Nope, it's yours," Lixi said with a smile. "I want you to have it, Greg. It will bring you more luck than me—it sounds like you need it with your Thursday curse and all that. Besides, all mine has ever done is sit in my drawer since I was a baby. I really don't think it has any powers, even with magic coming back. But I want you to think of me every time you see it. A sort of reminder that we're not so bad. Elves, I mean."

I put into my pocket, wishing I had something to give her in return.

"Thank you," I said. "That's really nice of you. But why are you talking like we won't see each other anymore? I mean, is Edwin releasing me or something?"

"I really don't know," Lixi admitted. "But I know I'll be leaving soon. In a day or two probably. He has another mission for me."

We started walking then, along a familiar route out toward the old exercise yard.

"What's your mission? Is it dangerous?"

"I can't say," she said.

"Can't say or don't know?"

"Greg, I don't really want to talk about it," Lixi said, telling me all I needed to know about how dangerous it might be: *probably very*. "Can't we talk about the usual stuff instead? Like the cool plays the PEE used to put on? Or all the funny accidental use of magic we've seen recently?"*

I laughed, but then lapsed into quiet melancholy. The fact was, I could tell neither of us really wanted to talk about the usual stuff knowing it might be the last time I would see her for a while. Maybe ever, depending on how things played out.

"Do you know, Lixi?" I asked, breaking the sad silence. "What Edwin is *really* planning? How he plans to strip only *most* of the world of magic?"

"So he told you more, then, huh?" she said.

I nodded.

"Well, only a little," I said. "Just the part where Elves keep all the magic."

"I can tell from your tone you don't agree with the plan," she said. "Which is fine. From your perspective, I probably wouldn't either. But trust me, Greg, it will be for the better."

"How could he possibly pull that off, though?" I asked. "I mean, what if he's wrong? About even being able to do it?"

"Even if I did know more about the plan and could explain it to you," she said, "I still wouldn't."

"What?" I asked with half-joking offense. "You don't *trust* me?"

Lixi laughed, but it wasn't her usual melodic laugh. This time it sounded empty, laced with anything but joy.

---

* The other day, an Elf who didn't know he had the Ability must have stepped through a natural release of Galdervatn, because one second he was just walking normally, and then a moment later green lights shot out like laser beams from his ears, nostrils, mouth, and eyes. He got so freaked out he ran, arms flailing in a panic, right into a brick wall. He suffered a nasty bump on the head but otherwise was okay.

"It's not so much a trust issue as it is being loyal," she explained. "If the Elf Lord ordered us not to talk about it, then I will obey those orders."

I nodded and decided to change the subject. If this was indeed one of our last few conversations, then I didn't want it to just be me trying to pry information from her.

"Thank you," I said. "For being so nice to me. For being an actual friend while I've been here. I mean, this is probably the best a prisoner has ever been treated at Alcatraz. Even Al Capone, who supposedly got special treatment back when he was a prisoner here!"

"He was a Dwarf, you know," she said.

I laughed and nodded.

"Yeah, I found that out just a few months ago," I said. "Which is surprising considering how much he loved money."

"You're shocked that not all Dwarves are altruistic saints who only value things pure and noble and nonmonetary?"

There was a long pause and then we both burst out laughing.

"Okay, point taken," I said. "I mean, I guess Dwarves can be a little self-righteous."

"Just a little," she agreed.

We stopped in the yard and sort of just stood there in the sunlight for a moment. I listened to the birds and the comforting sound of the water on the nearby shores of the island.

"So do you think there's a scenario in which we get to remain friends?" Lixi asked, breaking the moment. "I mean, no matter what happens with Edwin's plan."

I breathed out slowly, not liking all the places my mind was headed.

"Probably not," I said. "At least not friends in the way people think. I'm always going to remember how funny and nice you are. How much I liked hanging out, even as a prisoner. But I really doubt there's a future where we're, like, going on bike rides and getting together to play board games and stuff."

Lixi moved some dirt around with her toe in the yard, drawing an uneven circle.

"You're probably right," she said. "But you do have to admit that if Edwin's plan goes how he's envisioning, it's more likely to work out that way. I mean, the way he tells it, *everyone* will be friends . . . sort of."

"And you really believe that's possible?"

"You keep saying Edwin's plan won't work," Lixi said. "And maybe you're right. But let me ask you this: What's the Dwarves' solution? Do you guys even have a plan to help avoid disaster when there are magical monsters everywhere and no modern technology works and all the Humans are confused and terrified? I mean, what are you guys going to do to keep the world from descending into total madness?"

I opened my mouth instinctively, ready to lay out some sort of quick, defensive argument. But then I closed it again. Because, really, what could I say? She was right. If the Dwarves had a master plan, they hadn't really talked about it much. They were too busy deciding just how badly we would probably fail at any type of strategy. Sure, we were doing MPMs for now, but that wasn't a long-term plan. It was like sticking Band-Aids on an incision after a major surgery.

Lixi took my silence for what it was.

"So, see?" she said with a smile. "What's the harm in us trying? *Someone* has to try *something*."

I nodded reluctantly. Whether I agreed with Edwin's plan or not, it was still better than what the Dwarves had in mind simply by default. Because as far as I knew we had nothing.

Unless my dad suddenly snapped out of it and could finally tell us how he thought magic could bring peace.

We hung out in the exercise yard and talked about mostly meaningless stuff for the next hour. I think neither of us wanted to go back to conversations about the end of the world. Or her new dangerous mission. Or anything more significant than which Netflix shows we would miss the most in the new magical world.

As we headed back toward my cell, I tried to choke out a heartfelt goodbye, but Lixi stopped me before it even really got started.

"This isn't goodbye-goodbye," she said. "I mean, I don't leave for at least another day. I'll still see you tomorrow for sure, Greg."

I nodded and stepped back into my cell. The guard slid the door shut and the electronic lock engaged.

Lixi shot me one last smile and then walked away and out of view.

It wasn't the last time I ever saw her, but part of me now sometimes wishes that it had been.

CHAPTER 36

You Know Things Are Bad When the Dwarf Is the Voice of Optimism

Edwin stopped by to visit again after dinner that night.

"How's my favorite captive doing?" he asked as my cell lock buzzed open.

"Ha. Ha," I said.

"Gotta laugh about these things," Edwin said, but he wasn't smiling.

In fact, if anything, it almost looked more like he'd been crying. His eyes were red, nearly purple. And he looked less like the happy fourteen-year-old I knew he was and more like a hundred-year-old man who'd just been asked to take apart the Great Wall of China brick by brick and move the whole thing ten yards to the west just because.

"What's wrong?" I asked.

"Everything, dude," he said with such finality that I didn't even dare try to tell him things weren't so bad.

Which almost made me laugh for real. Imagine that: a

Dwarf telling an Elf that things weren't so bad and to look on the bright side.

"Should I be worried?" I asked.

"We all should be," he said. "I suppose without TV or Internet in here you don't know what's happening."

I shook my head. "How could I?"

"Magic," he said. "It's coming back more rapidly than we expected. The whole island system of Hawaii hasn't had power for three days. And not everyone can simply dismiss the monster sightings as hoaxes anymore. I mean, there was a full moon not long ago. By our estimates, unwitting Werewolves may have led to the deaths of thousands globally. The very fabric of modern civilization is starting to come apart. You see now why I need to do what I'm planning?"

It would have been hard for me to tell him he was wrong, given all he'd just told me. So I didn't. Because I wasn't even sure he was wrong anymore. If it was true that thousands had died from Werewolf attacks alone, then it would be hard to sit there and tell someone that magic coming back was good for the world. That it would bring peace. Even if Edwin's vision was misguided, he was right in that it would probably keep more innocent people out of harm's way.

"So what's stopping you if things are getting so bad?" I asked.

"I can't tell you that," he said. "I can't have you trying to stop me. I know you think you'd be doing the right thing, but you wouldn't be. So for all of our sakes, I can't say any more. But it will be soon now. I hope. I just need to oust my mole first."

"At least tell me what's happening with Elves?" I said.

"Why I saw Elves fighting one another in New Orleans. Are other Elves out to sabotage your efforts?"

"I can't, Greg . . ."

"You can and should," I said. "I assume I'm getting out of here eventually? Otherwise why treat me so well? Why try to convince me you're not the bad guys? And if that's the case, don't you think it'd be good for me to know? So I can explain to the Dwarven Council what's happening. Whose side to take . . . if it comes to that?"

Edwin put his hands over his face and rubbed his eyes. Then he sighed.

"There's no guarantee I can ever let you out of here, Greg," he finally said. "I mean I *hope* it will get to that, but I can't take that chance just yet. Not until I've succeeded. And that's not a sure thing. But I guess I will tell you more, anyway, because I do want to call you my friend again. And I want you to trust me again.

"As I'm sure you're already aware, when my parents were killed the Elven kingdom fractured. Many of my father's top-ranking advisers across the globe made plays for power. And among the Elves who felt I was too young, too sympathetic to Dwarves to take over my rightful position as heir, there was a split. In fact there were lots of splits over lots of things. But the point is, it created chaos and infighting and a lot of smaller groups with no real power. Especially not while they fought among themselves.

"Luckily, many Elves remained loyal to our code and followed me regardless of my youth. It was a small group at first, but it has steadily grown in the last few months. But as you would expect, so, too, did the other factions finally fight it out and come to some sort of resolution. One particular group emerged as the most powerful, absorbing all the rest, who still opposed me as Elf Lord. That faction is a strengthened version of the same rogue, radical nationalist group I suspected took your father all those months ago: Verumque Genus."

"Who's leading them?" I asked.

Edwin shook his head.

"I'm not sure," he said. "I'm guessing one of my father's old confidants. I have a few candidates in mind, but it would help if I could figure out who among my trusted advisers is feeding them information."

"For a time, I thought it was you leading that group, to be honest," I said.

"What?" he asked. "Why? And how did you even know about them?"

"Well, I didn't know much about them," I admitted. "Until I befriended your parents' former Rock Troll slave, Kurzol, whose real name is Stoney, by the way. After your parents, well, you know . . . um, one of their loyal followers took Stoney to New Orleans. While imprisoned there, he heard some rumors. About the new Elven faction planning something terrible and devastating that would lead to *universal annihilation*, as he put it. And he also heard that their leader was a kid. So, while I didn't want to believe you'd plan something so terrible, I thought it seemed possible, given your state of mind the last time I saw you . . ."

Edwin shrugged, showing me that he didn't take offense.

"That's interesting," he said. "I never considered that their leader might be young like me. I wonder if it might be a former PEE student? Well, either way, your Rock Troll was definitely right about one thing: What they're planning is really troublesome. And it definitely would lead to global destruction."

"So you know what it is?"

Edwin nodded slowly, like he sort of wished he were bliss-fully ignorant instead.

"They want to amass an army of monsters and basically use them take over the world," he said. "Violently. They want to ensure that they stay at the top of the socioeconomic food chain, so to speak. And in a New Magical Age, they see a mon-ster army as the easiest way to do that. That's who my squad was fighting in the cemetery. And also why the Verumque Genus were trying to capture the Moonwraith, rather than exile it back to the afterlife permanently. My small team showed up to stop them and your party's presence was . . . well, unex-pected. It complicated things. In the closing moments of the battle, my people found you unconscious and brought you back here."

"Who won the battle?" I asked, again thinking of my friends and what might have happened.

"They did," Edwin said. "At least in the sense that they got the Moonwraith and got away. Though we didn't suffer many casualties, we ultimately weren't able to stop them from getting what they came for. Which is why it's more imperative than ever for me to find my traitor. I *must* banish magic once again before the Verumque Genus succeeds. Before their army of monsters is so large that nobody will be able to stop them. I want to use magic to keep peace, Greg. They want to use it to dominate."

"There's no other way to stop them?"

Edwin shook his head.

"Not one that doesn't involve a massive war on a scale much larger than World War Two. Which is why I've been saying this all along: I need to succeed in stripping the world of magic or it will be the end of everything as we know it. But first I have to find out who has been leaking information."

We sat there and let his statement of doom sink in for a few seconds. My mind drifted back to New Orleans. I had a nagging feeling in the back of my mind that I was missing something.

"So . . . you never had *any* alliances at all with the Elves in New Orleans?" I asked.

"No, not at all," Edwin said. "We didn't even know they were there until recently—shortly before the battle in the cemetery. An Elven prisoner of theirs escaped and came to us with the information."

I nodded and figured he must have escaped when Stoney had since he'd told me they'd all broken out together. It almost made me wonder if it was the same Elf that Stoney claimed had been poisoned with the same substance as my dad. A substance I now knew was . . .

My heart suddenly slammed into my chest and my eyes went wide.

"Greg?" Edwin asked, alarmed. "What's wrong? Are you okay?"

"Edwin, I know who your mole is," I said.

His concern changed to confusion and then finally a look of annoyed skepticism.

"How could you possibly?"

"The substance that poisoned my dad was a variation of an ancient Elven Separate Earth potion called *Shawara Marar Yarda*," I said. "It was brewed personally for your dad. Only he and the brewer ever possessed any."

"So?"

"*So,*" I said. "If I obtained the batch given to your dad, then that only leaves the batch the person who brewed it had."

Edwin shook his head in frustration.

"Greg, I still don't see at all what this has to do with my mole."

"The only reason I went to New Orleans in the first place was to find out what happened to my dad and how to fix him," I said. "Stoney told me a fellow captive in New Orleans was drugged with the same toxin as my dad. Which, as we know, only *one* person other than your father ever possessed."

"How do you even know all this?"

"Because that one person, the person who made the poison, *told me* all of this, here, at Alcatraz," I said. "Dr. Yelwarin."

Edwin's eyes went wide for a moment, but then he shook his head.

"No way," he said. "She's been too vital to my efforts so far. She wouldn't—"

"Well, why wouldn't she help when she knows she's got the upper hand to stop it all in the end?" I suggested. "It's the only possibility, unless Stoney was wrong . . ."

"Well, you *are* trusting the word of a Rock Troll, Greg," Edwin said.

"Yeah, *I am*," I said. "Have you ever met a Rock Troll?"

Edwin tilted his head to the side and grinned, knowing I was about to win this argument.

"No."

"That's what I thought," I said. "So how can you just assume they can't be trusted? Or that they're unreliable? Just taking your old Elven books' word for it?"

Edwin shrugged, still grinning—though it was far from good-humored. It was more resigned and bitter than anything else.

"Well, Stoney is my friend, Edwin," I said. "And I trust

him. Dwarves don't trust others lightly, due to the standards of integrity we try to uphold among ourselves. You know that. But I trust Stoney. And so if what you said the other day was true, that you still trust me, then you have to believe me."

Edwin sat there for what felt like forever, but was perhaps mere seconds. His icy blue eyes bore into my own and then he finally nodded.

"It seems I need to go find my good doctor," he said, standing quickly. "Right away."

CHAPTER 37

——— ◆◆◆ ———

Greggdroule Stormbelly: Master of Lightning

The dreadfully familiar sounds of battle woke me the next morning.

Not just any battle, but an earth-shattering conflict that involved swords clanging off swords, terrible screams, howls from unknown creatures, and the unmistakable sizzling and flashing lights of magical energy from Elven spells.[*]

It sounded like the world was ending.

And it grew even louder when a huge Ogre smashed into the prison wall across from my cell, blowing open a hole in the building large enough to drive a car through. Beyond it, I saw a terrible, strangely beautiful sight.

The sky was dark with rain clouds and lightning flashed,

---

[*] Over the past few weeks of captivity, I'd come to find out (mostly from witnessing accidental displays of magic) that Elven spells were a little bit different from Dwarven spells. Ours involved earthly elements, like wind and plants and rocks, and theirs were more like psychedelic flashing light shows—almost like futuristic lasers.

illuminating raindrops like falling gems. There were creatures of all sorts beyond the crumbling wall, rushing past, battling with Elves. Yellow and red and green bursts of energy from Elven spells lit up the foreground. Screams and the ringing sound of swords filled the air as Elves fought other Elves. Hundreds of flying creatures blanketed the sky, and only during a lightning strike could I see what they were: scores of Harpies and Wyverns. In the frantic, glowing torrents of lightning and Elven magic, I also saw among the chaos Goblins, Orcs, Ghouls, Ifrits, and an array of other monsters I didn't recognize.

I knew right then it was the Verumque Genus (otherwise known as the VG) and their army of monsters.

I instantly knew they were there to destroy Edwin before he could take away their magic (and in the process their entire legion of enchanted beings). But a dark shape filled my vision before I saw anything more. I took a step back from the bars of my cell door.

It was the Ogre that had crashed through the wall.

He licked his thick lips hungrily and grinned down at me, saliva pooling at his feet in a steaming pile of slime. Ogres looked like something between a Forest Troll, an Orc, and a really ugly Human being. This particular guy was easily ten feet tall, had shaggy black hair tangled with dried blood and bits of flesh from its last meal (probably some hapless Human). He had a huge belly covered in a smock made from an array of animal hides, and his equally flabby limbs flopped about as he ripped apart the iron bars separating him from his next snack: *me*.

I backed into the corner of the cell.

"Let's talk about this," I said, for some reason thinking that maybe all this time around Elves had made me a more charming, persuasive person. "At least get to know me before eating me. It will make the meal a whole lot more satisfying, I'm sure. Ever hear of naming your food? I had an uncle once who named all his steers, even the ones he'd eventually be making into grilled steaks."

The Ogre laughed, his belly shaking up and down. Then he lunged forward with his right hand. It fell just short of me as his head crashed into the ceiling of the cell. Concrete crumbled around him. But he recovered quickly, and now having caved in part of the entrance, there was nothing in his way.

He stood back up and grinned, goopy saliva still oozing onto the floor.

That's when I felt it.

I wasn't sure if I was standing in a magical hot zone or if this was finally it: magic coming back in full force. But either way I could feel Galdervatn coursing through me. The more magic I'd performed over the last few months, the easier it was to tell when it was present, when I actually had the means to cast a spell. It felt sort of like confidence in a way, but you could tell the difference because having the essence of magic was a lot less logical. Like, confidence only went so far. Confidence alone couldn't convince you to try to leap across the Grand Canyon. But with magic, the *confidence* you felt had no limits. It truly felt like you could *do anything*, no matter how crazy or illogical or dangerous it would normally have sounded.

The Ogre lifted a fist and swung it down as if to crush me like a bug. But just as his hand descended, I summoned a spell I didn't even know I was capable of: a bolt of lightning zoomed in through the hole in the prison walls and connected with the back of the Ogre's head with a *crack* so loud it sounded like an Australian buloke tree being snapped in half.

He fell forward, hair ablaze, crackling and snapping from the collected congealed animal fats in its tangles.

I managed to dive out of the way as he crashed into my toilet and smashed it into a thousand pieces. Water sprayed from the broken, exposed pipes and promptly put out his flaming hair. It sizzled and smoked as the Ogre lay motionless.

I ran out of the cell and over to the ragged hole in the prison wall. The battle still raged outside. Bodies littered the concrete walkway and I didn't look long enough (nor did I want to) to see who or what any of them belonged to. Instead, I crouched back inside the cellblock and debated my options:

1. I could use this as my chance to escape. Find a way back to Chicago and inform the Council of everything that was happening (or about to happen).

2. I could stay and join the battle and try to help Edwin defeat the VG and their ghastly army of creatures.

3. I could curl up into a ball and whimper in fear until the whole thing was over.

As appealing as option three sounded, I eliminated it immediately. Part of me definitely wanted to flee, to save myself, to use this as my chance to escape. But at the same time, the other part of me felt like Edwin and I were *almost* friends again. At the very least we weren't sworn enemies anymore. But even beyond that I'd met a lot of genuinely nice Elves working at Alcatraz, Elves who were now in danger. And last, and maybe most important of all: Regardless of what I thought of Edwin's plan to *save the world*, there was no denying it was probably better than what the VG Elves had in mind. So stopping them seemed like the most important objective at the immediate moment.

It was settled: option 2.

I would stay and help Edwin.

Even if it likely meant one of these two outcomes:

1. We won and I would go right back to being a prisoner.
2. We lost and I would be killed in action.

CHAPTER 38

An Old Friend Goes Orc Bowling

My first problem, as I dashed outside to join the battle, was that I did not have a weapon.

My second problem, just seconds after running out into the rain, was that I was already surrounded by seven angry green Orcs armed with nasty-looking curved swords as thick as cars, battle-axes stained with blood and covered in cracks and chips (likely from chopping so many bones), and wicked clubs with sharpened animal tusks sticking out from the ends.

Orcs were larger than Humans, but only slightly taller (most were around seven feet tall). But they were a lot thicker—built like hairless gorillas on steroids. Their skin was all different shades of splotchy green and covered in moles. They had gaping mouths that never seemed to close and sported teeth like huge dogs. And they started hacking right away, without even giving me time to assess or plan or reason with them.

I managed to dodge the first blow.

Simultaneously, I summoned some magical vines that

pulled one of the Orcs off the ledge of the walkway and down into the bay below. But three of the other Orcs' weapons connected, my body turning to stone just a fraction of a second before impact. But unlike all the other times I'd used that defensive stone spell, which had been relatively painless, this time the blows actually still hurt.

Their swords clanged off my rock exterior, but rattled my teeth and sent me sprawling, dazed and wondering if they had managed to chop off a limb even though it had been stone. I looked around, my back and arm throbbing. I was still in one piece but already three other Orcs were swinging two huge axes and one massive spike-covered club down toward my head.

I knew this was it—I didn't have the energy for another spell. I could feel that much already. And even if I did, it wouldn't be enough. Dwarven magic alone apparently had its limits in combat with orcs. But just before the weapons hit and darkness came, a boulder nearly the size of a small house came flying in out of nowhere and obliterated all three Orcs like they were bowling pins. The boulder rolled off the ledge into the bay, leaving a smear of green blood and Orc parts behind it.

It wasn't until the three remaining Orcs were being slammed violently into the wall by a rocky shoulder attached to a massive, charging blur of gray that I realized who had saved me.

"Stoney!" I shouted.

"STONEY GUARDIAN GREG!" the huge Rock Troll bellowed as he easily flung one of the Orcs over his shoulder hundreds of feet into the air, like he was throwing away a piece of trash.

Then in a flash, my other friends were at my side. *All* of

them: Ari, Lake, Eagan, Glam, and Froggy. And all four of the Dwarves I'd met in New Orleans were there as well: Giggles, Yoley, Tiki, and Boozy.

Ari threw her arms around me and it was probably the best hug I'd ever gotten.

"You guys are okay!" I said, my throat choking up as I struggled to keep from breaking the Universal Dwarven Rule: *Dwarves never cry.*

"We're sorry we waited so long," Ari said, ignoring the rule as tears flowed down her cheeks.

"Come on, this way," Eagan said, leading us back inside the relatively quiet prison walls, away from the action.

The larger battle itself seemed, for now, to be relegated mostly to the exterior prison grounds. Which is likely what the VG wanted, with so many of their army either able to fly or too large to be effective in the cramped hallways of the prison.

We crouched inside Alcatraz, around the corner and near a cellblock adjacent to my own. The lights were off and the place was dark. I wanted to stop and explain to them what was going on, but before I had a chance I heard a familiar voice in my head.

Oh, how I've missed seeing your ugly mug, Greggdroule!

Froggy tossed me the Bloodletter, as the ax continued to rant.

Those slightly crooked, dirty-mud-colored eyes. Those yellowing and haphazardly arranged teeth! Your stringy hair! The smell, oh, and the smell! Never before have I missed a smell like that.

My heart leaped at the sight of it.

As the handle hit my palms, a spark of power surged through me. Whatever aches and pains I'd had were gone. And also, oddly enough, I now wanted more than anything to run back out there and lay waste to everyone and everything. To *both* sides of the battling armies. For putting me and my friends in danger.

Yeah, the Bloodletter added. *And also they held you prisoner! I mean, who does that? They kept you captive with a smile on their faces! Like they were doing you a favor!*

The ax was right: Why had I been so accepting of being a prisoner anyway? I should have been furious the whole time. Whether they'd treated me relatively well or not was irrelevant. I had been their prisoner—they'd taken my freedom. And the Verumque Genus, well, they deserved to be destroyed for obvious reasons. All I saw ahead of me was vengeance and fury.

My teeth were grinding together so hard I thought I might have chipped one of them. How had I been so blind to my situation before? It had to have been Elven manipulation and powers of persuasion.

No Elf will be left standing, the Bloodletter said.

Well, I'm not quite sure about that . . . I thought back.

You're not angrier only because they fooled you with their Elven charm, Greggdroule, the Bloodletter said. *But now that we're reunited, nothing will stop us from saving the world from the Elves. All of them.*

Okay, let's do this, I thought back. *Let's go destroy!*

Heck, yes! Rock and roll!

I started to get up, to go charging outside to unleash the chaos of the Bloodletter on both groups of Elves. But Eagan put a hand on my shoulder and stopped me.

"Whoa, wait just a second," he said. "What's going on here?"

In the heat of the moment, I forgot I hadn't filled every-one in. So I explained to them very quickly who the Verumque Genus were. And what their plan was. And why they were fight-ing Edwin, and what his plan was.

"We've got to stop them," I said at the end. "All of them. Edwin wants to strip the world of magic and the VG want to use magic to control an army of monsters to wreak havoc. Clearly, we can't let either happen."

"These are good points," Eagan said. "But I wonder what the Council—"

Tell him that the torpid Council can go eat a drungy borrloonger, the Bloodletter said. *We can handle this our-purbogging-selves.*

"Forget the Council," I interrupted Eagan, choosing not to be quite as harsh as Carl suggested. "What I want to know is, how did you know I was here? And why didn't you come sooner?"

"The Bloodletter led us here, actually," Eagan said.

"Really?"

"Aye!" Lake declared. "Tis powers nary be underestimated henceforth!"

That's right, I'm a boss, the ax boasted. *Don't ever mess with me or my Dwarf.*

"We didn't *want* to wait so long, really," Ari said, and I knew she meant it. "After the ax led us here, which was a long process itself, involving it glowing in different shades of blue and purple—almost like a compass—we had to send word back to the Council. They told us to wait and observe and only go in if we thought your life was in immediate danger. They didn't want to risk prematurely starting a war with the Elves."

I nodded, then stood up again.

"Okay, either way, enough chitchat, let's go end this," I said.

"Now you're talking!" Glam said excitedly. "It's Elf-smashing time."

"Wait, guys," Eagan commanded. "Greg, have you actually *seen* the size of the armies out there? I don't think we can take them. There are only ten of us, with Stoney, and likely close to a thousand of them all totaled. I think we're better off just try-ing to escape unnoticed. We can take this new information to the Council and let them decide how to handle the Verumque Genus. We don't have to save the day on our own."

"Guys, I hate to interrupt," Ari said. "But I don't think it matters. We don't really have a choice anymore, from the look of it."

We all stood up and looked around. On either side of us in the cellblock were two masses of monsters and Elves, cutting off both possible escape routes. On one side was a legion of Goblins armed with tiny hatchets and swords. Though only three feet tall at most, Goblins made up for it with speed, light use of magic, and ferocious relentlessness. There were likely a hundred of them in the cellblock in front of us, their shiny green heads bobbing up and down hastily like waves, and so the relatively small size of their weapons was not very comforting.

On the other side were at least twenty-five huge, vicious-looking beasts that I immediately recognized as Manticores. They were easy enough to identify from their unique appearance, which was exactly how they'd been described in our Monsterology texts. They had a massive body similar to a lion's (but spikier—and I knew from my studies that the spikes were laced with venom), with dark, leathery wings folded up on their shoulders like a Dragon, and long spindly tails with poisonous barbs on the end like a scorpion.

But the worst part was their head. A Manticore had an almost Human-like head. Had it just been a Human face on a creature's body, it maybe wouldn't have been quite so terrifying. But it was the *almost* part that made them especially, unnaturally Ghoulish. The face was structured like a Human's, complete with teeth that were surprisingly rounded for such a savage beast, and a pointed nose with two nostrils. But the face was stretched wider, distorted and waxy, like bad special effects in an old movie. And the mouth, framed by a wild lion-like mane, was always twisted into an ugly smile.

The venomous Manticores were flanked by about a dozen Elves wearing black enchanted armor with glowing green-and-gold runes on it. VG soldiers: all armed to the teeth with swords, bows and arrows, and wicked spears called halberds. The VG Elves smiled, knowing as well as we did just how trapped, outnumbered, and likely doomed we all were. And then one of them spoke, his voice familiar and chilling to the bone.

"Well, well, if it isn't Roly-McBowly Fatmont!" Perry Sharpe said.

By far the biggest bully at the PEE, Perry was a vicious tormenter of pretty much everyone, but especially of kids like me and Froggy. I quickly noticed now that his armor was different from the other VG Elves'. It was fancier. So I already suspected that he was the very same "adolescent" leader Stoney had heard about.

Perry confirmed this a second later.

"Like my new army?" he sneered. "Somehow I should have

known you and Edwin would still be working together! That kid always has been such a disgrace to the Elves—having such a soft spot for Dwarves. I mean, even when Dr. Yelwarin reported back to me that you were here, I didn't believe her! Oh! Oh my, and look, it's also little Froggy! The half-breed! Two for one!"

Froggy scowled and raised his throwing axes.

"Well, I'm just so happy we're outside the PEE now," Perry said. "So I can finally do to you both what I've always wanted to!"

A short silence followed as we stared up at Perry and he looked down at us. And the Goblins on the other flank shuffled their feet restlessly. After a time the silence actually got a little uncomfortable.

"Um, well, now what?" one of the VG Elves next to Perry asked.

"What do you mean *now what*?" Perry screeched at him. "Attack! Attack! Wasn't that clear? Attack and kill them all!"

And so it seemed we now had to join the battle, if there was going to be any chance of getting off this island alive.

CHAPTER 39

◆—➤➤◄◄—◆

Carl Is Finally in His Element

We drew our weapons and formed ourselves into a tight circle as the two armies closed in slowly on either side of us.

Glam's fists turned into boulders. Stoney roared and several of the Goblins took an uncertain step backward, their beady eyes actually displaying fear.

"Come on, guys!" Glam shouted with a huge grin. "Let's go have some fun! Glam SMASH!"

She charged into the sea of Goblins, her boulder fists swinging wildly from side to side, sending little green bodies flying up into the second level of prison cells. Something about it was oddly intoxicating to watch: little green limbs flailing as the Goblins soared into the air. Or maybe it was just the Bloodletter's ecstatic screaming in my head making me think that way: *WoooooooOooOOOOo! Come on, Greg, join the fun!*

He was right, I didn't have time to watch it rain Goblins.

The VG Elves and Manticores were already charging toward us on the other side. I readied the Bloodletter. It vibrated with glee.

Finally! I've been waiting a long time for this moment, Greggdroule.

His words kicked my adrenaline into overdrive. Magic surged through me. I suddenly felt like the most powerful being in the universe.

I easily dispatched a Manticore right away—after all, this wasn't an MPM, it was a real battle. Plus, I didn't even have time to think about it—the Bloodletter nearly moved on its own as I twirled around and lopped off another's poisonous tail just as it was soaring toward Froggy's back. Almost as an afterthought, like I was on autopilot, I used a Dwarven wind spell to deflect three arrows heading toward my friends.

The arrows clattered onto the concrete harmlessly.

In a way, it felt like the Bloodletter was doing most of the work as I jumped and spun and swung my ax. It felt even lighter than weightless—as if it was pulling me along. Like the Bloodletter and I were the same being, like my brain was switched off. Decisions didn't need to be made—they didn't even have a place in this battle.

Every limb moved on its own.

As I took out three Goblins surrounding an unaware Giggles Bitterspine, already tangled up in a sword fight with two other Goblins.

As I fended off two VG Elves charging at me with glowing swords.

As I smashed a Manticore to the ground just before it was about stomp on Yoley.

I figured it was only a matter of time before an unseen arrow pierced my back or a blade found its way past my many stone defensive spells. But I didn't care—all I could see before me were my enemies and the Bloodletter.

Find Perry, the Bloodletter taunted me. *Let's make him eat his words. Let's pay him back for all the times he stuffed you headfirst into the Souper Bowl.*

How do you even know about that?

Because we're one and the same now, he said. *When you fully embraced me as my owner at the start of this battle, when you accepted my power, we became one. Well, at least in a magically symbolic way, of course. You're still flesh-and-blood Dwarf and I'm still cold, merciless metal.*

I spun around, looking for Perry as the Bloodletter suggested.

But as I searched the chaos for him, a different realization hit me: Beyond the power of the Bloodletter's magic, our side should have been losing. We were outnumbered in this cell-block twenty to one. Then I recognized the main reason we were holding our own: Stoney.

He was a beast.

The Rock Troll rampaged through the crowd of Manticores, flattening everything in his path. He picked up two of them—even though they were nearly as large as he was—and used them as living battering rams as he took out a dozen more in less than five seconds. The VG Elves were furiously casting spells at Stoney, but they seemed to be having little effect.

At least at first.

I watched as their bolts of lightning and colorful balls of energy simply evaporated into Stoney's rock-like skin with weak sizzles. But after several dozen spells and thousands of blows from the Goblins' tiny axes and swords, and dozens of stings from the Manticores' venomous spikes and barbed tails, Stoney finally began to stumble, looking weak and tired.

He swayed backward and then crashed through a row of

prison cells. He obliterated them instantly and continued falling right through the outer prison wall. I stood powerless as a massive section of the old building collapsed onto Stoney (and half of the Goblin army), burying them all in rubble.

A scream of rage and panic erupted from my lungs as the Bloodletter dispatched two more Goblins.

I ran toward the pile of rubble, trying to summon any magic I could think of that would help unearth my fallen friend. But the collapsed wall had opened up our cellblock to the rest of the battle. Two Wyverns were already soaring toward me, screeching like Dragons (despite being a lot smaller) as they bared their sharp teeth. Unlike many different Dragon breeds we'd read about, Wyverns did not breathe fire, but I knew their bites were poisonous—they had a temporary but instantaneous paralyzing effect.

I dodged the first Wyvern, swinging the Bloodletter up toward its belly as I rolled.

The second one clipped my shoulder with a talon and blood spurted out onto the pavement. But I didn't have time to worry about a mere flesh wound. I jumped back to my feet and conjured up another bolt of lightning. It zapped across the sky and connected with the Wyvern in a bright flash.

The winged creature fell silently toward the ground.

I spun around, back toward the rubble pile, but it was too late. The larger battle had spilled inside now and my path was blocked by dozens of Edwin's Elves fighting an array of monsters and VG Elves. It would have been hard to tell the two sides apart if not for the VG Elves' matching combat armor. Whereas Edwin's army looked more ragtag, most not wearing any armor at all—which made sense considering this had likely been a surprise attack.

Then I somehow saw two things all at once, very clearly, amid the chaos:

1. Lixi was among the fighting Elves, battling three Orcs. Overwhelmed and outnumbered, her Elven blade was knocked from her hand by an Orc wielding a huge iron-and-bone mace. The force of the blow threw her backward and she slammed into a pile of bricks. The three Orcs lunged toward her as she struggled to sit up.

2. I heard Eagan screaming for help. My head spun as I looked back the other way and saw him being carried up into the sky by two Harpies (ugly creatures that were basically half woman, half bird, and all nasty—known to frequently carry away their victims for a slow and torturous death later), seemingly fighting over which one got to have (and later eat) their spoils of war.

And I knew right then and there that I only had time to save one of them.

CHAPTER 40

For Once, Greed Is Good (Sort Of)

The blind vengeance the Bloodletter had infected me with when I'd taken hold of its cold handle evaporated in an instant.

At the beginning of the battle, this would have been an easy choice: Save Eagan, let the Elf die. But now my thoughts flashed back to how kind Lixi had been during my time here. To how much fun I'd had hanging out and talking with her in spite of technically being a prisoner. And most of all, to how I knew she was a good person deep down, regardless of what any Dwarf would ever tell me.

How could I make a choice like this?

It's easy! the Bloodletter hissed. *Save your real, true friend. Not the lying Pointer that helped hold you hostage. Eagan wouldn't even be here if she hadn't made you a prisoner. Let the Elf die, she deserves it.*

My insides melted with dread.

The two Harpies were still greedily fighting over Eagan as they ascended higher and higher into the sky, and his cries for help started to fade. Lixi, however, was furiously kicking at the Orcs as they grabbed her limbs, seconds from possibly pulling her apart.

I knew now there was no real choice—circumstances saved me from the torture. Lixi would be the first to perish and so that made my decision clear. I didn't care in that moment that I was supposed to hate Elves forever and was foretold (as the Bloodletter's "Chosen One") to rise up and lead the Dwarves to glory. None of that mattered to me. What mattered to me was that I had a friend in trouble and couldn't just do nothing.

Besides: this was also precisely what Eagan would do.

I sprinted toward Lexi.

Greggdroule, no! the enraged Bloodletter howled into my brain.

I dodged two arrows and a Goblin swinging a sword on the way. I tried to summon a spell to help Lixi as I ran, but nothing was happening. Was she too far away, or was the Galdervatn fading? Perhaps this wasn't the final return of it after all. Or had my magic run out? Did it have limits?

Either way, it meant I'd have to do this the hard way.

Lixi had just managed to free herself from the grip of one Orc when another grabbed her neck and lifted her off the ground. She had maybe seconds left, and I was still ten yards away.

Before I even realized what I was doing, my shoe (of all things) was in my hand. And then it was soaring through the air a split second later. It connected with the back of the Orc's head. He grunted in surprise and turned around, still holding Lixi by the neck. The two other Orcs also spun around, their eyes glowing.

My shoe may not have been deadly, but it bought me the extra second I needed.

I was nearly there now, running full speed, and I leaped into the air, twirling my ax across my body, drawing a perfect half circle with it around my chest. The Bloodletter finished it, the three Orcs dropping to the ground half a second after I landed in the center of them.

I can't believe you made me save an Elf, the Bloodletter moaned.

Lixi landed on top of an Orc's body and then rolled off it in disgust. She kicked at his lifeless calf and then turned to face me. Her tear-filled eyes overflowed with affection and gratitude. But I didn't have time to respond.

I spun around, twisting the Bloodletter in a low arc—like an uppercut swing of a baseball bat.

And now you're going to go save Eagan, I thought to him as I released the ax handle.

The Bloodletter pinwheeled up into the sky, blade glowing blue.

If you had told me I could throw an ax hundreds of feet into the air like that I'd have laughed in your face until my cheeks were magenta and streaked with tears. I'd have laughed so loudly, it would have gotten awkward as you just stood there and watched me laugh like a maniac. And then had you added that I would hit two targets at a distance of at least fifty yards, while somehow avoiding a third object right between them, I'd have simply stomped on your toes for mocking me.

But somehow I knew that magic (whatever was left of both mine and the Bloodletter's) would guide the ax true.

The spinning blue glow disappeared into the stormy dark sky. Lightning was still flashing as rain continued to fall. A second later, there were two horrible shrieks of pain. The Harpies emerged from the clouds, tumbling back toward the ground in pieces.

A flailing Dwarf followed shortly afterward.

I sprinted toward where I expected Eagan to land, summoning the most powerful wind spell I could think of to soften his fall. But I was too far away and the already-gusting winds of the storm weren't helping. He slammed into the ground with a damp, thick THUMP.

A Human or Elf would have easily died instantly.

But if you recall, Dwarven bones are partially made from granite and diamonds. So instead of breaking, Eagan actually put a small crater into the concrete path down near the pier.

I ran down the incline and knelt next to him; he was bleeding, clearly injured, and unconscious. But he was still breathing. Had I saved him first and let Lixi fend for herself, he surely would have been almost entirely unharmed. The Harpies had taken him significantly higher in those thirty seconds I had used to save my Elven friend first (*but*, I reminded myself, those were thirty seconds she *definitely* hadn't had).

Look what you did, Greg, the Bloodletter called out from somewhere nearby. *Some friend you are.*

I didn't argue as I cradled Eagan's bleeding head.

Because the Bloodletter was right: *I* had caused this.

CHAPTER 41

It's an Uncomfortable Favor to Ask a Friend to Help You Drown Another Friend

Eagan lay broken (and maybe dying) down a shallow slope and mostly out of the periphery of the main battle up near the prison buildings.

I crouched there and waited as I saw my friends running toward us. My heart leaped when I saw Stoney trailing them, flinging away a few last Goblins like they were dead leaves. He was okay! Last I saw, he'd been buried alive beneath a collapsed prison wall.

But a quick look back down at Eagan killed whatever relief had swept through me. Ari also immediately saw how grave this was. She had several wounds herself, which looked pretty serious in their own right, but she paid no attention to them.

"We have to get him out of here and to a doctor," she said. "Our boat is down this way."

I nodded.

"Stoney, can you carry him?" I motioned toward Eagan.

The Rock Troll, who was also bleeding from a wound on

his head, nodded solemnly. His blood was thick and gray like clumpy paint.

"Gently," Glam said as Stoney knelt down to lift up Eagan, her dirty, bruised face racked with worry.

"STONEY RECOGNIZE WOUND SEVERITY," the Rock Troll thundered, lifting our motionless friend with one hand like he was politely and properly picking up a hot cup of tea.

Part of me still didn't want to abandon the fight. To leave Edwin and his people behind to have to take on the VG and their army of monsters all by themselves. But I also knew we had to get out of there. Besides, if we did stay to help, what would happen at the end? Regardless of who won, we'd be facing a pretty awkward situation. Plus, the Council needed an update—I'd discovered a lot about what the future had in store.

And so I stayed quiet and followed Ari, Lake, Glam, Froggy, the four NOLA Dwarves, and Stoney (carrying Eagan) as they climbed down to a hidden spot beneath the huge docks where a large tugboat was tied to a post. Two massive paddles, literally the size of trees, leaned against the cabin walls. Stoney nestled Eagan on a tarp near the back. Then he grabbed the paddles and plopped down in the center of the tugboat, ready to start rowing us out of there.

We couldn't use the motor because a huge surge of magic had clearly just hit this area, which meant that everything mechanical was now dead.

Just before we cut the line to the dock, a voice called out to me.

Um, aren't you forgetting something there, Maverick?

I looked up and back toward the shore. A blue glow near the rocks ahead of us caught my eye.

The Bloodletter.

Part of me wanted to just leave it there. But that would be irresponsible. It was too powerful to simply leave discarded on an Elven-occupied island. I hopped off the boat and ran over to the rocks and grabbed it, my hand finding the handle like it belonged there. It almost felt like I'd been missing a limb and hadn't realized it yet. Which was all the more disappointing and heartbreaking considering what I knew I had to do next.

For a second, I actually thought you were going to leave me behind, Greggdroule! Even after everything I've done for you.

I did not respond as I ran back toward the boat, cut the line, and helped my friends push us off from the shore. The large tugboat was basically full to capacity with ten Dwarves and a huge Rock Troll aboard. The water came up to just a few inches shy of the gunwales.

Stoney took up most of the room as he sat right in the center and rowed with the huge, makeshift paddles that appeared to have been made from a disassembled billboard ad for a business called *Trick Dog*.

As we pulled silently away from the island, the large battle still looming above us came into view. From the water, against the darkened backdrop of the stormy sky, it looked, well, *magical*. It would have been breathtakingly beautiful had I not known what terrible things were occurring up there.

And so it was simply breathtaking.

The hundreds of Harpies and Wyverns flew like black specks in the sky, their limbs and wings visible only in the flashes of lightning in the clouds behind them. Tracers of yellow and green and blue magic fired from the prison grounds at them, lighting up the sky like an expensive fireworks display.

Even more flashes of magic and fire bloomed on the island

itself, visible inside the building through Alcatraz's few windows. An explosion rocked the back half of the island and I wondered how long it would take for the police of the modern world to arrive. Shouldn't they have already? The battle had been raging now for at least an hour. Why had there been no Human response?

Was the modern world really already that far gone?

I had been cut off from everything for weeks, so I really had no idea.

But none of that mattered to me then. As Stoney slowly rowed us farther away from the island, and from the epic battle that might be laying waste to my former best friend, I was instead preoccupied with what I knew must be done now, right then and there in that moment. And it was not something I wanted to do. Rather, it *needed* to happen. For my sake. Maybe even for the sake of the world.

Don't do it, Greggdroule, the Bloodletter pleaded. *You can't.*

I have to, I thought back. *I know that now.*

But we make such a good team; surely you saw that back there. We were unstoppable together in battle. A powerful force that could change everything. That could win the war. The legends foretold as much. You and I, we are the Legend. The Legend of Greg and Carl. You're fulfilling my destiny. OUR destiny.

You're wrong, I thought back. *My destiny isn't in defeating the Elves. I know that now. I don't even have a destiny. Together, we create only violence and darkness. You're more like a curse.*

So what will you do? Huh? Invite them over for tea? Have that army of VG Elves and their monsters come on down to the Underground for a civil dinner party during which you'll eat avocado toast points and politely discuss your differences with good-natured jokes? Without me, they'll tear you apart, Greggdroule. All of you. I am supposed to be the savior of all Dwarves in their darkest moment. This feels like that moment, don't you think?

I didn't have an answer for my ax. He made a lot of good points, brought up a lot of problems without any obvious solutions. But they were solutions I'd have to figure out on my own.

Without the Bloodletter.

"Ari, I need you to do something for me," I said, breaking the somber silence. She looked at me, weary and curious. "Take the Bloodletter from my hands, and throw it into the Bay."

CHAPTER 42

A Boy Says Goodbye to His Magical Talking Ax

Thankfully, I was the only one on the boat who could hear the Bloodletter's anguished screams of rage and despair.

And perhaps also of terror, which nearly convinced me to change my mind.

If Ari had heard its screams, she probably wouldn't have stood up uncertainly like she did. But despite standing, she still hesitated.

"Greg . . . are you . . ."

"I'm sure," I said. "It has to be done. It . . . it corrupts me. It turns me into something I'm not."

"But you should have seen yourself in battle back there," Glam said, looking at me in a way I'd never seen before.

I looked around the boat, at all the faces watching me. Respect and admiration dotted everyone's nervous glances, even in spite of my decision to help out an Elf before Eagan. Or maybe they just didn't know about that? In the chaos of battle, they likely had no idea that I could have saved him first. They couldn't have, or else they wouldn't be looking at me like that.

Like a *hero*.

"A sight to behold, thee and thy ax," Lake said with obvious wonder and awe.

"It was incredible," Boozy Alemaul said. "Never seen anything like it. For a moment you looked like you could take on the whole monster army by yourself."

"The power you showed was, well . . ." Froggy added, before going silent with amazed wonder.

"You guys were like a superweapon," Giggles Bitterspine added.

"That monster army was awful," Ari said. "If that's our new enemy, our future, then we need you. We'll need the version of you we saw back there with the Bloodletter."

I realized what I saw in their eyes when they spoke to me: Deference. Respect. Admiration. Those were things I wasn't accustomed to seeing on people's faces when they addressed me. For a split second I was almost intoxicated by how special it made me feel. By the power and confidence that surged through me.

But it wasn't real.

"Are you sure about that?" I asked. "Because killing creatures so easily, even dangerous and savage ones, didn't exactly feel helpful to me. In fact, I hated every part of it, even as much as the Bloodletter's own joy overwhelmed me in the moment. That's the real problem. That Greg *wasn't me*."

You're wrong, Greggdroule, the Bloodletter said. *You should listen to your friends. Since when could you ever trust yourself over them?*

"He's right," Froggy said. "I've known Greg longer than all of you. As powerful as he was, as remarkable a fighter . . .

the look in his eyes wasn't the look of the same nice kid who befriended a weird loner like me when he didn't have to."

Ari nodded slowly, realizing just how right Froggy was. It was almost as if the power of the Bloodletter was so intoxicating that it could distort not only my perception, but my friends' as well.

The ax pulsed with energy in my hands, like a desperate last attempt to sway me. It felt so at home there that I wasn't even sure Ari would be able to wrench it from my grip at all.

"The ax corrupts my thinking," I continued. "Yes, it gives me power, but that's not who I am."

"But Stormbellys are destined to become our greatest, fiercest leaders in battle," Glam said, almost pleading, as if she knew the truth but just didn't want to accept it. "You're supposed to be our finest hero."

"No offense," I said, "but I don't care what I'm *supposed* to be. I'm tired of hearing about my namesake and my *destiny*. My life is not prewritten based on what my ancestors did thousands and thousands of years ago. I am me, Greg Stormbelly, and that's all I am. I will do my best to help the Dwarves, to save lives, to save Humans and even Elves from harm. I want the world to be better. But not through violence. The Elves aren't inherently evil, just as I'm not inherently a great warrior. It was only the Bloodletter's cursed magic that made me appear that way. It fills my head with blind vengeance instead of empathy and compassion. Edwin is still not a terrible guy; his thinking has just been warped by tragedy. He means well, even if his plan is deeply flawed. Understanding the nature of magic and ourselves is the answer to finding peace; war is not. Peace is not defeating others. I still believe that deep down. My dad was right. The Bloodletter's power over me will only end in misery.

For me, and for all those around me. It has put your lives in danger through me too many times. Please, take it from me, Ari, and throw it into the Bay."

She looked at me, still standing just a few feet away. At the tears streaming down my face. Then she lunged forward and pulled the ax from my hands.

Stop her, Greggdroule! There's still time. You're making a mistake!

I don't want to do this, I thought back. *But it has to be done.*

I had to look away as Ari flung the ax overboard. It splashed into the Bay and sank quickly into the murky, green depths. The Bloodletter's anguished voice trailed up toward me as we drifted away from its watery grave.

I loved you, Greggdroule.

I know, I thought. *You were . . . well, you were my friend. In spite of the tragedy you would have brought me, I'll always appreciate the times you helped me. They're too many to even list.*

Those moments aren't over, the Bloodletter said, his "voice" so faded now it was more like a whisper in my head. *You still need me. You'll see that in time. I will always forgive you for this. We were meant to bring peace into this world. Someday you'll know that. I just hope that by then, it's not too late.*

CHAPTER 43

This Time There Are No Ducks Wearing Hiking Boots

The mood was hardly celebratory when we finally made it back to the Underground in Chicago.

For one thing, the world had clearly changed forever. Magic still hadn't fully returned, confirmed by the fact that we weren't able to perform much during most of the trip home. But it was likely just days from happening now, not months or weeks. The panicked reports on the radio of dozens of monster sightings and other strange happenings were enough evidence of that.

The semblance of normal society still prevailed, but it was obvious that total chaos was just over the horizon. When we made it to the shore of the Bay, we found Boz Brightfinger (the Swiss cake roll–loving Dwarf from our second MPM in Wisconsin) waiting for us. Behind him was a huge cargo van that was supposed to transport all of us back to Chicago.

It took nearly four days to get there.

Twice during the long drive our vehicle was rendered dead and useless by a surge of magic. The first time was near

Henderson, Nevada, and the second happened just outside of Omaha, Nebraska. Each time it delayed us for over a day while we located a new vehicle that still worked and was large enough to accommodate Stoney. The only good news was that we found a Dwarven Healer within a small local branch of Dwarves just outside of Las Vegas on that first night of travel, and he, thankfully, was able to stabilize and treat Eagan.

Eagan was groggy and slept most of the drive back, but the doctor in Vegas told us that he should ultimately be okay. He'd suffered a severe concussion and some bruised ribs. Miraculously nothing worse, given how far he'd tumbled back down to earth.

Many grocery stores, restaurants, and gas stations we passed on the drive across America back to Chicago were closed. The owners and employees likely wanted to be home with their families in these uncertain and scary times. Most Humans still had no idea what was happening. Though some of the radio hosts had developed theories that were shockingly accurate. Some callers claimed extraterrestrial interference. Most people, though, were seeing this as some sort of biblical armageddon. Which was, in many ways, more dangerous than the truth.

Looters ran through the streets in some of the cities and towns we passed through. Law enforcement and National Guard units struggled to maintain control. It was clear to me that whatever my dad's solution was, I needed to figure it out quickly. The world could not keep going in this direction.

During the ride, we mostly stayed quiet, the mood somber. The few times we spoke, we talked about what lay ahead. About what we might find in the next town or city—at one point we even wondered aloud if we'd make it back to Chicago at all. But we also debated what sort of plan the Council might come up with to fight the Verumque Genus, ranging from tepid to extreme:

 Me: "Probably nothing, you know, because we're Dwarves."
 Ari: "Yeah, and then it will be up to *us* to save the day *again*."
 Glam: "No, they'll declare all-out war, I'm sure."

—✦—

When we finally made it home, my dad welcomed me with a tear-filled hug—after all, I had been missing, a captive like he had been, for almost a month.

I kept assuring him that they treated me a lot better than he had been and that did calm him down some.

It was good to see my dad again, even now that I knew there was probably no way to fix his condition. But it didn't matter as much anymore. Not after everything that had happened with the Bloodletter and the Elves. At the very least, I realized I should be grateful. After all, the Bloodletter did help me get more perspective on my dad's condition. It really was better than losing someone forever.

After my dad finally stopped hugging me, he gestured toward an envelope on my bed.

"It arrived earlier this morning," he said. "Hand delivered to the Cronenberg's Offal Delicatessen and Rotary Telephone Repair Shop storefront by an unarmed Elven courier."

Inside the envelope was a handwritten letter from Edwin:

Greg,

 I hope you made it back to Chicago safely. We saw your party escaping on the boat and did our best to distract the beasts of the Verumque Genus long enough for you to slip away. I want to thank you for remaining a true "friend," so to speak. You tipping me off about Dr. Yelwarin gave us just enough warning to survive the surprise attack. We eventually fended them off and they retreated, but both sides suffered heavily and I know this is not over yet. They will strike again. Can you believe that jerk Perry Sharpe is their leader? I guess it shouldn't surprise us, but I never thought he was smart or likable enough to lead an army. Unfortunately he got away . . . this time.

Anyway, I hope you saw the state of the world on your return. All flights have been suspended worldwide. We're on the brink of societal collapse. All these things should make it clear to you now that I am right. That I must succeed in my plan. The fate of the world rests in our hands, Greg. Please do not try and stop me. When this is all over, I really hope we can still be friends. Or at the very least, not mortal enemies.

"And?" my dad asked when I finally looked up from the letter. "The Council almost made me surrender the letter to them since it came from Elves. But I convinced them that that sort of tyrannical intrusion would be beneath us as Dwarves. Privacy and freedom are vital to our culture. To our integrity."

"It's from Edwin," I said.

I sat down and explained to my dad what my former best friend's plan was. At least, the parts of it I knew about: stripping magic from the world once again, except for a select group of Elves, who would then use that magic to keep the peace and restore the world back to a tranquil normalcy—as best as possible.

"It's not a terrible thought," my dad said, surprising me. "At least his heart is in the right place. But he's wrong. Magic returning in full is the only way to true peace."

"But . . ." I hesitated, afraid that asking the question too forcefully might set off another spell of delirium. "You keep saying that, but do you know *how*?"

My dad looked into my eyes and for a second I was sure he was going to start ranting about ducks wearing hiking boots or some other such nonsense. But his gaze stayed clear and sharp for once. It almost felt like something else inside him, something mystical (like magic!), was keeping him in check at the moment.

"I wish I knew fully," he said. "But I do know I'm right. You do, too. You must sense it every time you feel magic coursing through you. How pure and good it really is. How powerful. It just needs to be harnessed the right way. I believe that's why the Fairies banished it all those years ago—not because they felt that magic itself was bad, but because Elves and Dwarves and everyone else were misusing it for corrupt purposes. It was an escalating war that they saw no end to; we were past reasoning. Think about it, Greg: What makes the Bloodletter so dangerous? The fact that it's magical? Or is it because it's a weapon? It was made to kill, that's the whole reason it was created! It's not the magic itself."

"So it's really just as simple as we need to stop making weapons?" I asked skeptically.

"Yes!" my dad said breathlessly and for a second I thought

maybe this was one of his crazy spells after all. "But it's more than that. I mean, it requires a whole shift in thinking, but getting rid of weapons would certainly be a good start. Think about it: Dwarven spells by nature are not *offensive*. They're not suited for battle, but rather for protection. I'm not sure if you've noticed this, but Dwarven spells by themselves are not capable of killing. Had Dwarves not started forging weapons, magic would only be used for good, helpful purposes. It was our shifting nature that corrupted magic, not the other way around! And the same is true of Elves.

"Magic can be used to clear our minds of all the negativity. The gut reactions. The hate and anger that come with fear and jealousy and insecurity. These are the core emotions behind almost all that is wrong in this world. Of course, this isn't to say that magic can end the existence of *bad people*. Or evil deeds. Without the freedom to *be bad*, what is the point of living? But I truly know that magic can allow people to see things, the world, and the other living creatures around us more clearly. With more empathy and understanding. And when that happens . . . well, I think we'll all be surprised by just how quickly people—Human, Dwarf, Elf, or otherwise—stop *being bad* on their own. We won't want to create weapons or use magic for destructive purposes anymore."

I didn't know how, but I knew he was right. It made perfect sense: Magic itself has no violent tendencies, no inherent malice. We, people and creatures of all kinds, ruined magic's purity all that time ago, not the other way around. By creating weapons, instigating wars, making enemies. Magic was just another tool for living beings to use, no different from uranium, metal alloys, certain plants and residues: all resources that are misused in the modern world to make the same mistakes over and over again. I was more convinced than ever that my dad's theory was still correct. That magic was the answer to lasting peace on this earth. We just needed to use it properly for once.

All of which meant, in spite of Edwin's letter, we still had to stop him.

My dad must have been thinking the same thing, because he stood suddenly.

"Come on, let's go tell the Council about your friend's plans."

CHAPTER 44

◆─➤❖◄─◆

Always Butter Your Flag for the Lions

For a moment there, I actually allowed myself to feel hopeful. An obvious mistake for a Dwarf.

At first I was hopeful that my dad might actually be getting better. After all, he had been remarkably clear and thoughtful back in our apartment. But then, on the walk to the Dosgrud Silverhood Assembly Hall, he introduced another of his *Kernels of Truth*. All I could do was sigh in despair as he launched into an overwrought bit about the importance of soaking flags in melted butter before raising them up on flagpoles—his even more non-sensical reasoning being something about how it would make the pride easier to fight off (whether he meant a pride of lions or the emotion, I didn't know, and frankly, I didn't care).

Then I allowed myself to feel optimistic that we actually might be able to stop Edwin. After I explained to the Council everything I'd discovered about the Elves' plan while in cap-tivity (being sure to include the parts about them being very humane in their treatment of me), Dunmor nodded and said that he knew exactly how Edwin planned to pull this plan off. Which I hadn't expected—I'd figured I'd tell them the plan and they'd be just as clueless as I was about how Edwin thought he could achieve this feat, leaving us all hopelessly ignorant as to how to stop him.

But *of course* that's not what happened.

"He must believe he knows where to find the Faranlegt Amulet of Sahar," Dunmor said.

"But it doesn't actually exist!" Dhon Dragonbelly, one of the Council Elders, practically shouted.

"Preposterous!" Ooj added.

"It must!" a regular Councilwoman from the surrounding seats countered. "How else could the Fairies have banished magic all those years ago?"

"Even if it existed once," another Council member argued, "that doesn't mean it still does."

This was about to initiate another round of incoherent arguing among the Council, but Dunmor stopped it before it started by banging his rock on the table.

"Well, clearly Edwin Aldaron believes it still exists," Dunmor said once he had the room's attention again. "Out of an abundance of caution, I think it's safer if we assume not only that it still exists, but that the new Elf Lord somehow knows where to find it. There's simply no other explanation for this plan of his. We should now assume that Edwin plans to use the Faranlegt Amulet of Sahar to convert all magic to some other substance that he and his followers alone will have access to. It's possible he may even plan to destroy the amulet forever once he succeeds."

There was another rabble of debate and panic from the Council. I slowly raised my hand and the hall eventually fell silent as Dunmor again pounded on his stone table with the huge rock.

"More input, Greg?" he asked. "A detail you forgot, perhaps?"

"I mean, if he thinks he found it, then that means we might be able to as well," I said. "Let's not just give up so quickly."

"So where is it, then?" Dhon Dragonbelly demanded. "Your *friend* clearly has information we do not!"

"Okay, fine," I said. "But he got it somehow. What *do* we know for sure? I mean, what do the ancient texts or whatever say about its possible location?"

"Well, see, that's the problem," Dunmor said bleakly, sitting down in defeat. "Anything we know about the amulet is only according to ancient Fairy lore, which is information passed down verbally in stories—not in writing."

"So what do the stories say about it?" I said, not letting this go.

They may have wanted to ignore this like a bunch of Dwarves, but that wasn't me anymore. I wasn't going to let destiny make me act a certain way anymore. I was Greg, and only Greg, and would do whatever *I* felt was right.

"Well," Dunmor began, "before they banished themselves to the earth's core, the Fairies hid the Faranlegt Amulet of Sahar inside a charmed cave that lies within the magical realm of an unknown, remote forest. They supposedly used the last bit of magic left to enlist the ancient spirit of a half-Elven, half-Dwarven mage named Ranellewellenar Lightmaster to guard the amulet. Edwin must know the location of the forest and the cave. And now it's just a matter of getting there—something he theoretically cannot do until magic fully comes back. The cave is said to require magic for entry—one reason many Elves and Dwarves have long believed the amulet to be lost forever. A paradox.

"But now that we've been proven wrong about magic's return . . . then, well, it stands to reason the cave could eventually be accessible once again. May even be right now, as we speak. And so if Edwin really does know the location, and how to get past the spirit of the mage, then he will have everything he needs to implement his plan. And there is nothing we can do to stop him since we still do not even know the location of the forest, let alone of the magical cave hidden within. It could literally be anywhere in the world where there is, *or even once was*, a forest."

As Dunmor finished, the entire chamber seemed to exhale in defeat all at once, as if collectively punched in the gut by hundreds of invisible fists.

All was lost.

There was no way to stop Edwin if he indeed had found the location of the Faranlegt Amulet of Sahar.

And I knew he had. Replaying our conversations now in my head, I'd recognized that look on his face. Edwin's confidence was never false. I knew him too well to think he'd been bluffing. Even that one time I brought up the amulet he'd only grinned at me, and it was the same smile that always appeared on his face right before he swooped in and made the move that would checkmate me.

Edwin had all the information he needed to find the amulet. He was headed to that cave, and once he retrieved the amulet, all would be lost.

Plus, there was still the problem of the Verumque Genus. We couldn't forget about the threat they posed. Even if Edwin was somehow stopped, then what would we do about this other group of Elves? The ones amassing an army of monsters with plans far more sinister than anything Edwin had in mind.

See?

See now why I said it was a mistake to ever let myself, a Dwarf, get hopeful?

CHAPTER 45

An Unlikely Hero Emerges, and It's Not Me

After the Council Session, I went to see Stoney.

I wasn't sure if it was because I thought he could cheer me up. Or perhaps deep down I wanted to steal more of his "poop" so I could enjoy one last hedonistic spending spree before the world ended. But either way, just the sight of him somehow did cheer me up when I walked into his room.

He was sitting with his back to the wall, battle wounds all bandaged up, snacking on a huge stack of gold bars like they were popcorn.

"You got some gold!" I said, pleased that someone had brought him some of his favorite food.

"ARI CONVIVIAL CONTRIBUTION!" Stoney bellowed, his stomach bulging from the millions of dollars' worth of gold he'd eaten.

I laughed in spite of everything else going on.

"Nothing better, right?" I said.

"NEGATIVE!" Stoney said. "SOLITARY ARTIFACT SUPE-RIOR."

"Oh, yeah?" I asked, sitting down next to him. "What could be better than a pile of gold? I know if I was sitting at a table filled with hamburgers, which is my favorite food, my life would be complete right now."

"ROCK ONE!" Stoney bellowed. "ROCK ONE UNRI-VALED OBJECT."

I seemed to remember him babbling on about some special rock before.

"Oh, yeah?" I said. "Why is it special again?" I asked, and braced myself for Stoney's enthusiastic response.

"SCARCEST MINERAL. SOLITARY. ENDANGERED. UNIQUE. ALLEGED NONEXISTENT."

"Hah," I said humorlessly. "That sort of sounds like this dumb enchanted thing that's the key to—"

I stopped and leaped to my feet so suddenly that Stoney cried out in surprise.

"Stoney!" I nearly shouted. "Do you realize what you've done?"

He stared at me dumbfounded, his mouth hanging open, full of crushed, half-chewed gold bars.

"INCONTINENCE, GREG?"

"No, no, I didn't have an accident," I said, actually allowing myself to laugh again. "Come on, follow me. You're about to save the world, Stoney."

———◆I◆———

Partly because of my dad's celebrity status, and partly just out of the sheer panic and excitement in my voice, I was able to get the Council to reconvene on short notice.

Ari, Froggy, Lake, Glam, and Eagan were with me. We stood in front of the towering table of Elders, Stoney at our side. My friends had been just as excited as me when I told them what I thought Stoney might know.

Even the NOLA Dwarves—Giggles, Tiki, Yoley, and Boozy—were there, behind us in the spectator seats. They smiled at me encouragingly when I glanced back. They'd made the decision to leave New Orleans, to go with my friends to San Francisco to rescue me, knowing full well it might be a while before they got back home—if ever. But they were excited to finally be a part of the larger cause—which is also why Kimmy had given them her blessing.

"This better be good, young Stormbelly," Dunmor said wearily, taking his seat. "We have much to do."

"It is," I assured him. Then I turned to Stoney. "Go on, Stoney. Tell them about Rock One."

"ROCK ONE EXTRAORDINARY MINERAL!" Stoney shouted excitedly, causing several Elders and half the Council members to flinch. "STONEY COVET!"

I could see from the look on Dunmor's face that he was already losing his patience with this.

"Stoney, *what is* Rock One?" I asked.

"SCARCEST MINERAL," Stoney explained. "SOLITARY. ENDANGERED. UNIQUE. PURPLE GLEAMING MINERAL. RED SHIMMERING MINERAL. GREEN GLISTENING MINERAL. ORANGE SPARKLY MINERAL. VOLUMINOUS HUES. LUMINOSITY. ONE ONLY. ONLY ONE."

"And do you know where to find it?" I prompted.

"AFFIRMATIVE. STONEY PINPOINT," he said, pointing at his head. "LOCALITY DIAGRAM WITHIN."

I looked at the Council excitedly, expecting them to rejoice and immediately instigate a vote for a call to action. One that would pass unanimously, setting into motion a flurry of activity that would, hopefully, save us all.

But of course that's not what happened.

We were still Dwarves.

Instead, the whole chamber seemed to emit one loud exasperated groan.

"He's lost his mind!" someone quipped. "Like his father."

It seemed like my dad's celebrity had worn off even more in the past month. The full extent of his condition must have been getting more evident with every new episode because at least forty others in attendance laughed at this.

But that was of no concern to me right then.

"What on earth would this dumb Rock Troll and his dumb Rock One have to do with anything?" Ooj shouted at me angrily. "You're wasting our valuable time!"

"Give him a chance to explain!" Ari said. "You all owe Greg as much—more than that even!"

"Yeah," Eagan added. "We wouldn't know *any* of this without Greg. Not about either faction of Elves or their real plans. Greg may not want to accept the fact that he will be our savior someday, a true Dwarven hero, but surely by now you all must recognize that it *is* true."

"He's already done more for our cause than all of you combined!" Glam pitched in. "And he's pretty good at smashing stuff when he needs to . . ."

While their arguments that I was some kind of hero made me pretty uncomfortable, I still couldn't help but grin with pride that I had such great friends. I knew they would always be there for me, would always support me, no matter what my next plan was: whether it might be breaking into an Elven skyscraper fortress to rescue my dad, running off to New Orleans to investigate a rogue group of Elves, throwing the most sacred ancient Dwarven relic ever found into the San Francisco Bay, or wherever else this new insane life would take me next (to the moon for all I knew).

No matter where I went, I knew they'd be right behind me.

"We're with Greg, too!" Tiki shouted from the seats behind us. "He's the greatest Dwarf we ever met!"

The other NOLA Dwarves let out some hoots and hollers to confirm this.

"Okay, fine," Dunmor said with a reluctant yet clearly proud grin. "Greg, enlighten us. What does any of this have to do with our current problems?"

"Can't you see the connection?" I said. "Stoney's *Rock One* is the extinct mineral *Corurak* that makes up the core of the Faranlegt Amulet of Sahar!"

Finally some of the Council members and Elders perked up a bit.

"How can you be sure?" Dunmor asked cautiously.

"Think about it," I said. "Stoney said it's the rarest rock in the world. The last one known to exist. He also said the color changes. He also said it glows. And may I remind you: He used to be imprisoned by Elves. And *with* some of the same Elves who are now allied with Edwin. Rumors flew all around in those dungeons. And you're forgetting the most important part: Stoney says he knows where it is!"

This was met with a murmur of excitement and the beginnings of another chaotic debate. Some, like Ooj, clearly still didn't think this was relevant. But others, Dunmor included, appeared legitimately intrigued and excited.

"Stop!" I shouted, silencing them immediately, surprising

even myself with how commanding my voice sounded in the chamber. "This time, we will not ignore this Rock Troll or dismiss him as stupid or unreliable. Stoney can save us all. And I, for one, am going to listen to him and follow him!"

"Yes!" Ari and Glam shouted.

Froggy patted me on the back encouragingly.

"We're in, too!" the NOLA Dwarves added.

Dunmor pounded on the table with his rock and called for order.

The Council held a brief debate.

Then a vote occurred.

And for once Dwarves were not reduced to inaction by our own pessimism. For once Dwarves voted to do something to try to fix all of this.

For once, the Council voted yes.

As soon as the final vote tally was announced, Glam, Eagan, Froggy, Lake, and Ari smothered me in a cheesy group hug. Well, I say cheesy, but of course I mean that in a good way. The NOLA Dwarves rushed down from the stands to join in. Then Stoney moved toward us.

"STONEY PARTICIPATE GRATITUDE EXHIBITION?"

We quickly broke up the group hug and encouraged him to celebrate with us verbally—without any of his bone-crushing hugs. This made Stoney laugh, which only made all of us laugh. And the stunned and confused Council watched in silence as ten kids and a huge Rock Troll stood there and laughed giddily, even though we all knew that potentially grave dangers lay in our adventures ahead.

But we didn't care, because we'd be on those adventures together.

The details were planned that evening, since there was

no time to waste. Nobody knew just how close Edwin was to obtaining the amulet. To miss catching him by even an hour would be devastating.

And so we would leave tomorrow: a small band of Dwarven warriors, plus one Rock Troll with an important map in his head. We (sort of) knew where Edwin was headed next. And we knew what he was planning.

But the real question was: Could we actually beat him there and stop him in time?

Or would we keep being Dwarves and fail more miserably than Dwarves had ever failed before?

Don't miss the final book in

AN EPIC SERIES OF FAILURES!